THE OLD JUNE WEATHER

BOOKS BY ERNEST RAYMOND

THE OLD JUNE WEATHER

by

ERNEST RAYMOND

. . . is the curtain blue
Or green to a healthy eye?
To mine, it serves for the old June weather
Blue above lane and wall. . .

BROWNING

CASSELL · LONDON

CASSELL & COMPANY LTD
35 Red Lion Square, London WC1R 4SG
Sydney, Auckland
Toronto, Johannesburg

First edition 1957
Second edition, second impression 1973

I.S.B.N. 0 304 29159 5

Printed in Great Britain by A. Wheaton & Co., Exeter

CHAPTER ONE

I was thirteen and a half, and in one of the lower forms of St. Paul's School, when the magic of the great Classical English Novelists—Fielding, Smollett, Dickens, Thackeray —suddenly lasso'ed and enslaved me. Straightway I cast aside my Marryat, Henty, and Fenimore Cooper as 'kids' stuff' and read all the works of these mighty authors, even including *The Virginians* of Thackeray, which is saying a packet. I sank myself over head and eyes in their deep enchantments, sitting in my large attic bedroom under the roof of our house in Edith Road, and when my Auntie Flavia, with whom I lived, called up the stairs to know what I was doing, I answered 'Studying the Classics,' at which she withdrew, surprised but satisfied.

When I had read perhaps fifty of these fat, unbuttoned, richly fed, and well-wined novels, I decided that it was time more books of the same robust and jovial habit, prone to laughter but ready with the occasional tear, should be given to literature, and that the person who would write them was sitting here beneath the slates of Edith Road. That Dickens could never be done again didn't at that stage occur to me; so, with the enormous ambition of thirteen and a half, I hurried out to the shops in North End Road and bought a thick exercise book of over a hundred pages, price one and a penny.

Having no experience to write about, except my life at home with Auntie Flavia and Gael, or my life at school, I chewed my penholder over the thick exercise book and resolved that since other authors had written quite good school stories—Dean Farrar and Talbot Baines Reid—I would concentrate upon adult life—with the result that Auntie Flavia became the central figure in the story, and not an attractive figure, either.

For, at that time, I liked my Auntie Flavia less than

7

anyone else in the world, except Fowler C. A., at school. Other prominent characters in the book were my Aunties Gloria, Evelyn and Primrose, and they are not shown in a really attractive light, either. Except perhaps Auntie Evelyn. Auntie Gloria, indeed, could be said to compete with Auntie Flavia for the distinction of being the least lovable character in the book. Worse, the manuscript was illustrated with pencil sketches of Aunties Flavia and Gloria in their more displeasing moments; and these portraits would certainly have offended them. They occur above such captions as 'Our Hero is Ejected from Decent Society by his Auntie Hepworth' (why on earth 'Hepworth' for Auntie Flavia I have forgotten) and 'Auntie Candida is exceedingly candid with the Children.' The identity of Auntie Candida with Auntie Gloria is shewn by one caption where in a forgetful moment I had written, 'Auntie Gloria, *more suo*, Disapproves of Our Hero.' I was proud of *more suo*.

Auntie Evelyn is not guyed; she, on the whole, appears as a fairly comfortable person to have about you; but there is only one figure in the tale who is drawn with admiration and love, and that is my Uncle Lucy. He, under the name of 'my Uncle Knightly' (surely an admirable invention for so studiously courteous a person, and such a mischievously amusing one) strides into the pages as a tall old gentleman of splendid presence, and of character without fault. A verray parfit gentil knight.

Auntie Flavia and the other aunties being the daughters of the late and saintly Canon Middian, Residentiary Canon of Selby St. Alban's, and afterwards Bishop of Chesterfield, the manuscript is entitled irreverently (and again forgetfully) 'Sir Gervase Knightly and the Middian Girls.'

Of course it comes to an untimely and jagged end. For never a child in history (except one) has completed a novel, no matter how elaborately decorated the title page or how beautifully written the first thousand words. My book, begun so neatly, falters on unsteady feet into a void of thirty clean, blank, feint-ruled pages. Partly because Auntie Flavia, while possibly enjoying the portraits of her sisters, would have been incensed by the treatment of herself, and partly because a child of fourteen is capable of some small compassion, I had to hide my illustrated exercise book, and being, despite my dreams of greatness, completely unoriginal, I prised up a floor-board in my high attic room and put it to sleep there, covering its resting place with the carpet. I never dared show it even to Gael, though she was my fellow-conspirator in most games and cared for Auntie Flavia hardly more than I did. You see, my picture of Gael was not such as would please her.

All this took place in the year 1905, and from then till now, fifty years later, that manuscript has been seen of none except my wife and children who, having no reason to be hurt by it, adore it, though my wife usually exclaims 'Heavens, you must have been a horrible child!' It is a pompous and facetious bit of work, but it has one value, she declares; it is an awful warning of what eyes and ears children have—how much they are hearing and watching, how strangely and secretly they are pondering it all, and how ludicrously inadequate are the smoke-screens with which adults seek to cloud their chatter when the children sit at table with them.

No, but wait: I *did* show it to Gael after nearly forty years. I showed it to her in the year '39. Not before, because it had seemed to me that, even though nearing fifty, she still craved admiration and resented any breath of disparagement; but one day in '39 she came running to me with the news that a play-producer called Agostino Procuro—or some such name—wanted his favourite dramatist to make a play of what he was pleased to call 'one of the world's great love stories.' He was positive he could sell the film rights, he said. This excitable little impresario had come to her seeking, not her consent, since this was unnecessary, the story being safely in the public domain, but her goodwill and her help, since she must know more about it than anyone now living. (He had not heard of me.) 'One of the world's great love stories'—this set us contrasting, in a long and agreeable chit-chat, the public view, or posterity's view, of all famous lovers with that, say, of their relatives, their servants, and any children in

9

the house. On the word 'children' I decided to show her that shocking manuscript, so unjust in parts, so perceptive in others; and to my surprise she only roared with laughter at the picture of herself, having developed her humour in fifty years. She did add, however, 'My, what a little beast you were! And I was quite fond of you. In a way.'

'But why ever didn't you go on with it?' she asked.

'Because nothing exciting ever seemed to happen in that house in Edith Road,' I explained. 'I wrote it for a few months, and then retired from authorship for want of anything really interesting to write about.'

'Nothing ever seemed to *happen*!' she almost screamed. 'Nothing interesting! And then in 1906! . . . Oh if only you had known!'

Yes, if only I had written for one year more. If only I had known the revelations that were coming to us—the story that would resolve all the mysteries of our rather mysterious household in Edith Road.

This is the story.

CHAPTER TWO

In the house lived Aunt Flavia, its mistress—Miss Flavia Middian to the outside world; Gael Harrington; myself, Travers Winfrith Ilbraham; and our two servants who seemed so old to us, Lizzie Blake, the cook, who really was old, and Mrs. Willer, the house-parlourmaid, a plump and lively widow of forty-nine. Lizzie had been with us all our lives; Mrs. Willer but a few months. Very rarely Uncle Lucy would come, surrounded by mystery, to the fine room reserved for him. He would come quietly over the water from his home in Paris, and remain with us, *en tapinois* as he would say, for only a day or two. To the few people who perceived his visits he was known as Mr. Grenville. Lizzie and Mrs. Willer generally spoke of him as Mr. Lucius, though his real name was Louis, and 'Lucius' was only Aunt Flavia's playful embellishment of the name. You will have noticed that among the 'ladies and gentlemen', as we called ourselves, to distinguish us from the servants, no two surnames were the same. Certainly our immediate neighbours noticed this, and 'Very odd,' they said among themselves.

Edith Road, in West Kensington, is a long grey, quiet suburban road, all of whose houses are a light grey brick with stucco dressings. There's nothing in it but these mottled grey façades, between the flags of the pavements and the slates of the roofs. At one end, in the misty blue distance, and closing the long vista, are the red academic towers of St. Paul's School, that famous foundation which has its roots in England's greatest humanistic age; at the other end, crossing the road's mouth, runs all the vulgarity, din and blaring hideousness of North End Road, that winding artery which was once a country lane and now, indifferent to nature, to beauty, to taste, to all high human aspirations, to everything but loud self-advertisement and eager profit-getting, is a shining fruit of our present industrial age.

So there we were, with Dean Colet's great foundation at one end, and a rattling, clattering, roaring industrialized highway at the other, and our long, grey, genteel road stretching, in some perplexity, between. In our day all of us in Edith Road thought of ourselves as 'ladies and gentlemen', but already one or two of the houses had been cut up into 'maisonettes' and, unless I am imagining it now, the road had been touched by the first melancholy of decay.

As for our house, it stood somewhere near the middle of the north side, its number being—no, I will not give you its number lest I embarrass its present population with my record of things that once happened within it; I will say only that it is not far from No. 73 and stares obliquely at the corner of Trevanion Road.

My schoolboy manuscript begins on a summer afternoon in 1905. I must have learned something from my Classical Studies, because the opening chapter is skilful. It brings all the characters of the drama on to the stage, and truly I cannot do better than take a leaf from the book of that rather obnoxious child.

It was Auntie Flavia's birthday, and her three sisters, Gloria, Evelyn, and Primrose, were coming to tea. Auntie Flavia told nobody her age; 'twenty-nine and a bit' she would say with a laugh, if asked; but Gael and I guessed it as fifty-something, and in fact this was her fifty-sixth birthday. The day was a Friday in July and Gael and I should have been at school, but Auntie Flavia, often goodhearted, often amazingly unscrupulous, and always delighting in a party, had said, 'Of course you must be at the party. I'll invent some excuse. Sickness or something. Toothache, perhaps; but don't worry me about it now. I'll write the excuses in the morning.'

'We don't go to school on Saturdays,' I reminded her.

'Oh, what does that matter?' she demanded, irritated by such precision. 'So much the better. I shall have all the week-end to think of something. Now go and make yourself tidy. You know what your Auntie Gloria is.'

When sufficiently tidy, I stood at our Playroom window, which was a window on the second floor, and gazed at our long empty street and at the quiet grey houses opposite. Down in the hall a clock struck four.

'Four o'clock,' I announced to Gael, 'and the Middian Girls are at hand.'

My use of that title, 'Middian Girls,' plunged Gael into talk about the saintly Bishop Middian, their father, whose photograph in its plush and silver frame stood on the grand piano in the drawing-room and often held Gael entranced, so beautiful she thought him, so adorable.

'Oh, let's go and look at him,' she exclaimed when her enthusiastic words had inflated anew her delight in him. 'The drawing-room must be ready now. All ready and waiting.'

I was as anxious to see the drawing-room as she the bishop, so we both ran down to it. Yes, Mrs. Willer had prepared and polished it well: it was tidy and shining for a party. The dust sheets which usually shrouded piano, sofas, and bureaux had been peeled off; the drugget had been rolled away from the Indian carpet; the holland and lace-fringed blinds had been suffered to spring upwards between the gold brocade curtains; and all the hundred and one knick-knacks, ornaments, fans, feathers, bull-rushes, and ferns had been carefully dusted for company.

And as we knew, it was not only for the aunts that the room had been thus put on parade for inspection. Always our drawing-room was brought back to life, like Lazarus out of his graveclothes, when *he* was coming.

'The Willer has done her job very adequately,' I said, looking around.

But Gael, who affected to despise my schoolboy humour —chiefly, I think, to snub me, because sometimes, before she could stop herself, she had smiled at a pomposity of mine—Gael ran to the piano to gaze at the bishop in his frame. 'Gosh, isn't he lovable?' she said.

I gazed too at the seated figure, graceful and elegant in white rochet, black chimere, and pectoral cross.

'They called him saintly, even when he was only a canon,' she said.

'And yet he produced five enormous daughters,' I submitted. 'He couldn't have been all that saintly.'

'Yes . . . that's true . . .' she mumbled, ruminating. 'Yes . . . I can never understand about that and the clergy.'

'Seems it's legitimate for them . . . within reason,' I surmised. 'Funny that he should have been thin, and all his daughters orotund.' This fine word I imagined to be a handsomer brother of 'rotund'.

'Orotund?'

'Yes. Fat as houses,' I instructed her.

'Funnier still that Auntie Gloria should be the only one like him, ghastly as she is.'

'Look!' I broke in. 'The Royal Standard is flying.'

I was staring at another photograph on the velvet tableland which was the piano's top. This was a picture of Uncle Lucy taken nearly thirty years before, and coloured. His face and dress were very different from those of the shaven and silvery churchman, but in this portrait they more than held their own against the bishop's beauty. His hair, moustaches and rippled imperial were a light brown in those days, and he stood there, tall as a Viking, in the splendour of court dress. Gold oak-leaf embroidery tapered down from wide shoulders to neat waist; his long legs looked shapely indeed in white kerseymere knee-breeches and white silk hose; and they in turn tapered neatly to black buckled shoes. His hand rested on the gilded hilt of a short sword, and his beaver cocked hat, bordered with ostrich feathers, stood on a carven table at his side.

Posed so long ago, the figure had a certain stiffness, as if, unseen, a stand and clamp had held the neck rigid for a long exposure.

'H.M. will shortly be in residence,' I said. I always called that old and stiffly coloured portrait the Royal Standard because it only appeared on the piano, when Uncle Lucy was coming to visit us. Then Auntie Flavia would 'put it out for fun.'

There were photographs of the other aunties arrayed on

the piano, and one of Auntie Flavia as a little girl in the comic dress of the fifties; but never one of her in the freshness of young womanhood. This didn't strike us as strange; we supposed it to be because people didn't display pictures of themselves in their own houses.

'Now then, you two young imps! What are you doing in here? You're not doing anything misch'eevous, are you?' Mrs. Willer had sped into the room, in her full afternoon dress of black frock, white cap and bibbed apron, a uniform which, designed for a young parlourmaid, always looked incongruous on her big, bulky, middle-aged figure. 'Your aunties are coming. You know that.' She was carrying a three-tiered cake-stand.

'I should say we do,' I agreed.

'Well, for pity's sake don't get in my way, but lemme get on wimmy work.' In her impatient vivacity Mrs. Willer never had time to sound a dental before a labial; always her 'got my' became 'gommy' and her 'want my' became 'wommy.' 'Now lemme see that everything's set to rights. You know that your Auntie Gloria sees everything. Her eyes are all over the shop. Hammy that dish.'

'It's a good job,' I said, 'that she isn't bringing Brendaheim and Walterstein with her.'

Auntie Gloria had two grown-up children, Brenda and Walter, and I always amended their names in this fashion, because I liked to fancy they had long noses like Jews.

'Now then, none of your parts, Master Travers!' This astonishing phrase was Mrs. Willer's way of saying 'Now don't be impertinent' or 'Now don't start misbehaving.' To this day its aptness eludes me. 'Brendaheim and Walterstein indeed! Whoever heard the like? I'm sure Miss Brenda and Mr. Walter are two very nicely behaved young people. They been properly brought up. Mr. Walter is a particularly civil-spoken young gentleman; and if you're half as nice as he is when you grow up, you'll be lucky and I'll be surprised. Now look, Miss Gael dear, there's a shammy leather in that bureau. Get it for me, there's a ducks. These here spoons aren't all that they might be yet. Lor, your auntie hasn't half semmy a job, polishing all the silver in the house! But everything has to be absolutely perfect when *he's* coming. Upstairs, downstairs, everything got to be set to rights, like we was expecting royalty or something. You should see what the mistress herself has done to his room.'

I had seen, because I had peeped into it. There upstairs the room that was always kept for him stayed swept and polished and dressed for his coming. It was the largest room above stairs with the grandest brass bed and the most monumental furniture. The wardrobe was like a walnut mausoleum and the washstand before the deep-curtained windows like a marble-topped altar. Sometimes I had heard it whispered that all this furniture was his own.

'Gosh, to think that he's on the train, or on the boat now!' said Gael.

But Mrs. Willer continued in her own line of country. 'I don't wonder we've got to set everything to rights for him. Liz says he's been accustomed to the best all his life. She says they had forty servants in the home he come from. Forty servants and fifty bedrooms! Will you only think of that? Stewards, butlers, footmen, and the Lord knows what else. Not just an old cook and an old parlourmaid. It's a mercy he only come once in a blue moon.'

'Now then, you two children, what are you up to in here? You know you should be up in the Playroom.' Auntie Flavia had come into the room almost as speedily as Mrs. Willer. 'I told you to stay there till they come. What are they doing, Mrs. Willer? Travers, why are you so disobedient? Why have you come here?'

'I came,' I said, 'to see that everything was in good order for the afternoon's rout.'

'Well, go upstairs and wait till you're sent for,' she ordered, unwilling to have her displeasure deflected by humour. 'And you too, Gael.' Not a doubt that her voice always changed when she spoke to Gael; its pitch dropped, its tone softened. 'Run upstairs, dear, and wait.' But suddenly she seemed to repent of her harshness to me, for she said, 'No . . . all right . . . stay here now, if you'd like to. You're tidy, aren't you?' And she straightened my tie and my hair almost caressingly. 'There now. You look quite nice. Sit down like a good boy.' Gael it was unnecessary to tidy; she'd been rearranging her two brown pigtails, and prinking the broad yellow ribbons that bound them, and re-settling her yellow dress in front of the mirror for the last hour. So Auntie Flavia said, 'Yes, you'll both do,' after giving another gentle push at my heavy forelock which *would* fall over my brow.

At fifty-six Auntie Flavia would have been a good model for what is now called 'The Outsize Figure' or 'The Mature Woman.' Personally I should have called her very fat, and I did so until Gael and I were taken to see her eldest sister, Auntie Constance, who lived at Torquay in widowed wealth and comfort. Her we found to be considerably fatter—'mountainous', as we said, 'and beyond a joke,' and thenceforward she stood for us as the ultimate canon of fatness, which our Auntie Flavia failed to reach by quite a wide margin.

This afternoon Auntie Flavia was dressed for the party as surely as the drawing-room was. And Auntie Flavia in full parade dress was very different from Auntie Flavia in her daily fatigue dress. For during much of the day, being an impatient, restless, woolgathering woman, she was happy to stay in a loose dressing jacket with her feet in worn slippers, and to let her copper hair, streaked with grey, hang in two lazy plaits. But now, this afternoon, she wore a blue gown whose lace yoke ended in frills like a cape. Her skirt in its lower part was flounce upon flounce, till the last flounce sang on the floor. The copper-and-grey hair was brushed up and rolled, Pompadour fashion, over a pad, whence it waved away to a chignon big as a sponge.

And I knew that she was dressed for more than the party. She was dressed for *him*.

As far as was permissible in those days, her face was powdered and rouged. The fatter and older she grew the more she powdered and rouged, and the more she applied something called 'lip-salve' to her mouth and laid blue shadow on her eyelids, so that her brown eyes could look, as she would say, 'as if they'd been put in with a smutty finger.'

Many a time I've heard people say of her, 'How pretty she must have been, with her small features, that auburn hair, and those soft brown eyes.' It was difficult for a child to see this lost beauty, but I caught glimpses of it on afternoons like this, when she was dressed for company, and a necklace of pearls ringed her throat beneath the sag of her second chin.

'Auntie, why did he wear court dress?' Gael was staring again at the picture of Uncle Lucy. 'Do tell us. You never will tell us.'

'Because at one time he had to attend occasionally at court. I've told you so, often.'

'Yes, but why? Why?'

'Mrs. Willer, go downstairs and be ready for them, will you?'

'Yes, ma'am.'

'All's very nice up here, Mrs. Willer. You've done it beautifully.'

'Thank you, ma'am.' And she went.

I perceived at once that this dismissal was the result of Gael's question.

Nevertheless, Gael persisted, 'Why did he have to attend at court if he was only Mr. Grenville?'

'Because he was in Parliament for a little, as you know. How often have I told you?'

'Do all members of Parliament have to go to court?'

'Oh, don't worry me. I've other things to think about. Where's that silver sugar basin? Has Lizzie——'

'But Winnie Clynes says that only the most important members wear gold embroidery like that. Was he important?'

'Don't worry me, I said!' She suddenly stamped her foot. 'I can't tell you more than I know.'

Gael, who didn't like having a foot stamped at her, said sulkily, 'But you must know more than you tell us. Travers says you do. Why did he give up being an M.P.?'

'Oh, don't *pester* me!' she cried. 'Leave me alone!' It was the shout of an angry woman to a child. 'I'm not going to tell you any more. So there! I don't know any more.'

And now I must explain that just as Auntie Flavia,

except at parties, was careless of her appearance, so, when no strangers were around, she was utterly careless of her temper. I would go further and say that she enjoyed dropping the reins and letting it gallop away with her. Gallop and steeplechase and even leave all solid ground and fly on high for a while. She made me think of the Sea of Galilee. Or of the Lake of Como. Both these lakes, I had learned in a Scripture lesson, could be a flat calm one moment, and then lo! a wind swept down through the encircling mountains and all was raging storm. So with Auntie Flavia. In a moment, at a single offending word, she could resolve upon a storm. And, once started on a storm, she liked to develop it thoroughly; she whipped up wind and waves till there was a hurricane blowing and nothing was safe on her sea.

§

But here a *caveat*. I fear lest these my first pictures of Auntie Flavia should read unfairly because I am still under the influence of that schoolboy's heartless manuscript, having read it again but an hour ago. So let me say here and now, before I write one more word of my tale, that long after the manuscript was closed and forgotten, I realized that she was capable of deep affection and a passionate loyalty, where she loved. For a long time my perceptions into her true nature were limited by my dislike. And my dislike sprang from fear, because when her passions ran to temper, she could shout at me, bending towards me with threatening eyes and angry, thin-lipped mouth. After such an attack, studying her fascinated, I would think that, even in repose, her mouth was grim and soured and slow to forgive; I know now that it would have been kinder and more perceptive to call it frustrated and sagging and sad.

§

We were both a little afraid of her when she lost her temper and shouted, so Gael didn't pursue her questions in the drawing-room this day. Not that there'd have been much time to do so, because almost immediately there came a sharp knocking at the front door. It was a ratta-tat-*tat* that stopped every movement in the room as completely as if we were figures on a cinema screen and the projector had ceased to turn. It was an imperious knock: the knock of one who liked to be obeyed. And as we stood still the bell shrilled down in the kitchen. It rang there in powerful support of the knock.

'Come back, Travers! Come back, Gael!' cried Auntie Flavia. We were rushing towards these sounds. 'Stay where you are. It's your Auntie Gloria.'

'Oh, law!' I said, and agreed to stay where I was.

'You know she's always the first to arrive. She likes to be here on the dot because your Auntie Evelyn's always unpunctual. It's a lesson for her, and for us all. I was never punctual. Sit down properly and look nice; look well-behaved. And for goodness sake stand up when she comes in.'

We all sat. In silence, Auntie Flavia fingering the frills on her yoke.

And in that silence we heard the deep-throated voice of Auntie Gloria addressing Mrs. Willer in the hall. 'No, no, my good woman, I don't want anybody to show me up. Goodness gracious, no; not after all these years, ha, ha. You stay there. I know what stairs are. And we're neither of us as young as we used to be. Or as light and slim, ha, ha.' Anyone hearing that voice knew that its owner took pride in her heartiness and humour, but two of a trade will never agree, and I, as a purveyor of humour myself, thought her brand completely embarrassing. I suffered shame for it. I blushed for it.

We continued to sit in silence and to listen to her heavy steps coming up the stairs.

She came in sight, and we rose. She stood framed in the doorway that she might discharge at us more humour. 'Ah, the Family assembled! For the great occasion. And manners! Such manners from the Young. The perfect little lady and gentleman.'

Embarrassing. I looked away. I looked at the houses across the road.

Auntie Gloria was the largest of the Middian Girls, but whether she was fat I find it difficult to say; because while her hips were enormous, and would not have seemed small on a prize shire mare, all above her waist seemed narrow and sloping. Thus she had the shape of a bell, all below the waist being the bell itself and all above it the 'ear' or handle. Sixty-one, and 'done with all frippery,' as she would loudly assert, she wore a severely tailored suit of dark broadcloth whose long buttoned coat reached to her calves—if you could imagine her having such things within the long trailing skirt. Her one concession to beauty was a spray of nodding violets in her black straw hat. All this harshness of taste was a pity because, with her bold features and her large black eyes, she must have been once, and could have been still, the handsomest of the handsome Middian Girls.

She came forward to kiss her sister. Since she disliked all sentimentality (as she declared six times a day) her kissing of a sister almost exactly resembled the Kiss of Peace which, after the Agnus Dei at High Mass, the Priest gives to the Deacon, and the Deacon to the Subdeacon. That is to say she placed both hands on the recipient's shoulders and inclined her face towards the recipient's left cheek, and nothing much more.

Next she came to me. She did not kiss me, and I was glad of this, because her deep masculine voice was matched by a sprig of masculine grey hairs which sprang from a mole on her chin. She contented herself with wringing my hand like the bell for tea. If it had been a bell to bring in all the nuns from Cloisters she could hardly have shaken it more vigorously. Then she threw it away. Meanwhile her eyes swept my clothes from Eton collar to black pumps. 'So smart you are; the perfect little gentleman!' As every word in this sentence, except the definite article, was an offence to me, I drooped my head, and she remonstrated, 'You're not afraid of me, are you? Not a boy of your age? My gracious, aren't you growing tall? One day you'll be as tall as———' But here she stopped. 'How old are you, child?'

'He's thirteen and nine months.' In Gloria's presence Auntie Flavia always answered for me, as if I were deaf and dumb or an idiot.

'Thirteen. And you're already taller than little Gael! Gael dear, you're six months older, aren't you?'

'Seven, Auntie.' Gael had no such shyness as mine. On the contrary she had a fine sense of what are now called 'public relations' and believed that all her customers should be kept pleased, and be encouraged to recommend her.

Having given her the Kiss of Peace instead of wringing her hand and throwing it away, Auntie Gloria sat on a hard chair with her reticule on her knees. She looked round the room and leaned down and scratched an ankle (having done with feminine graces). In the silence she was clearly about to say, 'No sign of Evelyn or Primrose yet,' when a knock at the front door snatched this criticism from her.

Voices down below: the voices of Auntie Evelyn and Uncle Arthur.

'She's brought Arthur with her, has she?' Gloria, so sharply deprived of a criticism, spoke irritably. 'Why doesn't that silly little man get some work to do? Instead of just following her round everywhere like a dog.'

To Gael at my side I muttered behind unmoving lips, 'Good night! The lady has brought her appendage.'

'*Shut* up!' whispered Gael, and would not smile.

If Gloria was the tallest, Evelyn was the shortest of the Middian Girls. And, to my eye, the prettiest, because her wavy white hair crowned a face that, at fifty-three, still seemed as round and pink and girlish as Gael's. Unlike Gloria, she had certainly not 'done with beauty.' Not for a moment. The round face was carefully powdered and pinked; her dress of a brightly patterned silk fitted perfectly to her plump body; and her hat, black on top and white below, sat cocked on the right side of her hair with a bird's green wing pointing to the sky from under the upthrust brim. Evelyn's hats were always a wonder and a joy to us.

Besides being the prettiest she was also, in our view, the pleasantest. Evelyn's and Gloria's garments bespoke their natures: Evelyn's as gay and colourful as a June afternoon among the roses; Gloria's as sunless and brusque as a clouded autumn day with an east wind blowing.

'Now then, Gloria, it's no good sitting there and looking as if I was unpunctual,' were Evelyn's first words. 'Today I'm a lesson in punctuality. I said to Arthur, "We'll be there as the clock strikes just to teach Gloria not to look down her nose at us." How are you, Constance—Flavia, I mean? Happy birthday, my dear, but how disastrously old we're all getting. Bless you a lot.'

She turned towards Gael who had come close to her, full of good public relations. Head to one side in a joyous welcome, Evelyn put out both hands towards Gael. 'And you, Brenda, Walter, Arthur, Em'ly, Margaret—confound it!—what's the child's name—Gael! How are you, Gael?' Evelyn's gushing nature made her rush her words, and since in the genial hurry she could seldom remember names, she would run over all the names in the family till memory rejoiced her with the certainty that she had alighted on the right one. She came sailing through a scatter of names to the one she required, much as she would come sailing past all other guests in a room till she arrived at the person she wanted to kiss. Brenda and Walter, as we know, were Gloria's children; Emily and Margaret were Evelyn's maids.

Gael put her head on one side and did her public relations stuff very effectively, kissing her auntie.

'And you, Travers—ah, got that right first time—how are you? My word, how tall you're getting. And only thirteen, isn't it?' She turned to look with a kind of secret mischief at Flavia and Gloria. 'Doesn't he begin to remind you of . . . of *Someone*?'

Quickly Flavia checked her with a frown, but Evelyn was not repressible. 'It quite frightens me sometimes,' she said, and was rescued from further indiscretions by the entry of Arthur, who had tarried in the hall, doubtless to

23

arrange his tie and moustaches in the hat-stand mirror. 'Ah, here's my Arturo. Say all the right things, Arturo, and then sit down.'

Arthur Pressworthy was the neatest little man. He was small and spare, and looked unusually spare by the side of his rotund little wife, but you felt that he didn't intend this smallness to prevent his resemblance to a copper-plate engraving of the Perfectly Dressed Gentleman. Indeed it was possibly the prime cause of his clothes. In summer he walked the pavements in a trim grey suit with his grey hat to one side of his grey hair, and his cane swinging from two fingers. If instead of a cane an umbrella dangled from the fingers it was rolled as thin as a rod. Indoors, as now, having the comfort of neither hat nor cane, he substituted for them a neat and springy strut in his walk and an up-and-down rising on his toes when he halted for speech. Today the stiff line of his grey bow-tie was matched by the line of his neat grey moustaches, which he often touched and twisted. To me, always watching, these moustaches seemed too wiry, masculine and military for so small a man.

'Well, Flavia dear,' he said, rising up and down on his toes before her. 'Your birthday! May it be the happiest of happy days. Gloria is already in her place, I see. Young Gael, Young Travers, my compliments to you. Primrose not arrived yet?'

'Did anyone ever know Primrose to be in time?' asked Gloria, able at last to score a hit in that direction.

'Perhaps she thinks,' he said, now rising up and down on his toes before Gloria, and misquoting, 'that Time was made for slaves, and Man has Forever.'

'Well, I haven't Forever, ha, ha,' declared Auntie Gloria, who, proud of her hard sense, had little patience with poetical nonsense. A dogmatic, decisive, blunt-speaking, and damnably silly woman, my Auntie Gloria.

'Now sit down, Arturo,' called Evelyn from her distance, 'and don't talk a lot of nonsense.'

Arthur, well accustomed to these happily thrown instructions, this remote control, from his wife, sat down on the brink of a chair, put both hands on his knees, lifted one hand to smarten up the wings of his bow tie, put the hand back on his knee, and attempted some good social talk with his hostess.

Primrose arrived soon after this. Her entry was the least impressive because she was the only one of the Middian Girls who suffered from diffidence and social timidity. Still a spinster at forty-eight, and never approached by a man, she was sharply conscious of her virginity, and this consciousness had bound her round with doubts and fears, so that she was as self-suppressed as her sisters were self-assertive. As a rule she said only what she thought people would think she ought to say; and when, as sometimes happened, she strove to be gay her humour seemed forced, insecure, and quick to retreat. Her general unsureness had affected her posture and clothes as well as her talk. Her figure had not expanded like her sisters'; rather had it shrunk a little, though without leaving her angular. Impossible for a Middian girl to be that! She stooped, and on this stooping figure her mildly gay dress hung as straight and loosely as a garment on a hanger.

'Well . . . and about time too, Primrose,' laughed Auntie Gloria. 'You're only twenty minutes late.'

'Oh, I'm sorry. Am I late? Sorry, Gloria. Is it really as late as that?'

'It's twenty-past four, I think. Unless that clock misinforms me.'

'All right, all right; you needn't go on about it. I expect you're a little late sometimes.'

'Twenty minutes is hardly little.'

'Oh, do leave off going on.'

'No need to get angry, Prim,' Evelyn chided. 'Gloria was only teasing you. She was being jolly.'

'I'm not so sure. . . . Gloria's always getting at me.'

'Go along with you! You shouldn't be so sensitive.'

'Now tea,' said Auntie Flavia promptly and brightly, wanting only good fellowship at her party.

I have read in a learned German work that every chicken-run can show hens of dominating personality—*grandes dames*, as it were—who peck all the others, and some who both peck and are pecked, and least one who is merely pecked by all. In our hen-run I should have classed Primrose as this last unfavoured bird if it hadn't been that every now and then she could rebel and peck back sulkily.

§

'So *he* is coming again?' asked Gloria over the rim of her teacup, and all her disapproval of him was in the words.

'Yes.' Flavia seemed to defy her sister, but merrily, with this single syllable.

'When?'

'This evening.' Three syllables no less defiant. 'But you needn't hurry, my dear. He won't be here till late.'

'Coming for the birthday, I suppose?' This was Arthur: Arthur leaning over the cup which he held so neatly before his breast. For Arthur must always insert his voice into any talk, and the sisters had now been talking together for a long time without remembering him.

'Not for the birthday only. Have some more cakes, my dears.' Flavia, loving a party, was always a good hostess, fussing over her guests and calling them 'my dears'. 'Primrose, have another sandwich. This time he's going to stay'.

'*Stay?*' A word of alarm from Evelyn.

'Well, for quite a time.'

'That's something very new, isn't it?'

'Yes, Evelyn, it is.'

'But isn't it rather a risk, Gloria dear—I mean Flavia dear?'

'I should think it very unwise,' opined Arthur, after sipping from his cup as if sampling the truth.

Flavia shrugged and laughed. 'He says he's suddenly begun to feel old and is entitled to some cosseting and some endearments before he dies.'

'Ever hear such rubbish?' asked Gloria of her cup. She was as ready to scorn other people's humour as to think highly of her own.

'And he says he need trouble less about the risk now, because his days won't be long.'

'H'mm.' The sound came down Gloria's nose; a bassoon note that was the opposite of a laugh. 'Well, I don't know. . . . When I think of all. . . . I simply don't understand you.'

'I know you don't, my dear, and never will.' If Gloria wanted to quarrel about him, well, Flavia's hand was lightly fingering the hilt of her sword. 'Travers, pass your Auntie Primrose those cakes. She's got nothing. Don't just sit there eating all the time.'

'How long since he last appeared?' Evelyn pursued.

'Not since Travers's birthday last year. He hardly ever misses that.'

'He was always fond of children,' Primrose suddenly announced from her neglected chair.

'And that, oddly enough,' said Gloria, 'has been true of some of the wickedest men in the world.'

'He's certainly not one of them.' Flavia's blade was now an inch out of its scabbard.

'He'll return to Paris in due course, I imagine?' said Arthur, deeming it was time he spoke again.

'Naturally,' said Flavia. 'Where else?'

The five talkers had long ceased to think of Gael and me as other than insensible furniture. They were giving no more heed to us than to the two huge Chinese vases standing in the corners or to the old faces watching from the frames on the piano.

'I wonder how he spends his days over there,' said Evelyn. 'Paris is adorable for a holiday, but——'

'Paris, like patriotism,' put in Arthur, who always wanted to be witty but generally sounded no more than ponderously sententious, 'is often the last refuge of a scoundrel.'

'Oh, do keep quiet, Arturo—don't interrupt me—Paris is perfect for a holiday, but to stay over there for ever with that revolting Channel tossing up and down between you and your country—it must be like being on the other side of death.'

'Don't be so absurdly sentimental, Evelyn.' Gloria laid down her cup on an occasional table.

'I don't think Evelyn's remark was sentimental at all,' Arthur declared. Usually his custom was to agree with the most powerful person in the room until he felt, after a time, that he wasn't being listened to seriously, or that some words could be construed as an offence. And a discourtesy to his wife in the presence of her husband could certainly be construed as an offence. 'For him, after all he did and was, Paris must be rather like Limbo.'

'Of course it was sentimental. You're both being absurd.'

'I'm not being anything of the sort. To take a different view from you is not necessarily to be absurd.'

'All he did and was! A commonplace offender who made his country too hot for him! Good gracious, we here know what we know, and I intend to say what I think;' to which she tagged on a strange sentence. 'No matter who's present.'

'*Commonplace?*' Evelyn snatched at the word. 'That's no word to apply to him. To him of all people. When you remember his dazzling brilliance——'

'Dazzling fiddlesticks.'

'—and all that he might have done and become, if *that* hadn't happened; and, above all'—Evelyn's voice took on a sudden honeyed richness as if she were relishing a wonderful memory—'when you remember how lovely he was to look at——'

'All I remember, Evelyn, is that he broke our dear father's heart.' Just as the devil can quote Scripture to his purpose, so Gloria could use the most sentimental phrases when it suited her.

'Well, that's an absurd exaggeration,' said Arthur, in whom the word 'absurd' was still rankling.

'It's not an exaggeration at all. Not at all. My father was a saint, and for *that* to happen to him was like death.'

'I quite agree,' said Primrose, but nobody was listening to her.

'Stuff!' Arthur scoffed. 'Bishop's hearts are not as frail as that.'

'I'll thank you not to say anything against my beloved father, Arthur.'

'Arthur is allowed to speak, I suppose?' said Evelyn, who was inclined to regard her Arturo as a pleasing but possibly fragile little possession which shouldn't be clumsily handled.

'Arthur intends to,' said Arthur.

'And when you think,' continued Evelyn, 'that if ever a man was born with a golden spoon in his mouth, it was he; that he had every advantage of birth and wealth and terrific talents—be quiet, Arthur; don't interrupt—and influence—such influence! Think who his godfathers were. And then again his looks. What a gift from the gods. I'm sure he was descended from the Vikings.'

'He was certainly good looking,' murmured Primrose.

'The Vikings, my dear Evelyn,' Gloria corrected in superior tones, 'came from Scandinavia, and so far as his ancestors were anything but English, they must have been Norman.'

'And the Normans were descended from the Vikings,' Arthur almost shouted, delighted thus to trump her ace.

This blow from history, unexpected, certainly rocked her for a moment, so she dodged aside from it. 'All I know is, I don't forgive the man who did that to my father, whatever Evelyn and Flavia may do.' (No mention of Primrose.) 'And it may be nothing to you, Arthur, but please to remember'—she looked away from us all, out of the window—'he ruined the life of one of us sitting here.'

They were launched far into the deep now, and we two sat listening with watching, staring, fascinated eyes. We knew them well, and knew they would go rashly on, because Gloria was so confident of her superiority that she couldn't imagine she was ever unwise; because Evelyn, easy-going and vivacious, ran her likes and dislikes on the easiest rein; because Flavia might be secretive about many things, but if her temper was aroused, she had no control of it, and desired no control of it; and because Arthur must always assert his views into any talk. Let them go on. They were talking of the dark but peopled past out of which we had come. We were two orphans sitting in the bright light of today without a history, but the roots of our being, undisclosed to us, must be somewhere in the dead darkness of yesterday, and we had vowed to each other that we would come upon them one day. Only let these talkers go on; we would listen.

'Commonplace!' resumed Evelyn. 'Why, people still talk of him to this day. After all these years. Arthur and I were at Milly Fowler's the other day and a woman mentioned him. She did, didn't she, Arthur darling? I heard her asking if he was still alive, and, if so, what became of him. And would he perhaps appear again. She little knew whose ears were starting out of her head a couple of yards away. A wretched woman was talking to me about her vicar, and it made my head ache, trying to answer her and to listen to the other creature at the same time. One thing I heard: she said his fall was like the fall of a tower.'

'Sentimental rubbish,' sneered Gloria.

'I don't think it was rubbish at all,' said Arthur.

'Be quiet, Arthur. *I'm* talking. That tower in the Bible that fell on a lot of people and slew them. I forget where. But, Gloria sweet, you must admit that he towered above most with his brilliance.'

'I prefer common decency to brilliance.'

'And all said and done,' continued Evelyn, for my aunts in spate listened only to themselves, 'what did his sins amount to except a weakness for a pretty face? And what a price he had to pay for that! What a price! And you've got to allow that it was an exceptionally beautiful face.'

'I can't think what you're all coming to. To speak of behaviour like his as a "weakness"——'

'Of course I know he was rather inclined to love them all. And I expect he does still. After all, he's only in his late seventies. Thank Heaven, Flavia, you've nothing beautiful in your kitchen. Mrs. Willer'll hardly keep him awake. Or old Lizzie either.'

'I find nothing in all this to laugh at,' Gloria persisted. 'For my part I have some standards. I see nothing to admire in a man who obviously hadn't a scruple in his system and was an outrageous liar into the bargain.'

30

'He was certainly a good liar,' said Evelyn, but with appreciation rather than disapproval.

'His life was one long lie.'

'Oh, come!' objected Arthur.

'And he may have been as brilliant as the noonday sun, but I shall still call him a wicked and unprincipled——'

But Flavia's face, which had been irritably turned from the talk ever since that word 'commonplace offender,' now swung round upon Gloria. Her eyes were shining with tears and her thin-lipped mouth shaking with them. I knew the signs. A sufficient wind had come through the mountains, and the smooth lake was stirring and about to become a tumultuous sea. She rose, thrust the cake-stand away, and the first words she hurled at Gloria were like the first rush of a wave. 'You think it clever to talk as you do. Well, I think a remark like that's just cruelly unfeeling. How you can bring yourself to utter it in my house I don't know. The real truth is, not that you're just outspoken, but that you take pleasure in wounding——'

'I quite agree,' muttered Arthur. Had he not been called absurd? Which was wounding.

'If I think a person's wicked, I intend——'

'As if I haven't suffered enough in my life. You rejoice to hurt me. Always. Plenty of other men have done what he's done and not had to pay his price——'

'*Oh*, no; *oh*, no!' fired Gloria, like two quick shots from a double-barrelled gun. 'The things that came out in court were too atrocious.'

But Flavia wasn't going to listen. 'You hate him because you're one of those who take advantage of your sex to insult any man, but it didn't work with *him*; you got as good as you gave that time, even if it was wrapped up in the most courteous words. I remember. I was there. For once in a way someone was twice too many for you, and you've hated him ever since. You don't care how much this sort of talk hurts me. You go on and on with it. Few people have been called upon to suffer as I have done, merely because I tried to give some comfort and happiness to a man who needed it terribly. I know I gave him happiness when he was cast out and alone, I gave it to him, I know; I gave it——' this deeply pathetic sentence, which she must have loved, caused her to break into a storm of tears, but a cataract of weeping never halted Auntie Flavia from speech; rather it swept a whole new detritus of words down with it. 'I gave him back a desire to live—he used to say so—a desire to live—and I look upon it as one of the best things I ever did in my life. To my dying day I shall not be ashamed of it, even though he . . . even though . . . and I'm sure I've given up my life to these two children. Anything might have happened if I hadn't stepped in to save them. Have I not made them the one object of my life?'

In her storms Auntie Flavia would thrash about in the most irrelevant waters for affecting sentences that would justify tears. No one had been discussing us children. Her mention of us, however, swung her round to where we sat, frightened and staring at the loud quarrel, Gael with tears in her eyes. 'Go away, you two children. You should not be listening to this sort of thing. Go *on*, I say!' She stamped her foot, and I, who had risen, shied timidly from the noise of it. But then a moment of pity made her say, 'Here, take these cakes and go. Go up to the Playroom and enjoy yourselves;' and we had to go out of that sun-bright drawing-room, leaving the storm in being, and never knowing how Auntie Gloria met it. The door slammed on us, and we stood in the windowless darkness of the landing between the first and second flight of stairs.

'Fierce raged the tempest o'er the deep,' I said to Gael; and she, angered now instead of alarmed, said, 'Oh, hang! Why couldn't we stay? I love it when somebody tells Auntie Gloria where to get off.'

§

We did not go up to the Playroom; instead we ran across the landing to our cave beneath the second flight of stairs. Since the landing was windowless this cave under its tilted roof was very dark. Its close stagnated air smelt of old dust and cobwebs because it had not in a dozen years been visited by a broom. This dark and secret place we called our 'Anarchists' Cave.' The aim of Anarchists, I had read, was to emancipate the individual from laws and rules enforced by people quite different from himself and so enable him to be all that he wanted to be; and as the ambition chimed with my own dreams, and was a view not without interest to Gael, I had founded the Edith Road Anarchists. And here in their cave the Anarchists would sit in privy conspiracy, plotting espionage, secret manœuvres, petty treasons, and complete liberation one day.

Today we plumped down on to its bare floor, Gael lifting up carefully her skirt and a petticoat, and sitting, I think, on her drawers. Our heads almost touched the underside of the stairs. And in the darkness she scoffed, 'Well, if that's their idea of a party!'

'It was not whoreson jolly,' I agreed. 'But interesting. The talk had points.'

'It certainly did. Why did she say he was wicked?'

'Because she's a hairy old beast.'

'He's not wicked. He's sweet. I hate Auntie Gloria sometimes.'

'I do always. It's simpler.'

'The only one I like is Auntie Evelyn. She stood up for him. She's easily the decentest, and, what's more important, she's the prettiest.'

'She's not bad, but I'm not all that smitten with her. But then, you see, apart from Uncle Lucy. I don't like anyone very much. Not even you.'

'Is that supposed to be funny?'

'No. Merely the unfortunate truth.'

'You're frightfully witty, aren't you?'

'Yes, I think so.'

'Well, it's a good job that you think so, because no on else does. I love Uncle Lucy and I won't have him called wicked. I love him and I love Mr. Appledore.'

Mr. Appledore was the vicar of our church. He was Gael's latest idol, with the result that she was now much given to prayers at different times of the day. Whenever and wherever possible, in bedroom, playroom, or train, she

33

said what she called her 'Offices', reading them from a tiny black manual entitled *The Garden of the Soul* which Mr. Appledore had given her. For several days she pursued me with the manual and the insistence that I should say something called 'Sext' at noon; but I declined. Now, in our cave, she began to tick off on her fingers the persons she loved. 'Uncle Lucy . . . Mr. Appledore . . . Auntie Flavia, after a fashion . . .'

'Personally,' I interrupted, 'I find it much simpler to love only one person.'

'And Aunt Evelyn, quite a bit. . . . Did you notice that the old beast said something about awful things that came out in court?'

'You bet I did.'

'Do you think he's been in prison?'

'Oh, *no*.' I revolted from this. In my mind I saw the dignity on his figure and face, the quality of his clothes, the courtesy of his manners, the excellence of his French, and found it difficult to think that anyone so obviously a gentleman could be put in prison.

As if she'd read my thought Gael rejoined, 'But they do put gentlemen in prison sometimes. . . . And ladies, too,' she added, delighting to state the astonishing.

'But what could he have done to get into Quod? He couldn't have stolen—he'd never steal—I wouldn't myself —at least not enough to get me into prison. And he couldn't have murdered anybody or he'd have been hung.'

'Oh, I do think it's a dirty shame they won't tell us anything. I asked Auntie Flavia yesterday if I had any real aunts and uncles, and if I was an only child, and as usual she just said, "I'm not *going* to be bothered. You'll know one day," and when I went on she flared up and shouted, "Leave me alone, I tell you! Don't pester me," and she *ran*. Ran away. So what can one do? That's what always happens.'

Yes: what always happened. And these sudden loud rages could momentarily frighten me, turning my cheeks pale and even jumping tears into my eyes; but at the same time their very warmth and bitterness ripened my determination to find out all. 'The Anarchists will have to find out everything,' I said.

'They haven't found out much yet. We still don't know anything about your father and mother, or about mine.'

'For my part,' I said knowingly, 'I'm fast beginning to suspect there never was a Mr. Ilbraham.'

'But you must have had a father of some sort. Me, too.'

'No doubt. But whether your old man's name was Harrington I take leave to question.'

'Well, whether his name was Harrington or not, I know one thing: I know he was a gentleman.'

'Why?'

'Why? Because I *feel* a lady. One just *feels* these things. Don't you?'

'Oh, yes,' I said. I certainly felt a gentleman.

'Sometimes I feel as if my father had been someone *very* distinguished. Oh, it's swinish of them not to tell us. What can we *do*?' She thumped the floor with her fist. 'Do, do, *do*?'

'Well, for a start——' I jumped up and crashed my head against the underside of the stairs. 'Damn and blast! Agony and death. For a start let's go down and try pumping Lizzie and Mrs. Willer.'

'We'll get nothing out of them.' Nevertheless, Gael rose too, carefully evading the roof.

Creeping past the drawing-room, where the Aunts' voices were still a loud tangled miscellany, we did a winged flight down the stairs to the hall; and thence down the basement stairs, steep and narrow, to the kitchen parts. The kitchen was a large clean room whose furniture seemed limited to the black-leaded range, the bare scrubbed table, the wide dresser, and the row of shining dish-covers that reflected our sun-filled area and the momentary sparrows or pedestrians on the pavement. For Gael our kitchen held some alarm because of the black beetles that, on occasion, came walking across its linoleum shamelessly.

This evening Mrs. Willer sat at the table cleaning t¹ : silver with a pink powder, and Lizzie sat by the range in her rocking chair with a newspaper on her lap. Warmth from the range came like a welcoming influence towards us, its breath laden with the smell of roasting beef.

Lizzie. Always I have but to read or hear that name, and I see our Lizzie rocking in her chair before a background which consists of her kitchen range made glossy with blacklead; the steel fender below it shining like swords; and above it the high black shelf holding a parade of upturned saucepans with their handles pointing down at us. From one corner of this shelf dangled a fly-paper speckled like a battlefield with the bodies of flies, mostly dead but some still quick and brandishing their legs in their small mute censure of the universe.

'Now then, you two young imps,' said Mrs. Willer, without looking up from her spoons. 'Thought you were with your aunties.'

'We were hoofed out,' I explained.

'What for? Misbehaving as usual?'

'No. Auntie Gloria was rude about Uncle Lucy and there was a row.' I fiddled with a kitchen knife on the table. 'Gosh, you could kill someone with this.'

'Ah! About Uncle Lucy.' Lizzie nodded, rocking in her chair. It was an 'Ah!' full of thought. They were nods full of meaning. 'And so you came down to worry us?'

'Precisely.'

'Precisely!' Mrs. Willer echoed the pretentious word and held up a spoon to the light. 'That child's a proper comic,' she told the spoon.

'And I'll lay,' Lizzie sighed, 'that you'll want some bread in the fat.'

'Yes, please,' said Gael.

'Oh dear, oh dear. Never a moment's rest.' Lizzie got out of the chair (which went on rocking) and drew the meat-pan from the scorching oven. She cut slices of bread, put them in the sizzling fat, and tossed them on to a plate for us. 'There you are. That'll be sixpence, please.'

Lizzie must have been nearly seventy. Her hair was thin and grey; her face with its lines looked twenty years older than Mrs. Willer's (and indeed was all of that), but in height and girth she was much smaller than her fellow servant. She had been with Auntie Flavia for more than thirty years, and in the Bishop's service before that, so we knew, as we watched her shutting the oven door, that her slight wrinkled body must hold all the secrets of our house. She could have answered all our questions. But she never did, partly out of a real loyalty, partly because she knew that any betrayal must come to her mistress's ears and would mean, at her age, dismissal into penury. A later incident made it clear to us that, not even to her daily companion in this basement, had she done more than hint proudly at things which she knew well and could uncover if she cared.

Sometimes, proud of this secret knowledge, she would steer very close to it, but always she beat away to windward and out to sea before she had quite touched it.

Gael sat herself beside Mrs. Willer and said, 'I'll polish for you, shall I?' The good public relations which would prepare the well for pumping.

'Yes, if you like, dearie. Everything has to be shone when Mr. Lucius is coming.'

Gael glanced quickly at me, because this had slightly opened the door for us. 'He's going to stay this time.'

'Is he, and all? Hammy them fruit knives, please. What else did they talk about up there? I'll lay Miss Primrose never said much. She always seems afraid to be the least bit jolly lest she should say something wrong.'

'It's her pudor,' I said. But this pleasing word was wasted on the company, because I alone had met it. So I tried something else, my own parody on Wordsworth's 'Peter Bell', which I'd learned in 'Repetition' at school. 'Our Primrose by the aunties' side A yellow Primrose did abide, And did do nothing more.'

'Now none of your parts, Master Travers,' said Mrs. Willer, polishing hard. 'If you get any sharper, you'll cut yourself.'

'Gracious, the children of these days!' came from Lizzie's rocking chair.

'What time will he arrive?' Gael insinuated this into Mrs. Willer's ear.

But it was Lizzie who answered. 'Not till late. Very late. And don't start asking me for why, because I don't know. He comes and goes how he likes. As you know.'

The door had opened a little wider.

'And we shall be in bed, I suppose?' Gael lamented.

''Course you will. At ten or eleven all good children are in bed.'

'But I shan't be asleep,' I said. 'How long have you known him, Lizzie?'

'Ever since I first met him.'

'Don't be silly. When was that? Do tell us.'

'Well, if you must know, and to tell the honest truth——'

'Yes?'

'—it was exactly seven days after the week before.'

'Oh, shut *up*! The week before *what*?'

'Before I clapped eyes on him, silly.'

'Oh, you are poisonous, Lizzie. Was it before I was born?'

'Long enough before that unhappy event. And now let's leave it at that. Ask no questions and you'll hear no lies.'

'Before Travers was born, or me?' asked Gael.

'Before either, naturally. Now stop being a Miss Inquisitive.'

'Do you remember us being born, Lizzie?'

'I wasn't there, believe you me.'

'I was born in France,' said Gael proudly.

'I know that.' Lizzie rocked the knowledge with her in her chair.

'And I in Italy,' I acclaimed, not to be outdone by Gael. 'In Florence.'

'That's right.'

At this point Gael pushed the door wide open. 'I sometimes think that Travers and I are really brother and sister.'

'Don't be ridiculous. How could that be?'

'Why not?'

'Well . . .' Her little black eyes looked at us, and in them one could see that sharp prurience often to be noticed

38

in old and unwed women when, guiltily but pleasantly, they touch the subject of sex. 'You're scarcely eight months older than he is.'

'What difference does that make?' I asked. ' I don't see.' And this was true. Queen Victoria was dead; her sun was some time set; but she still reigned over our street in a kind of long evening afterglow; and that reign had denied all such knowledge to me. For a year I had been studying Latin and Greek within the red academic walls of the great school at the end of the road, but I had learned nothing there that would lead me to Lizzie's meaning.

'Well, if you don't see, you don't. Besides, aren't your names quite different? Ilbraham. Harrington.'

'Yes. And who was Mr. Ilbraham?'

'That's something I've never been told, so don't ask me.' In a forgetful moment, rocking there, she repeated this sentence, varying a word. 'That's *one* thing I've never been told.' The obvious implication was that she'd been told most other things, and, perceiving this, she said hastily, 'If you want to know these things ask your auntie. It's not my place to go answering questions.'

'Do you like Uncle Lucy?'

'Yes, of course I do. So far as I ever see him.'

'I'll tell you who doesn't like him.'

'Who, Master Know-all?'

'Old Sycorax, Brendaheim's dam.'

But this wonderful series of syllables was quite wasted, for Lizzie said only, 'What *is* the child talking about? Is he swearing?'

'*I* think,' declared Mrs. Willer, pausing in her cleaning as for an important announcement, 'that Mr. Grenville's the perfect gentleman.'

'He's all of that,' agreed Lizzie behind lips nearly closed, as if there were a hidden significance in her words.

'He was in Parliament once,' Gael reminded her proudly.

'I believe he was. For a little.'

'Who was?' asked Mrs. Willer, interested. 'Mr. Grenville? No one ever told me that.'

'It was all of twenty-five years ago,' said Lizzie, with her head down.

'Well, I never! Mr. Grenville in Parliament!'

'Mr. Grenville—ha!' For the hundredth part of a second her 'ha!' laid a doubt upon the name. That was the nearest she steered this evening towards the dangerous rocks of truth, and instantly she put the helm over and veered away from them. 'Yes, he was in Parliament for a little. Or so I've heard.'

§

I lay in bed in my attic room, awake. I could not sleep for listening. The house was quiet; the maids were in bed, too, because it was long after ten, and in our sober and orderly street ten was the normal end to an adult's day. But down in the dining-room on the ground floor I knew that Auntie Flavia sat listening, too. Listening for the hooves and jingle of a hansom cab or for the grating tyres of a four-wheeler. I heard no sound of her, but I could see her there, perhaps sewing, perhaps reading, but ever and anon lifting her head to hear. The summer night was cold, and she would be sitting between table and fire. And at any sound on the metalled road she would put down sewing or book and go to the window.

I lay with eyes open staring at the blue jewel of gas-light, which I was allowed because, despite my love of pompous jesting, I was a nervous child, subject to night fears and dark dreams, to calling out in my sleep and even, at one time, to sleep-walking. Maybe this nervousness was partly caused by my perception that Auntie Flavia, try as she might, couldn't feel for me what she felt for Gael and thus I had a buried sense of lovelessness, up there in my large attic, unless Uncle Lucy was in the house. I know I was fully happy once he had come through our front door. For both of us, Gael and me, his visits were an avatar, a visitation of glory. Glory came into the house with him. If there was any hope of his arriving before our bedtime we would watch and watch from our Playroom window for the first sign of the four-wheeler, or the hansom, that might hold him within. Even on this birthday occasion, though we'd been told he'd be very late, we watched from the window in hope, till it was time to go to bed.

Here was a sound. Coming this way. Harness bells and soft purring wheels. A hansom. I sprang from bed and ran on bare feet to the window. A thin grey mist, strange for a summer night, hung in the street, and each of the gas-lamps, in its vaporous tissue made a large yellow asterisk like the halo of a saint in our grey and ungodly world. Here and there in the houses opposite a window showed a glow behind a Venetian blind, but for the most part the ranked houses stood there with all eyes shut, asleep on their feet. Only at the far end was there a yellow radiance of life, for there the busy North End Road ran by, and some of its shops, and all of its taverns, were still open.

The hansom went purling past to the grey stillness at the road's other end, and I, chilled, went quickly back to bed.

In its grateful warmth I almost slept, but now—another cab, and I was out and shot against my window pane like a pea from a pea-shooter.

A four-wheeler this time, with two portly gladstone bags on top. And beside it a ragged man padding—padding along the empty pavement with a flapping of feet; a man who, anywhere between Victoria and West Kensington, had seen those bags and come running in company with the horse to earn a sixpence by helping to lift them down.

The cab bent towards our pavement and stopped before our door, at which the bony horse stood nodding his head as in dubious approval. Now I had to stand on a chair to see clearly from my dormer window. Out stepped the tall, familiar, beloved figure. By the light of the cab lamps I saw that he was wearing his long black overcoat with astrakhan collar and the tall black felt hat that always looked like a cross between a top-hat and a bowler. I saw him pay both cabman and ragged runner—generously, it was plain, because they were being effusive with their good nights and good wishes. As far as I remember, the ragged man added his blessing.

Auntie Flavia must have been at her window as soon as I was, because our front door opened before these amiable exchanges concluded.

Uncle Lucy came up the steps and under the pillared portico; and straightway I left my window and ran down one flight—down the next—and the next—till I was just above the hall and could see and hear them both.

The black-and-white-tiled floor of the hall, uncarpeted, seemed to send up its bare porcelain coldness to me as I leaned over the banisters in my nightshirt. The hanging gas lantern, with its squares of leaded and stained glass, threw coloured lozenges on the walls, and by its pale light I saw the tall figure holding its hat before it like an open guide-book lately consulted. He bowed to his hostess and presented her with a bouquet of roses and carnations in a large cone of white paper. When he'd put a gentle kiss on her brow, he unbuttoned the long coat so that I saw its lining of heavy brown fur.

'Oh, what lovely flowers!' Auntie Flavia spoke low in her emotion. The voice which had been so harshly raised against Gloria was now the softest caressing breath. 'But they're beautiful!'

'Just a small thank-you in advance. They may even be premature. But I seemed to remember that no one in the world ever fussed over anyone as you do. Especially when they're tired and melancholy and slightly suicidal.'

'But how late you are, *chéri*. So late.'

'I had dinner with Jack Fanshawe at the Ambassadors'.'

'At the Ambassadors'! But, *Marcus*'—not for years did I realize why she sometimes varied the nickname Lucius with this of Marcus—'did no one recognize you?'

'After twenty-five years? No, my dear. I think not. After a quarter of a century, who remembers? A new generation has arisen which knew not Joseph. Besides, look at my white hairs.'

I looked and saw them, silver in the lantern's light.

'Yes, but look at *you*.' She was gazing with a teasing

42

smile at the white moustache and imperial. 'Did anybody ever look like you?'

'An old ruin, my dear, like hundreds you can see in workhouse or asylum.'

'Well, a most recognizable ruin. Like Glastonbury, perhaps, where you and she were so happy once.'

'More like Stonehenge. In its great antiquity. She was with me there, too, once upon a time, my poor lost Lottie.'

' Yes, poor Lottie . . .'

'She was beautiful.'

'And so were you. Evelyn says you were like a Viking.'

'Too kind. Too kind. Well, this is a Viking raid. And this time you will not be able to expel me so quickly.'

'But how wonderful! How long, how long, will you stay?'

'I do not know. I feel I must be fussed over properly for a while. It is clear that I begin to break up. I now talk to myself aloud. I walk along the road doing it, and people turn round. In the Champs Elysées.'

'That's nothing. We all do that sometimes.'

'Do we?' He seemed relieved.

She was helping him off with the coat. 'But have you come to the Arctic that you wear this coat? It is summer. Are we Esquimaux that you come dressed like this?'

'My dear, the silence of your country, if not the cold, is almost Arctic. I have come to the Silent Island. After the Gare du Nord and Boulogne Harbour, oh, the silence! The silence of Folkestone and Victoria and the Coffee Room at the Ambassadors'. Your cold and quiet island.'

'Yours, too.'

'Hardly any more.'

'Now, enough of that. Come. I have whisky and sandwiches and a fire for you here.'

They disappeared into the dining-room and I rushed happily back to my bed, there to delight in thoughts of tomorrow and to sleep at last in untroubled peace.

CHAPTER THREE

UNCLE LUCY was sleeping late in the room always reserved for him. It was nine, and we were finishing breakfast, when we heard his tread upon the stairs. He appeared in the doorway and bowed to us seated at the table. 'I am most deplorably late and I apologize unreservedly. Miss Gael, you will pardon me, I trust. And perhaps you will intercede for me with your kind auntie.' In his hand were two small brown-paper parcels of which he seemed ashamed, since he held them a little way behind him.

Gael rushed and flung her arms around him, at which he exclaimed (for she'd arrived with something of a crash) 'Damn.' Then stroked her hair and said, 'Thank you. A charming child.'

She pranced up and down before him, crying, 'Uncle Lucy. Uncle Lucy. Uncle Lucy,' to which he retorted, 'Not at all. Not at all'—not denying his identity but demurring at the approval implicit in her ecstasies. He stooped and kissed her brow.

'Sir Travers,' he said to me over the top of her head. I had run behind her but, unable to commit anything so unmasculine as a hug, I just stood there, dissatisfied and jealous, in this secondary position. He would sometimes call me 'Sir Travers,' only anticipating, as he put it, the honour which a grateful nation would certainly accord me in the future. 'How do you do, Sir Travers?' He only bowed over me as we shook hands, but there was a pressure of love in his grasp, and in mine, too, even more in mine, responding. 'Gracious mercy, how tall! What are you now? Eighteen?'

He looked down on me, smiling. His eyes were an Arctic blue, and the more Arctic, perhaps, because of the snowy white eyebrows above and the curly white moustache and imperial below. His face was long and lean, with strong-boned features, at the top of the long strong-boned body. In these last years the long body stooped a little; he liked to deny this indignantly, but if forced to agree at last, he would say, 'Well, perhaps . . . perhaps. Have I not borne the burden of existence for seventy-seven years and pondered deeply on it all the time, with a drooping head?'

'I will ring for your bacon and eggs,' said Auntie Flavia.

'No, no,' he protested, but approached the table notwithstanding. 'Let me incommode no one. A cup of coffee . . . a crust . . . perhaps a pat of butter.'

'Did you sleep well, Lucius?'

'So far as any man can in a universal silence.'

He sat in his place, put the two parcels on the floor beside him, and spread his napkin on his knees. But at that moment Mrs. Willer came in bearing a hot-water plate on a tray, and at once, laying the napkin aside, he rose and bowed to her. Always if he passed Lizzie or Mrs. Willer in Edith Road he raised his hat to her as convincingly as if she were a princess of the Royal House; and to anyone remarking on this he liked to quote Saint-Simon's statement that Louis XIV, the *Grand Monarque*, passed no woman, not even a housemaid, without uncovering for her. 'How are you, Mrs. Willer? It is good to see you again.' It was he who insisted that we must always give Mrs. Willer her surname and title, in view of her widowhood and her girth. 'You keep well, I trust?'

'Yes, sir. Thank you, sir.'

'I . . .' He sat down again. 'I have brought you a small gift.' He produced one of the parcels, shyly, from the floor.

'Oh, *sir!*'

'It is nothing, nothing. Just a trumpery piece of silk. From the Rue de Rivoli.'

'From Paris, sir?'

'Yes . . . yes . . . the Rue de Rivoli is in Paris.'

'Oh, thank you, sir.'

'There is a little something for Miss Lizzie, too. A mere nothing. A few cambric handkerchiefs from the Rue

45

de la Paix. Perhaps you will do me the kindness of taking them down to her.'

'Oh, she *will* be pleased. If you'll just gimmy the parcel. . . . It *is* good of you, sir.'

'Not at all. Not at all.' He brushed a knuckle under the white moustaches, this way and that, to left and right. 'In each parcel there is a small bottle containing a soupçon of liqueur. Crême de Moka, I think, and Huile de Rose. They may help you through the labours of another day.'

'Oh, thank you indeed, sir.' She uncovered the hot-water plate before him.

'Too kind. Too kind,' he said, looking down on the bacon and eggs.

Mrs. Willer retired, and he had begun with knife and fork when Gael cried out, 'Oh, but you haven't said Grace!'

'What?' He rested on knife and fork. 'Grace? Oh, yes, Grace—to be sure, yes, I forget everything these days. Grace certainly.' And he bent his head over the bacon and eggs and said, 'Bless, O Lord, these Thy great gifts of which we in our extreme unworthiness are about to partake. Amen.' A couple of mouthfuls and he announced, 'For your auntie there was a small gift which I gave her last night. For two mere children naturally there is nothing.'

And naturally we disbelieved this.

'At least I don't think there is. After I have taken some sustenance we will go and look.'

While he took his sustenance Gael talked with him merrily and impudently. I sat gazing at him as a Hindu might sit in meditation before an image of Brahma, the source and goal of all things.

When he had done, and brushed the napkin under his moustaches this way and that, he said, 'Yesterday was, I think, your kind auntie's birthday. A great occasion, surely, and one which should be celebrated with some seriousness. You will wish to attend a matinée with me, I take it, and have tea and an ice or two afterwards.'

'Oh, yes, yes!' we cried. And both of us added, 'Can it be the Hippodrome?'

'The Hippodrome?' he teased. 'Where is that?'

'You know. You know. You took us there last time.'

'The Hippodrome . . .?' He appeared to be probing deep in memory. 'Hippodrome . . .? Ah, yes, I remember something.'

In those days it was only about five years since the London Hippodrome had risen in terracotta magnificence at a corner of Cranbourn Street. It still justified its name. and fulfilled its founder's intentions, by providing circus shows and animal acts on its sawdust ring between stage and auditorium. The ring could be transformed into a lake by flooding it with water from the Cranbourn stream which flowed then—and still does, they tell me—under the Hippodrome stage. Then there were 'water shows,' such as when a one-legged diver plunged from the glittering roof into the lake, or when a whole hunt in pink jackets, and with hounds belling, galloped through the water from the stage to an alleyway through the auditorium. Beneath the auditorium, as in the Colosseum at Rome, were cages for the circus animals: lions, tigers, polar bears, and seals— to say nothing of snakes and anacondas.

'No, not the Hippodrome,' said Uncle Lucy. 'Your kind auntie will hardly be amused by a Boxing Kangaroo. Or the Bucking Donkey.'

'Oh, but their kind auntie won't be able to go,' bewailed Auntie Flavia, who so loved a 'theatre outing' and a 'tea outing.' 'She has promised to decorate the church for the festival.'

'What? Are they celebrating your birthday in church? How right.'

'No, don't be absurd. It's our Patronal Festival. Oh dear . . . what a shame. I can't possibly come.'

'Then I shall have the burden of these children alone?'

'I'm afraid so. Oh dear. . . . And it's ages since I've been to a theatre. I never seem to go now. But I can't —I mustn't—I promised Mr. Appledore—no, I can't, I can't.'

The relief, the delight! Within me I cried, 'Oh, hurray!' Put Uncle Lucy, Gael and me together, and that equalled happiness. Add Auntie Flavia, and the sum totalled less.

'Very well. So let it be.' He assumed the expression of a strong man stoically resigned; and he buttered another slice of toast.

'But you must enjoy yourself, too—your first day home.' Auntie Flavia insisted. 'Oh, I *wish* I could have come. It *is* a shame. Personally I love a bucking donkey. But you——'

'What do I matter? It is they who matter now. My life is over.'

'Of course you must go to something you'll enjoy,' cried Gael, and she jumped up and flung her arms around him in a compassionate embrace.

'Lord!' he murmured. 'How like her mother she is.'

'Lucius! Hush!'

'You've got to be happy,' said Gael; and I agreed, though sad to see the Hippodrome receding.

'This Hippodrome it shall be.'

'But won't you be utterly bored after a time?' Gael worried.

'Not wholly. I always enjoy the darkness of a theatre, even when I've ceased to be interested in the stage. One can always sit there in the darkness and commune with one's tormented spirit.'

We'd heard things like this before, so we didn't treat his torments seriously. 'Then it *is* the Hippodrome,' cried Gael, prancing up and down on her toes.

'Yes. But how shall we get there? It is a great distance. By a *voiture de remise*?'

'A *what*?' I demanded, foreseeing some exciting new experience.

'A hired carriage from the livery stables.'

'No, please,' begged Auntie Flavia. 'Gael is always sick in a cab.'

'Yes, that is true. She is fearfully and wonderfully made.'

'You will go like three sensible people on the top of a bus.'

§

And on the top of a bus we went. We wanted to go on one of the motor buses, a few of which could now be seen in the Kensington Road, but Uncle Lucy submitted that it would be safer to be drawn by 'two intelligent horses than by all that fidgety and excitable ironmongery.' So we all sat together on the front seat of a horse-bus. Gael snatched the outside seat; pulled the rainproof apron over her lap, rather for fun than in fear of rain, since there were none but white clouds adrift over London; then rested her elbow on the rail to study the pageant of London running below.

Little comes back to me of that Hippodrome show. I recall Uncle Lucy's horror when I pushed towards my stall in front of Gael. 'Mr. Ilbraham! Really! First the lady. Then the old man. And last of all Mr. Ilbraham, surely.' I remember an astonishing performance by an 'Armless Wonder' who played a violin with his toes, and I see a picture of Uncle Lucy, sitting between us, very still and quite unemotionally, with his gloved hands resting on his stick. Once or twice, so silent he was, I turned to see if, perhaps and alas—for I didn't want him to be unhappy— he really was communing with his tormented spirit, but I saw a firmly disciplined grin beneath his moustaches and decided that all was well. There was a dancing show in the Can-Can style, with a row of girls kicking high their black-stockinged legs, and waving them around in a froth of petticoats, and since ever and again this granted the audience a glimpse of their black suspenders and pink thighs, and since I still didn't want Uncle Lucy to be unhappy, I turned to see if he could approve of this. But his tight-lipped smile was a little wider, and his eyes, besides quietly submitting to amusement, had sometimes a keen prospecting look which drew him forward from the back of his seat. One finger passed a knuckle to left and right under his moustaches, as if to establish contact with the smile; and again I felt confident that his meditations need not disturb me.

At the close of the show, when the house lights went up, I disappointed him again. I failed to aid a lady in front who had draped her jacket over her stall. 'Mr. Ilbraham, what are you about? Help the lady on with her coat.' But this I was too shy to do, and he did it himself, despairingly.

We came out with the throng into Cranbourn Street, and he said, 'Now I take it you will require a cake or two and an ice. Let us find a patisserie. In Piccadilly there will surely be one of a sufficiently high tone to appeal to Miss Gael.'

'Oh, yes, come *on*!' shouted Gael, pulling at his hand.

'*Doucement, doucement!*' he pleaded. 'I am old.'

Along Coventry Street and Piccadilly we went, with his hand lying on my further shoulder, not in search of support, but in affection. I could feel the love there. If Auntie Flavia loved Gael more than me, he partly filled up any gap in my heart by loving us both, but me (as I could but feel) the more. Perhaps in jealousy Gael continued to hold his other hand.

And so we three walked on, through the crowd in Piccadilly. He might assert that life was over for him, but this didn't prevent his eyes from swinging towards every pretty face that approached us, or his head from turning through an arc of twenty or thirty degrees that he might enjoy the sight as long as good manners allowed. He was quite frank about it. 'I love to see them coming along,' he said. 'But you must understand that my interest is mainly aesthetic. Just that and an old man's affectionate tenderness. Nothing more. As the excellent La Bruyère has it, "*C'est une grande difformité dans la nature qu'unvieillard amoureux.*" I merely feel—ah, look at this one with her mamma. Charming. Charming. The mother less so. But oh, my dear boy, don't stare. No, no, *please!* Never stare. Not all are beautiful, of course; not all are like your little companion, Gael. Women should be beautiful—that was the idea—but nowadays there are honourable exceptions. Your Auntie Gloria, for example. That terrible woman.'

'I hate her,' said Gael, currying favour.

'No, no; you must not hate anybody. We are all sinners. And I one of the worst. Ah, this would seem to be a pastrycook's.'

We went into the glittering shop and sat by the plate-glass window fronting the street.

'Here,' he said, 'you can exchange glances with the passers-by like goldfish in a bowl. Pass me the menu, Win.' More often than 'Travers' or 'Mr. Ilbraham' he liked to call me 'Win', from my second name, Winfrith.

He was still consulting the menu when a young slim waitress of dark Mediterranean beauty came to his side.

'Yes, sir?' she inquired.

He looked up from the menu, saw her beauty, and was momentarily incapable of speech. Returning to the peace of the menu, he said, 'Bread and butter, children? No. I take it the answer is No. Certainly not. Some of your excellent cakes, mademoiselle—plenty of them—cream ones, if possible—and ices later. For me? Oh, a cup of tea. No more.'

'Yes, sir. Thank you, sir.'

As she went away he commented, 'Very sweet,' and he watched her elegant movements till they were lost to him behind a service door.

We had eaten three or four of the cakes when a man, passing on the pavement, looked in, saw Uncle Lucy, and abruptly stopped: a man in a brown frock-coat with a forked grey beard that reached almost to the heavy watch-chain on his white waistcoat. He turned about and came into the shop.

'Monsieur Grand'Ville!' So only can I render his delighted exclamation. '*Mon dieu, mon dieu!* Monsieur Grand'Ville! But there is but a week since I see you sitting on the Boulevard des Italiens with a *petit verre.* Is it not so? What is it that you do in England?'

'My sister,' said Uncle Lucy, 'is ill. Very ill indeed. But this is splendid. Sit down and join us. Gael, this is Monsieur Duhamel, who lives near me. In the Avenue de la Grande Armée, is it not, monsieur? Win, pull out

51

Monsieur Duhamel's chair for him! Dear, dear. Come, come. Always look after your guests. Yes, I had a telegram saying she was very ill, so I came post-haste. I have just come from her. . . . From her bedside,' he added to increase the pathos.

'It is not serious, I hope?'

'Well . . .' Uncle Lucy hesitated, as one who would not exaggerate or answer carelessly, but speak the exact truth. 'I think it may be all right. She is better today. But she has given us an anxious time. Congestion of the lung. It is always serious, and of course she is not young —only a year and what?—three months—younger than I am—so it has left her very feeble. But she is being well cared for, and one must just trust. . . . And you, sir: how comes it that you are here?'

'*Les affaires.* I have business over here, as I think you know. I come often, and just now I am glad to come. It is too hot in Paris.'

'You will take tea?'

'No, only a very small cup of coffee. It is necessary that I hurry. Ah, that is a beautiful blonde young lady behind the counter. Her face so grave. *Exquise.* The perfect Anglo-Saxon type, *n'est-ce-pas?* I will sit here, where I can see her. And these young people—who are they?'

'This is Mr. Travers Ilbraham, a little ward of mine. And this is Miss Gael Harrington. Another young ward— to be exact. One of whom I am particularly proud.'

'But, Monsieur Grand'Ville! You collect the wards, is it not?'

'No, sir: they are thrust upon me. And I have only these two, I thank God. But there they are, for better or worse, and since I am staying in my sister's house, not far from where they live, I felt it incumbent upon me to take them out to tea. They like to call me Uncle, but it is an honorary title. Charming children.'

'They are not relatives?'

'Well, no. . . . Ilbraham, this young man's father, was my greatest friend. That is all. He was the same age . . . at the same school—Harrow: you may have heard of it . . . and at the same university—Oxford; New College, Oxford.'

'The same age? Then if you will pardon me, he did well to have this young gentleman, who is not more than thirteen, I think.'

'Oh, . . . *mais, monsieur!* He was not all that old. What was he? In his sixties. In Paris you think nothing of that.'

'And he is dead?'

'Yes . . . yes . . .' He said it very sadly. 'It would be too much to say that he died in my arms, but I was there when he died. Indeed . . . I helped the others to close his eyes. It was a very great blow to me, because I certainly counted him my best friend. But still . . . Ah, well, one must just accept these things . . . just accept . . . Eat up the last of those cakes, children. Come, you can finish those few.'

'And this young lady? She is *un vrai type Anglais, n'est-ce-pas*? Her father is——?'

'I am afraid her father is dead, too. That is how I came by her. Colonel Harrington I did not know so well. He—but here is your coffee, sir.' He had to pause in his story while he studied the beautiful dark waitress laying the coffee on the table and walking gracefully away. As well that he paused, for M. Duhamel, having also perceived the waitress, was not available for uninterrupted listening, till she was gone from sight. 'The Colonel was a much younger man than Ilbraham—very much younger—and—er—he was killed in our recent war with the Boers.'

'So?'

'Yes, he fell in one of General French's attempts to relieve Kimberley. At Magersfontein, I think. But there: I suppose these battles are of interest only to us. And they are all over now. That the Colonel died fighting bravely, I am sure.'

'And her name is Gail, you say?'

'Gael. With an "e." Her mother was Scotch. One of the famous Clan MacGuffrie. They come from Inverness-shire—no, to be exact, I suppose it's really Ross and Cromarty. Yes, Ross and Cromarty.'

'Golly!' whispered Gael.

In that Piccadilly tea-shop never could two people have listened with more open-mouthed interest. That Gael's father was a colonel and had died in war but five years ago was something we had never heard. Nor did it seem very likely. For Gael would have been nine years old then, and surely they would have seen something of each other. And my father his greatest friend at school and university? Could it be true? . . . But that sick sister. And her home near ours. And Harrow, when we knew he'd been at Eton. And New College, Oxford, when we knew he'd been at King's College, Cambridge. We continued to listen, eating or gaping.

'Ilbraham and I were quite inseparable,' he was saying. 'We were engaged in the same business for a while. Here are your ices, children. . . . Yes . . . well——' The waitress was now gone—'I couldn't know Colonel Harrington so intimately because he was so often away on his military duties. Is your coffee as you like it, monsieur?'

'Perfect. And Madame Ilbraham, the boy's mother? She must have been much younger?'

'Yes . . . she was young.' Do I imagine it now, or did his voice, as he said this, lose its ease, and all his lies their fluency? I remember that he looked down upon the table-cloth and fingered a crumb and put it away in an ash-tray. 'Quite young.'

'And she is dead too?'

'Yes . . . yes . . . she is dead. Dead. . . . Queens have died young and fair.'

So sadly did he say this that not even the inquisitive M. Duhamel cared to question him further. Instead he glanced with compassion at Uncle Lucy over the top of his cup, and laid the cup down, as if it were the symbol of a subject that must be abandoned. One finger forced a path through the grey scrub of his beard; finger and thumb played with a sheaf of it, meditatively, while he turned and glanced at me; and then he fell to speaking with Uncle Lucy of people and places in Paris unknown to us. This, I think, was the first occasion on which I felt, as I ate my ice and listened, a slight but real sadness that all the life of one I loved so well lay hidden in mists from me, whether it was in the streets of Paris with all the people he met there, or down the long road of his past, which stretched backward into unimaginable years and was peopled for me with nothing but spectres, silent, indistinct, nameless, and losing more and more definition as they faded into the farthest haze. But the sadness perished in the taste of the ice.

Not many minutes later M. Duhamel, having finished his coffee, looked out of the great window at the bright summer evening. '*Qu'il fait bon*,' he said. 'There is nothing like your London in this early evening light. For an hour she is beautiful as Paris. She is enchanted, is it not? I go. I go.' He rose and bowed and, after a last look at the beautiful grave face behind the counter, took his long beard out into Piccadilly and out of our lives. Gael waved to him through the window, bowed unconsciously as he bowed to her, and immediately turned to Uncle Lucy. 'Was my father really a colonel and killed in the Boer War?'

'Did I say that?'

'Yes, of course you did.'

'Well, no. That was a little entertainment to go with his coffee. You mustn't mind what I said. I do not know the man well and found his questions impertinent. The situation was palpable. At fourteen and a half you are on the point of becoming a beautiful woman, Gael, and that's enough to unsettle any Frenchman. He needed to know who and what you were, even if he'd no hope of anything else to help him; so I gave him a little to quiet his nerves.'

This was an explanation so thoroughly satisfying to Gael that she cared not to disturb it with another word; and it was I who spoke next. 'Then wasn't it true about *my* father?'

'What did I say about him?'

'That he was at the same school and the same college,' Gael thrust in, though the subject was mine. 'And that you were inseparable and in business together.'

'Yes . . . well . . . there were elements of truth in that.'

'And my mother was Scotch.'

'Did I say that? No, I don't think that was true.'

'Oh, do tell us more,' I begged.

'Yes, tell us more.'

'No, my dears. One day . . . one day.'

'Mr. Ilbraham married Travers' mother, did he?'

'Naturally. How else. . . .'

'And what was her name? Auntie Flavia will never tell us. She only gets in a paddy if we ask.'

'No . . . please . . . you must not worry me either. I am too old. It was a very sad matter for me—and for your kind auntie. Try not to worry her about it. One must always be kind. Another ice, each of you? Yes, I think so. Certainly. Waitress!'

Two more ices we had, each of us; but that was all we could manage, though he pressed us to more. We shook our heads.

'Not if you had some more tea to wash their predecessors down?'

'No.' A firm answer from both.

'Or perhaps a hot buttered scone to push them well down?'

'No.' I rather wished he'd stop.

'All right then. The debate is over. Come. Who goes home?'

We had risen to go, and I was two steps from the table, when Gael exclaimed, 'Gosh! We never said Grace.'

And at once she bowed her head over the dirty cups and plates and moved her lips rapidly. Uncle Lucy obliged by bowing his head and closing his eyes for a suitable space. I, less devout than either, just watched them, and was glad when we all got out of the shop.

'Where now?' asked Uncle Lucy in the brightness and bustle of Piccadilly. 'Let us go by St. James's Street and Pall Mall to the Park.'

'Yes, let's,' cried Gael, seizing his hand.

'And we will go home by the District Railway. It is useless to take a four-wheeler if Gael is always sick in one.

And after cream and ices she might . . . yes, a gentle walk in the evening air is probably what is best.'

He lit a cigar, passed it to and fro beneath his nostrils to enjoy its aroma, and, placing it between his lips, was equipped for the walk. We crossed the road; and on the pavement of St. James's Street his hand passed along my back and found my shoulder. We walked towards the old grey battlemented palace, passing the famous clubs. He was looking up at these—at the Devonshire and White's, at Boodle's and Brooks's and The Thatched House; and all the way he was silent, drawing at his cigar. Sometimes he sighed.

We turned left into Pall Mall and passed the Oxford and Cambridge, the Junior Carlton and the Reform. And i was on the pavement outside the dark Italian palace of the Reform that he slowed his pace so as to look up at its long range of windows all the way. Then the Travellers' and the Athenæum, and he looked at both of these too, silently.

Round by the Athenæum we turned into Waterloo Place and went down the Duke of York's Steps to the Mall. Not a word did he say, as we passed the Horse Guards and the Treasury, and Gael and I, not insensitive to his new sadness, kept quiet, too. Up the steps into Downing Street, and he looked long at No. 10, turning his head to see the last of it; and I, wondering, looked up at him and saw on his lips a small smile. It might have been a smile of acceptance and resignation.

Crossing Whitehall, we came to the corner of Parliament Street.

We had delayed long in the tea-shop, and it would be but an hour before the sun went down. The sky, this July evening, was a blue dome of light with a froth of high clouds at side and zenith and a lavendar glow at its rim. The slanted shadows lay long on the roadway, and the parting sun, its bright sorcerer's eye trained on the Houses of Parliament, laid an enchantment on their crocketed stones and put a ghostly lamp in each of the windows that looked its way.

In this idealising light of a London evening the towers and spires of Parliament stood aloof and dreaming, and they stopped Uncle Lucy in his slow, sad walk.

He came to a complete halt, with one arm along my shoulder and his other hand held in Gael's. And there we stood like a group of statuary at the corner of Parliament Street and Bridge Street. He was looking past the old Indian bean tree to the windows of the Ministers' rooms and beyond these in imagination, as I must believe, to the windows of the House of Commons and the Star Chamber Court. We stood there at gaze for a whole minute, and I felt his fingers gripping and ungripping my shoulder, spasmodically and unconsciously.

'That is New Palace Yard,' he said, 'and those are the Ministers' rooms.'

'You were in Parliament once, weren't you?' said Gael.

'For a while,' he answered, still gazing at those windows. 'Long ago. Come, we must go home now.'

§

In the swaying Underground train between Westminster and West Kensington I began to suspect that it was not Gael but I who was going to be sick. The train bestirred those cakes and ices into some dissatisfied mixture that beat on its prison cell demanding escape. I was shocked at this development and loth that Gael, the one usually teased for this weakness, should have the laugh of me. I longed to get home before the climax so that I could hide my shame behind a bolted door.

I turned my face from Gael to the window, but the switchbacking pipes along the tunnel walls and the clouding steam and stinking black smoke bade fair to expedite the climax, so I turned again and looked with caution at Uncle Lucy, but he was consulting his evening papers, bought at Westminster, and one was a pink paper and the other a green one, so I had to look away. Nor was the smoke of his cigar any help.

Each new station brought hope of survival—Sloane

Square, South Kensington, Gloucester Road—I might yet be saved—but at West Kensington the act of stepping down from the carriage was too great a disturbance and I voided all—no, not all, but much—on the platform before a stream of hated citizens hurrying home.

Uncle Lucy looked at the mess and said, 'What a waste;' then patted my head, with a 'Poor Win. Poor dear. Do it thoroughly while you're about it. Always remember that what's worth doing at all is worth doing well.'

'It's nothing,' I said, as one who would deny even feeling sick.

'No,' he agreed. *'Ce n'est rien.'*

Gael walked quickly on, hoping that none of the citizens would know of her association with Uncle Lucy and me.

I now felt delightfully better and ready for the walk home, but on these occasions it is not one's heart or will that is master of the hour, but one's alimentary canal; it plays cat-and-mouse with one's happiness, setting it free for a little while and then striking again; and, a minute later, half-way up the platform stairs, I stopped and stood menacingly still.

'Oh, not again!' pleaded Gael.

But the issue was not with me. I was but a passive channel. The predetermined fulfilled itself, promptly.

After this, however, I felt splendid again; it was as if righteousness and peace had kissed each other, and I walked in tranquillity up Edith Road, only wishing that Gael would not keep on turning to look at me.

At home I was put to bed and told to lie still, which I was glad to do because I did not feel sure that there might not be a third instalment to this tale.

Uncle Lucy, having delivered the casualty at the front door to Mrs. Willer, saying, 'Look what I've done,' went straight back to the shops in the North End Road and came home with two syphons, two lemons, and a bottle of acid drops. These he brought to my bedside and after mixing me a lemon squash which he declared to be 'always the best thing to sweeten the offended entrails; the soft answer that turneth away wrath,' he asked, 'Would there be anything else you require in your great sickness?'

'Only a pencil and paper,' I said, 'so that I can make my will.'

'That is an idea, certainly,' he answered without a smile, for his brand of humour was full brother to mine. Its elder brother, perhaps. 'An excellent idea, but I surmise you will last till the morning when we can send for the attorney.' He left my bedside for a moment to turn down the gas flame so that from being a butterfly's wings it became no more than a shining bead of blue and mauve. Then, coming back, he laid his hand on my brow and advised, 'Now rest. Sleep if you can. You have nothing to worry about, for the grievous fault was mine.'

§

That Uncle Lucy was fond of Auntie Flavia I knew from the gifts he brought her and the 'my dears' he addressed to her, but I could also see that he, a man of moods and much addicted to brooding, was often driven to escape from her talk; for she, like all the Middian Girls except the diffident Primrose, was a torrential talker. It may be that it was this gay chatter which drove him from our house that night, but I am inclined to think (I shall never know) that it was one of those little quarrels or 'rows' that were not uncommon between them. The towers and many-windowed façade of the Houses of Parliament had summoned him to a mood of melancholy and it could be that while he was thus possessed Auntie Flavia had said an unsuitable thing. For whenever she 'said the wrong thing' (her own description of any such tactical failure) he would go into a silence out of which, quite often, he could not drag himself for days. And tonight, rather suddenly, all voices ceased downstairs in our house. Silence; a strange silence. And not long afterwards I heard his footsteps in our tiled hall, slow like those of a saddened thinker. The front door shut behind him; and the steps went along the pavement—I know not where. There had been no talk of any social engagement; he had no friends in our neighbourhood; and I am persuaded that he walked the streets alone, wandering perhaps up the Kensington Road towards the Palace and the Gardens, with his stick dangling behind his back.

Always, whether happy or hurt, he liked to walk the streets alone.

I was wakeful after my sickness—indeed, as I have told you, I was often an odd, uneasy sleeper. In bed in the dark my hearing was quickened like a blind man's so that I could hear a mouse in the wainscot far below after all the household were abed, or a crack of some cupboard door, two floors down, which jumped my heart out of its rest and set it hammering lest that creak were the tread of an intruder on the stairs. And tonight I simply did not want to sleep till I knew he was back in the house, making it safe for happiness again. Auntie Flavia came up to her bedroom and shut her door, perhaps because she was in temporary disgrace, and miserable, and dared not sit up for him. All had been quiet for a long hour when I heard his key turn in the front door. The door closed gently, but not so gently that I didn't hear the latch click.

He came up the stairs to his room beneath me, very slowly. I could imagine him coming, tread by tread, a hand on the banisters for support; pausing sometimes as if his head were bent with memories and a particular memory had halted him. Into his room he went, but then, as if remembering his duty to an invalid, he came out and climbed with an exaggerated softness my attic stairs. He crept into my room, high on tiptoe and, reaching my bedside, looked down on my pillowed face. I pretended to be asleep, not wanting him to be unhappy about me. Gently he re-arranged a blanket, and quietly opened the dormer window that my sleep might be healthy. Then he tiptoed out like a trespassing child.

CHAPTER FOUR

ALWAYS on Sunday mornings we had Family Prayers before breakfast. When Uncle Lucy was there he insisted on presiding. This was not wholly insincere because he had a real feeling for Christianity and would have greatly liked to be a more obedient disciple of so noble a religion than his weaknesses had ever permitted, but, all the same, I fancy his sharpest motive was a pleasure in the richness of his voice and in the perfection of emotional expression with which he read the lovely words of Bible and Prayer Book. He loved the words of Bible and Prayer Book as if he had been their father. So this morning he sat himself at the head of the dining-room table with Auntie Flavia on his left and Gael and me on his right; but when Lizzie and Mrs. Willer came in he instantly arose and drew out chairs for them at Auntie Flavia's side and bowed with a grave reverence as if he were the flunkey and they the guests. And why not: at such a moment was he not the servant of the servants of God? Returning to his place he glanced at the card 'Come unto Me' which Mr. Appledore gave to those of his parishioners who wanted to read a passage of Scripture daily. Today's reading came from the Acts of the Apostles and he read it, not only with power, but with some pathos because it chanced that at one point it held something which could blow like a wind on a personal memory.

'Tidings came unto the chief captain of the band that all Jerusalem was in an uproar. ... Then the chief captain came near and took Paul and commanded him to be bound with two chains; and demanded who he was and what he had done. And some cried one thing and some another among the multitude; and when he could not know the certainty for the tumult, he commanded him to be carried into the castle. And when he came upon the stairs so it was that he was borne of the soldiers for the violence of the people. For the multitude of the people followed after, crying, Away with him.'

This line was so dramatic that Uncle Lucy repeated it in sheer appreciation of the drama, though it was not so repeated in the text.

'Away with him.'

Mrs. Willer had never before heard Uncle Lucy taking Prayers, and, for sure, had never heard the Bible read like this, with dramatic pauses and sudden full chargings of the voice, as if it were Shakespeare or 'Dangerous Dan McGrew.' She sat staring in astonishment at the reader. So possessed by wonder was she that she was quite unready to kneel when we all knelt and she remained seated and staring for a second or two before she perceived her mistake and her lonely position, whereupon she muttered 'Oh' and 'Pardon' and promptly flumped down upon her knees. Then murmured, 'Oh, sorry' when she realized she should not have said 'Pardon' in the midst of Prayers.

A heavy-bodied woman, the impact of her genuflexion was so hurried and unrestrained that the floor lodged its protest and Gael giggled, keeping the giggle behind locked lips and sending it down her nose. It came down louder than she wanted and she looked in alarm at Uncle Lucy. But he was too engrossed with his sacred occupation, too inspired by the beautiful prayers, to have heard this unfortunate and secular sound.

Lizzie, of course, had been quite unaffected. Having heard Uncle Lucy in action many times before, she had sat all the while with her scoured hands upon her lap, her eyes down upon them, and her thin, closed lips working in and out and up and down. Lizzie looked indeed as if her thoughts were far away—perhaps with days when she was young and would listen to the saintly Canon Middian reading the Bible in his Cathedral, while Miss Flavia, Miss Gloria and his other daughters sat primly together in the long, echoing, stone-white nave.

The reading done, Auntie Flavia in tears, and all of us on our knees, Uncle Lucy consulted a prayer-card of Mr.

Appledore's, 'The Beauty of Holiness'—consulted it long, and probably with a personal interest; then led us in an Act of Faith, an Act of Adoration and an Act of Contrition with Good Resolutions. After the Lord's Prayer as the just finale, we all rose in our places, bent our heads in a silent Grace (Uncle Lucy's being by no means the briefest) and sat down again, but not before he had bowed to the maids as they retired.

'Mr. Appledore's going to give me some more prayers soon,' said Gael, 'now that I'm fourteen.'

'Our Gael is quite a little saint,' he said, unrolling his napkin.

Gael looked pleased with his statement, but I thought, Good lord! A saint! Good heavens!

'You are coming to church, aren't you?' she demanded of him, to maintain this attractive character.

'Most certainly. Do I not always attend you to church?'

'No, not always. You make excuses sometimes.'

'Not excuses, my child. Explanations.'

'Same thing,' declared Gael.

'It isn't,' I affirmed. In my pedagogic and purist fashion just now I was rejoicing to detect whether statements were precise or not, and it seemed to me that neither Gael nor Auntie Flavia—more especially Auntie Flavia—cared a hoot whether their talk had any nice precision so long as it occupied the air. 'An explanation and an excuse——'

'Oh, you shut up,' advised Gael, and turned back to Uncle Lucy. 'Mr. Appledore's going to let me take a Sunday School class of infants, now that I'm fourteen.'

'My God! Yes, a saint . . . but how terrifying she'll be as a matron.'

'Oh, *no*.' Gael went quite white, so sudden and painful the fall.

'And that reminds me.' He was speaking now to Auntie Flavia. 'That terrible matron, their Auntie Gloria, she's not dead yet?'

'My gracious, no,' laughed Auntie Flavia. 'She's never been more vigorous.'

'And she still goes about like a roaring lion, devouring my character whenever she can?'

'She doesn't love you, I must admit.'

'Oh dear, oh dear! And she's only sixty-one. It'll be years before she dies.'

'Evelyn's always very nice about you. And Arthur, too. He'll never hear a word against you.'

'That's only because he's a Radical in politics, and that old hag's a Tory.'

So there they were again talking together, unmindful of, or indifferent to, the ears and watching eyes of us two children. Auntie Flavia told a lie about Mr. Herbert Cluffe, unworried by the fact that we should know it for a lie. Mr. Herbert Cluffe was a large, fat, well-dressed middle-aged man, high in the Civil Service, who came two or three evenings a week and sat with her in the dining-room. There they talked, and he drank whisky and soda, and she whisky and sparkling lemonade. He had been her chief male friend as long as we could remember and Uncle Lucy knew of his existence well enough, but for some reason or other Auntie Flavia always instructed us never to mention his frequent visits.

The 'Cluffe Man' was a favourite jest of Uncle Lucy's who supposed him to be no more than an old flame of Auntie Flavia's, long ago cast out and now seldom seen. 'Seen anything of Cluffe lately?' he asked.

'No, not for a long time,' she answered, though we sat there knowing that he'd come with flowers and gifts only two days ago on her birthday eve.

'And he's still an old bachelor at fifty?'

'So far as I know. He certainly was when I last saw him.'

'And when was that?'

'Oh . . . months ago. . . .'

'Never a mistress in half a century?'

'Good gracious, no! No, that I find impossible to believe. Bless me, no. Not dear Herbert Cluffe.'

'But, my dear, how has he *managed* all these years? How does he manage now? How do any of these puritanical English gentlemen manage? I do not know. And the

65

whole French continent doesn't know either. I take it he sins quietly and unhappily, here and there. Well, well! And they're all over the place, these sad fellows whose stable was Rugby or Cheltenham or any other English public school. Win's school. A strange, troubled, pensive fauna that proliferates on this island and nowhere else. I find them rather charming in their way. Don't you? And pathetic, because their awful puritan tradition has forbidden them to take other than covertly half the beauty of life. And yet they don't commit suicide!'

'Don't be absurd, Lucius.'

'They just go on dutifully with their work. Splendid . . . *magnifique* . . . *mais ce n'est pas la vie*.' He appeared to think further on this last point for he added, '*Non . . . non . . . ce n'est pas la vie Parisienne*. . . . I always was a stranger in their midst. Though I must hold that it is really they who are exceptional, and not I. They are the result, Win'—he turned to me—'of the blight laid upon this lovely and lively country during the last hundred years by a few grim German monarchs and the excellent Dr. Arnold of Rugby. Once the English were a nation of *bons vivants* loving good eating and fine drinking and, best of all, lovely women——'

'Sssh!' whispered Auntie Flavia. 'Not all this to a child of his age. Poor little sprat.'

'They loved art, Win, and admired intellect, and were unafraid of natural joys. Now they are alarmed by art, ashamed of intellect, and repressed and aloof and silent because they dare not speak the truth about themselves. I like to think that I resisted the blight from the beginning. Perhaps I am the original England—a strange relic of the old merry England which was once on these shores. A kind of Ancient Monument in a state of ruin, like one of those derelict palaces lost in the forests of Yucatan.'

Much of this exuberant outburst, immediately after Prayers on a Sunday morning, I have forgotten, but I do remember that he was suddenly addressing me on the subject of Women—mainly, of course, for Auntie Flavia's entertainment.

'You must begin to watch out, Win. You must look alive. They are all around you and they are dangerous creatures. And quite maddeningly unreasonable. They go all out to make themselves seductive, and then are angry if we are seduced. They say it was we who seduced them.'

'Quiet, Louis! Upon my soul! Remember they are only children.'

'One should not be afraid to speak the truth before children. Be not deceived, my dear Win. All women are Nature's Great Lie. Outwardly they are made to look soft and round and smooth, while within they are as hard as iron, and their judgments and opinions have cutting edges like a tenon saw. The truth of this is revealed when their usefulness to Nature has passed. Consider your Auntie Gloria.'

'I agree with you entirely,' I said. 'Such is my experience.'

He bowed in acknowledgment. 'And bear in mind that they have nothing inside them which, with any precision, can be called conscience——'

'Really! Lucius! Dear!'

'Allow me to finish. They may have somewhere inside them a certain hot-potch of highly adaptable rules, but it's not conscience. It's too mutable and amenable for that. And, anyhow, it's not the real truth of them. Whatever they may pretend—about us men, for example—they are really bored by the virtuous and much prefer the sinners.'

'Undoubtedly,' I said.

'Heavens above and heart alive!' murmured Auntie Flavia. 'I don't know what the world's coming to.'

'Undoubtedly,' he agreed, keeping the talk to the men. 'And furthermore, speaking generally, my dear Win, they alone are responsible for the disgusting snobbery of the world. Men have no great interest in it. They care little whether the fellows they are teamed up with, in work or in play, are aristocratic, middle class, lower middle class, working class——'

'Which are we?' I interrupted, seeing a sudden vision of Edith Road. 'Lower middle class?'

'Good *God*, no!' he cried. 'Oh, no, *please*'; and he recovered but slowly from this suggestion. 'Oh, dear.' He passed for his comfort a knuckle this way and that beneath the white moustaches. 'Lower middle class! My God!'

§

A few minutes later we all rose from the breakfast table for the Sunday Morning Gloom. So I called it, but not Gael, to whom Sunday was as Saturday to me; a day in which she could play the game she loved, which was not cricket in the garden, but worship in a pew. How she loved saying the prayers, singing the hymns (in her fresh young voice), opening her Bible to follow the lessons, and gazing, whenever seemly, at Mr. Appledore.

After breakfast, and before I was violently brushed for church, we had to go up to the Playroom and learn the Collect for the Day and some verses from the Epistle or Gospel. In about half an hour Auntie Flavia would come and 'hear us'—or Uncle Lucy would, and then what might have been weariness and strain became a lark.

Auntie Flavia's religion was of the austerest. She associated only with persons whose lives were untouched by scandal and she held that children should be guided along all the straitest ways that the Church enjoined. Her religion had such a hold on her that it hung superstitions like chains around her—not that she fully believed in all of them, but that she thought it safer to treat them with respect in case they were true. Thus she was perturbed if she saw anything but a Prayer Book lying on a Bible; much as she loved the theatre, she would refuse (sometimes with tears) an invitation to a play on a Friday; and if she spilled salt she flung a pinch of it, over her left shoulder, into the face of the Devil behind her. I think she fully believed in the Devil. Actions to be avoided lest they induced a malevolent response from him included bringing white may into the house, passing someone on the stairs, opening an umbrella in the hall, seeing the new moon through glass,

68

and helping another to salt or drinking his health in water. She was capable of screaming and getting quite angry if she saw we'd done any of these hazardous things.

Always Sunday brought into my life a secret misery which was hardly less than a sick horror. I had to get my top-hat, brush it with a curved brush till its pelt was smoothed out and shining and then walk through the streets to the church door, dreading lest the 'street boys' should come singing behind me, 'Where did you get that hat? . . .'

This walk to church in a shining topper—the memory of it drops my heart even as I write.

How different Gael: she strained like a greyhound in its slip to be on her way to Divine Service. '*Come* on!' she cried this morning when she was ready dressed for the public view, in her yellow frock and a large flopping Leghorn hat which was as much a joy to her as my hat a grief to me. '*Come on, do!*'

'Why this urgency?' Uncle Lucy inquired, rising from his easy chair in the dining-room.

'Because she's in love with Mr. Appledore,' said Auntie Flavia, who, also fully dressed, in black gown, black hat and veil, was drawing on her gloves, while her Prayer Book, Bible, and smelling salts rested on the table. The smelling salts went always to the pew's ledge, with Prayer Book and Bible. These were the days of the Church's pride, and our St. Margaret's would be so crowded on a warm Sunday morning that, as likely as not, some woman would crash down in a faint behind us, much to my interest, though I was forbidden to turn round and look at sidesmen and verger hoisting her off the floor. Then Auntie Flavia, hearing these Samaritan movements, would immediately sniff at her little bottle of ammonium carbonate lest the like should happen to her.

'But—pardon me,' Uncle Lucy pursued. 'How can she be in love with a man four times as old as she?'

Gael provided the answer. 'Because boys are awful. They're so dull and usually at sixteen or seventeen they're hideous. Mr. Appledore is beautiful. So now come on.'

'I see,' said Uncle Lucy. 'I now understand.'

'Come on, Trav. Have you got your Bible?'

'Oh, hell, no!' I mumbled and moved to go and get it, but after a few steps, no one noticing me, I abandoned the mission.

'Have you got yours, Uncle Lucy?'

Uncle Lucy said, No, alas! he no longer possessed one; and she said, 'Well, you can look over mine.'

He bowed in gratitude.

We set out, I with Dread for my companion, and comforting myself with the thought, 'All things pass. . . . All things pass. . . . Everything'll be all right in ten years' time. . . .' But my apprehensions were wasted today because not a soul cast a second glance at the silk hat, and no rude boy came behind, asking where I'd got it. From uneventful roads we stepped into the subfusc silence of the church, Uncle Lucy holding open the door for us with the solemnity of a doorkeeper in the House of the Lord, and then coming humbly behind.

§

It was true that Uncle Lucy was nearly always ready to come to church with us, and for long I wondered why, because his way of life, unlike Auntie Flavia's, was certainly not all that the Church prescribed. Light broke upon me some years ago when I was reading Sir Thomas Browne's *Religio Medici* and came upon words that seemed to paint the very picture of my Uncle Lucy coming into church behind us with his silk hat held before him like a guidebook—or perhaps a Prayer Book—opened at the proper page. 'At my devotion,' wrote old Sir Thomas, 'I love to use the civility of my knee, my hat and hand, with all those outward and sensible motions which may express or promote my invisible devotion. At the sight of a cross or a crucifix I can dispense with my hat. I could never hear the Ave Maria bell without an elevation, and at a solemn procession I have wept abundantly.' In a word Uncle Lucy loved all grave courtesies and stately ceremonial. And to this I would add that he hungered for the perfect in all things and rightly perceived that holiness was the noblest perfection of all. I am sure that he knelt in our church listening to the prayers and wishing he were good.

§

Sunday evening in our house could sometimes take on the quiet grey charm of an old Quaker dress. The house would be still, from attic to basement, because one of the servants would be taking 'the afternoon off' and the other have gone to church, Evening Prayer being the service, in the eyes of our world, which was especially designed for the servants, tradespeople and working classes. The long street outside, from end to end, from the North End Road to the empty towers of St. Paul's School, would be a channel filled with the obligatory Sabbatarian silence. And because Auntie Flavia must not touch her needlework on a Sunday, or we play our evening game of bézique with Uncle Lucy, she would lead us upstairs to the grand piano in the drawing-room and, screwing up the piano stool, sink her broad buttocks on to it.

'Draw the curtains, Gael darling,' she would say as she placed on the music-rack a worn volume of *Hymns Ancient and Modern with Accompanying Tunes* and by its side a flat red volume of *Old Songs of England.*

'Travers, light the two candles.'

This I loved to do, and to see the reflections of their flames rooting deep in the ebony of the piano and their pale radiance falling on the pages of old-fashioned music.

Uncle Lucy would often attend us to the piano; and he did on this day, saying, 'Yes, it will do something to alleviate the melancholy which is with me always, and especially on Sundays. I don't know about you, but with me a Sunday, by one o'clock, seems to have been going on for a villainous long time. Even in Paris on a Sunday the memories of old London Sundays can well up from the deeps and weigh me down by about four in the afternoon.'

Auntie Flavia adjusted her piano stool again, set reading-glasses on her nose and, having persuaded the hymn-book after a third effort to stay open on the rack, leaned forward between the candles to peer at the notes. We three, Uncle Lucy, Gael and I, stood behind her to sing—and to lean forward also should it be necessary to refresh our memory of the words, a contingency which happened to Uncle Lucy more often than to us. She began to play our favourite evening hymn. Taught only as a child by her eldest sister, Constance, she played clumsily, striking the keys with the flats of her middle fingers and the sides of her little fingers. But she hammered out the tune, and we all sang, our accompanist leading us in her high soprano which, though ageing, had some sweet notes still.

I am convinced that Uncle Lucy sang with us, not only to relieve his boredom, but also because his voice was still deep and strong, and only seldom slipped into a crack or ran into a wheeze (for which, when it happened, he apologized). Sometimes, rejoicing in his voice, and ours, he would bend forward to conduct this little choir with both his index fingers, but at other times he stood erect and sang as if to himself, sadly, with his eyes upon the gold brocade curtains which Gael had drawn across the windows.

Beyond those windows the gloaming would be low in Edith Road, and at any minute the lamplighter would be crossing from gas-lamp to gas-lamp, on his humble but god-like task of raising with a single touch of his wand a flower of light where none had been before. 'The day Thou gavest, Lord, is ended'—never can I hear the notes of our opening hymn, but it is Sunday again in Edith Road, and the candles on our piano defend a corner from the en-croaching dark, a corner occupied by the figures, long lost, of Uncle Lucy and Auntie Flavia, with Gael and me as children beside them.

The hymns first, in our reverence for Sunday, and then the old songs. But as a gentle decline from praise and worship to songs of profane love, we sang first 'The Holy City,' and 'Miriam's Song.' These made a great appeal to Uncle Lucy; he knew their words by heart, and his old voice was really splendid as he sang enthusiastically, with head erect and eyes on the far wall, 'Jerusalem, Jerusalem,

lift up thy voice and sing' or 'Sound the loud timbrel
o'er Egypt's dark sea! Jehovah has triumphed—His people
are free!'

Now, having done our duty by Heaven, we felt free for
the songs of love; for 'Early one morning, just as the sun
was rising,' and 'When other lips, and other hearts, Their
tales of love shall tell.' These tender songs Uncle Lucy
sang with much expression, Auntie Flavia with thoughts of
her own and her voice low, and we children quite un-
feelingly. You should have heard Uncle Lucy doing full
justice to the pathos of 'Remember the vows that you made
to your Mary', or 'When I am dead, my dearest, Sing no
sad songs for me.' I have known Auntie Flavia, who wept
so easily, her melting point being low indeed, stop singing
and let her lips quaver, her eyes moisten, and a tear fall
on the piano keys, as he sang gently, bending down to read
forgotten words, while we sang with an innocent harshness
facing all ways because we knew the words well:

> Oft in the stilly night,
>   Ere Slumber's chain has bound me,
> Fond Memory brings the light
>   Of other days around me. . . .

She brushed her eyes with a knuckle; and an unspoken
agreement passed between Uncle Lucy and us children
that we must all show tact and pretend that no one was
weeping anywhere. If she was not perfectly recovered by
the end of the next song, he would either loudly encore
his own performance, or encourage us with prods and
grimaces to demand other favourites; and we obeyed,
calling noisily for 'I dreamt that I dwelt in marble halls'
or 'I'll sing thee songs of Araby.'

'Yes, yes! Araby,' Uncle Lucy cheerfully endorsed, as if
everyone stood on the top of happiness and high above the
vale of tears. 'And then "Scenes that are brightest".'

CHAPTER FIVE

THE other evening, half a century after these events, I went to look at our house in Edith Road. Like many other houses in that long straight road, once so prim and dignified, it was now divided into three or more tenements. The window curtains were different on every floor because they belonged to different households. Our green window-boxes, housing their somewhat under-nourished geraniums and marguerites, were all gone from the sills, and the two lime trees behind the area wall, which had been but sapling babies in our time were now two sturdy youths. I stared at the curtained windows of the kitchen, where Lizzie would sit with her secrets, rocking them proudly in her chair; at those of the dining-room on the entrance floor, where Uncle Lucy would sit after dinner with his long cigar and play bézique or beggar-my-neighbour with us; and at those of the drawing-room above where the aunts would gossip so loudly and dangerously, and we on a Sunday would sing our hymns and songs. Above these were the windows of the Playroom, and I saw in my dream the faces of two children watching, watching, for the four-wheeler or the hansom that would bring Uncle Lucy—and happiness—out of the North End Road.

A working woman, followed by a child, came out of Lizzie's kitchen into the area and emptied some refuse into a bin; ever and again shadowy figures passed across the windows of the Playroom; and while I still loitered there, loth to leave the house and my thoughts, a young couple mounted the eight white steps and entered by just kicking at the communal door which hung unlatched. Then I saw again the black-and-white-tiled floor of our hall, unchanged, if less clean and in places loose. The young couple went up our staircase, bare now because a communal route; and a few moments later they flung open the dormer windows of the attic, once my bedroom and the dim-lit scene of my night fears. They looked out, side by side. Newly-weds, no doubt, and renting the cheapest flat of all.

The door swung to, on its own, slowly, rebuking my curious eyes.

And I amused myself wondering if a house was ever visited by the ghosts of those who were not yet born but would come to it in the far future; or if any of these many tenants of today, as they stood in its dusky tiled hall, or climbed its stairs, ever felt, like a passing breath, some dim suggestion of things that had once happened in it. I couldn't believe they did. The people of the past, with all their ambitions and passions and memories, were gone like ghosts in the sheer brightness of Today. And it seemed, not strange, but sad, that no one in the house today had any knowledge of what the dark passages knew, and the treads of the stairs, and the cave under the stairs.

It is possible they had heard of us, because Uncle Lucy had been a very famous man, and his fame was later revived; but what did they know, for example, of that day when this house, their home, was besieged, invested, on all sides, by reporters, press photographers, and staring crowds; when all the eyes in all the windows of the road were upon it; when night fell around it and still the men of Fleet Street, not to be abashed or turned away, attacked its door with loud knocks at one and two in the morning?

§

It would be far from the truth to suggest that I was unhappy in that house if Uncle Lucy was not there. I was very fairly happy. For nine-tenths of every day my buried insecurity was unconscious or forgotten. It was only after Auntie Flavia had lost her temper with me and shouted at me, or when I was lying in my dark attic room and the house was still, that it forced a few unhealthy weeds above ground. If Auntie Flavia had a low melting point, she had also a low detonating point, and once this was reached, her explosion was a loud, reverberating and continuing business.

75

She would lift her voice and stamp her foot and pace around and shout at me again. Then I would wander away, longing to be alone; and, when alone, I would enter like a prisoner into the innermost cell of myself and there feel a small, rich melancholy and enjoy it. In such a mood I might go wandering about the silent house, up and down the stairs and along the airless passages, gently pushing open doors and hoping to come upon something that was wrong for me to see.

Beyond doubt, at thirteen years old, I could give Auntie Flavia much cause for irritation, being often slack and dilatory and sometimes moody and rebellious, so she felt justified in opening upon me with every gun she'd got (which, I can see does any tired, disappointed, and ageing woman a power of good). It was '*Will* you get dressed;' '*Will* you take some care of your clothes. *Look* at those knickerbockers! How can I afford to be forever buying you new things?' '*Will* you listen when I'm speaking. And don't sulk whenever I say anything to you.' Fury could release her words from all cold inhibitions, and once she cried out at me, with tears in her eyes and voice, 'You're the last person in the world who ought to be rude and ungrateful to me. I've given up my life to you two children—and to you especially. I did more than anyone else saw fit to do. If you only knew, you ought to go down on your bended knees and thank me.'

Only once did she allow herself to say this curious thing because, while she enjoyed an occasional frenzy, she had no desire to be cruel. She could be patently sorry when she'd hurt me. She might bring me sweets then, or go out of her way to do something especially kind.

Besides my slack and loafing ways I had certain childish habits which could chafe her almost to the detonating point. Then it was '*Will* you stop scratching your head' (which I found difficult to stop because I enjoyed it as much as she enjoyed her rages) or '*Will* you stop biting those nails' (which again I found difficult to do, because it seemed to give me peace).

Gael could exasperate her too, but I could see that her angry chidings of Gael were braked down, and muted, by a love that she could not give to me. Some hidden revolt mingled with her desire to be kind to me.

Still, let me not imply that my guardian and I were nearly always face to face on either side of a quarrel. I remember many happy and absorbing hours when she sat with us in the Playroom, sewing or mending, and told us long stories about her beloved father when he was the saintly Canon of Selby St. Alban's, and she and Gloria and Evelyn and Primrose, and the distant Constance, all lived with their parents in an old stone house in the quiet Cathedral Close. They were always known as 'The Canon's five famous daughters.' Famous, because all five girls were handsome and because they were always so high spirited and 'up to terrible pranks', which contrasted amusingly—if a little shockingly—with the sanctity of their father and the sobriety of the Close. They loved to make fun of anything solemn. Sometimes their tricks were so irreverent that the people of the Close called them, affectionately, 'The Canon's five mad daughters'. Constance might be the eldest of them, but it was Gloria who was their leader. 'You would hardly think it now, but she was enormously lively and mischievous then. Primrose too: she was the baby of the family, of course, and perhaps a little over-awed by Gloria and the rest of us, but she was always ready for any new frolic that Gloria might be arranging or any fresh irreverence which we were plotting together to liven up the Close. Whether it was because she was the youngest I don't know, but she had the shrillest laugh of us all. The house was forever echoing with her screams of laughter, and it was one of Father's jokes that Primrose must really "moderate her cacophony, or she'd wake all the dead beneath the floor of the Cathedral, which would be most embarrassing." . . . *Dear* Father!'

It was certainly difficult for us, as we sat listening with fascinated eyes and begging her to go on with her stories, to see this screaming girl in the present bound-up and self absorbed Primrose, but I had no difficulty in seeing Auntie Flavia as one of the good Canon's most frisky and eager daughters. She might be well past fifty but there was something gay and childlike about her still. She loved a 'treat' or a 'jaunt' or 'a little bit of festivity'.   It might be a party, an excursion, or a theatre; and if a theatre, it might be pantomime, serious play, or Wild West Show: no matter. Having no taste, she cared little what the show was, so long as it took place in theatre, hall or circus ring.   Her range was thus unbounded and she would take us, her feet as eager her spirits as high as ours, to see Hamlet played by Irving or a melodrama such as *The Worst Woman in London* at the Lyric Opera House, Hammersmith; and we would enjoy both entertainments, all three of us, equally well.

Nor must I forget that she was always good to me when I was in bed with some illness.   Then she would delight to bring me—and here, alive again, was the old Middian mischief—some surprise gift, slyly disguised, of a book or a puzzle or a set of fretwork tools.   And if I was looking really ill, and lay still and quiet, she would even in her pity, stoop down and kiss me, which she could seldom do at any other time.

CHAPTER SIX

ONE memorable day during that summer visit of the migrant Uncle Lucy, as we all sat at luncheon, he spoke in riddles to Auntie Flavia. Somewhere in the riddles, and in a careless moment, he spoke the name 'Lottie', which I'd caught on his lips once before. The meal over, he lit his long cigar, passed it under his nostrils to savour its fragrance, and said 'Come' to Auntie Flavia. Together they went out into the half-darkness of the hall and stood there by the stairs' foot, talking secretly. Then suddenly he called out, 'Chaps!'—he liked to call us 'Chaps', though one was a girl—'Get your cricket stumps. We're going for a long drive to Putney Heath. Your kind auntie and I have something we want to see there, and you can play while we are about our business.'

'Oh, good-oh!' cried Gael, jigging up and down on her toes. 'But what are you going to see?'

'Never you mind, madam. That's no business of yours.'

'When do we start? When do we start?'

'We start as soon as we can obtain a conveyance.'

'Travers,' said Auntie Flavia, 'would you like to nip along to the Livery Stables and order a fly.'

Usually my answer to this frequent query of hers, 'Would you like to nip along to the grocer's' or 'the dairy' or 'the draper's' was 'As a matter of fact, there is nothing I should like less, but in my general amiability I will consent to do so.' Today, however, excitement obstructing humour, I said only, and crudely, 'Not half I won't!' and was gone from our house with the wings of Mercury on my feet.

The fly, a one-horse open carriage, was soon against the kerb before our house, and we were getting into it. All four could have sat inside, two facing two, but by consent of the driver, which Uncle Lucy insisted that I must first bespeak in the most courteous terms, I sat on his box-seat and shared his heavy blue rug with him.

We went spanking off, along Edith Road and round the red walls of my school, and along Hammersmith Road towards the Suspension Bridge and the river. Over the river, which smote us with a smell of mud and the sea, and then we ambled along between rows of clean little cosy homes; row upon straight row of them—then round by Ranelagh Club, and we were on the first of the commons. In the walled and leafy Roehampton Lane it really seemed that the country was embracing us and that Roehampton on its hill was a village set among wide green landscapes. The afternoon was grey but heavily warm, and when the Lane, after passing the Jesuit College, began to rise so that the old horse slowed its steps, Uncle Lucy immediately suggested that it would be a nice courtesy to this, our humble brother, who was drawing us so excellently, if we all alighted and relieved him of our weight. But the coachman, a merry fellow, turned his ruddy and well-weathered face round towards us and declared that the horse was extremely sensitive and would be aggrieved if we hinted that he couldn't pull us up Roehampton's low hill. 'Like me,' he said, 'he don't like people noticing his age. The young gentleman up here has already hurt his feelings by passing remarks about the way he uses his feet.'

Uncle Lucy perceived at once a humourist of his own metal and responded in the same coin. Without a smile, but rather with an expression of shocked disapproval, mingled with compassion, he said, 'Oh, no, Win. Surely not. "Be ye not like to horse and mule which have no understanding",' which wasn't very appropriate but was the only quotation he could think of, and at least mentioned a horse. 'There's no nobler animal, Win, than a horse. One of my best friends'—he added this rather wistfully—'was a horse.'

'The young gentleman said he swung his feet rather like the young lady when she's running.'

'Oh, what *lies*!' shouted Gael, looking up suddenly from her seat.

'Oh no, Mr. Driver. Not Mr. Win. He wouldn't hurt anyone's feelings, and certainly not one who's so kind as to drag us up this hill.'

'Mind you,' consented the driver, giving the horse a friendly flick with his whip, at which the animal capered, 'I'm not saying he isn't a trifle cow-hocked, but I wouldn't say it in his presence.   No.'

'You've just done so,' I triumphed, with all a schoolboy's imperception that the obvious is never witty.

'Ah, but he knows I only do it in fun,' said the driver and tickled the horse's flank again.   The animal repeated its caper and even—or so the driver declared—gave us a quiet horse-laugh.

And thus, in high good humour, we all went up Roehampton's tilted lane.

We alighted at the top of the Lane where it abuts on Putney Heath; and while Uncle Lucy cast his eyes over the heather and gorse to find a pitch for our cricket stumps, the driver flung his rug over the horse's back, hung a sweet-smelling nosebag over its nostrils, and went and sat in the back seat of his carriage, much as a bath-chairman on the sea-front will enjoy the sun in his chair.

Uncle Lucy and Auntie Flavia watched us pitch our stumps on a rough site by the Curling Pond and then, saying, 'Have a nice game,' went off in the opposite direction. They went back towards Roehampton Lane, and so strange was this that the game we played was not cricket but 'The Edith Road Anarchists.'   We threw a glance at the driver, thirty yards away, and, perceiving that he had drawn his top hat over his eyes and shut himself away for meditation, or for sleep, we promptly drew stumps and followed the adults from afar off, like leopards stalking their prey.

'I've a feeling they'll lead us to a clue,' said Gael; and I agreed, saying, 'It is possible, because of a surety it is all very mysterious.'

They turned out of Roehampton Lane into a side street, and, losing sight of them, we ran, soft-footed, to lessen the distance between us.   We peeped round the corner of the side street.   It was a curving road of large gabled villas, each in its own garden.

Our two adults, walking along the empty street, stopped to gaze at one of the houses on the opposite side.   They stood gazing at it, and talking together. Once Uncle Lucy appeared to shake his head, as in melancholy but humorous resignation.

This again was so odd that we longed to spy closer and learn more. But how? We could not see how, till they crossed the roadway and passed between the carriage gates of the house. Then we ran, as soundlessly as leopards on the pad, to a pier of the gates and peeped round. The tall grey house was manifestly empty. Its windows were dirty and veiled by broken Venetian blinds; its garden was overgrown and bedraggled. The privets along the garden railings, no longer clipped into a trim, straight hedge, had grown into untidy sprawling trees, so that we were able to creep and crouch along them till we found a peephole under their branches.

Uncle Lucy and Auntie Flavia stood side by side in the high uncut grass of the lawn. They were gazing at the house's door with its pretentious Gothic porch and at the blinded windows within their ornate and pointed arches. Since they were not six yards from my spying eyes, my heart thumped with guilt. They were talking low, and close together, as if feeling guilty too; and I could not at first hear any word they said. But soon Uncle Lucy went from her side and walked towards a window on the left of the porch; he peeped between the tumbled slats of a Venetian blind and, turning towards her, spoke so that I could hear. 'In that room she used to wait by her fire, sometimes till three in the morning, listening for the sound of hooves coming up the hill.'

We could not hear her reply; nor did he listen to it. He looked again through the blind and said, 'The white marble fireplace is still there, and as pompous and ugly as ever—but her fire, my dear, has long gone out.'

'It's been out for twenty-five years,' she called back, with something like a laugh.

'Yes; and now her grate is red with rust. But there are ashes there still.'

'Not hers,' she laughed. 'The place must have been occupied fairly recently, or there'd have been more weeds on the drive.'

'Nevertheless,' he said, as with a shrug and a spreading of empty hands, he came back towards her, 'I feel that if we stayed here till dark we should see her face at the window looking out to see if he was coming.'

'That's so likely!'

'Why not? After all, he has come.'

'But it's hardly time yet for her to be looking through that window. When she is dead, perhaps. . . .'

'Has the house really a haunted look,' he interrupted, turning to look at it again, 'or do one's thoughts put it there? Is it only there for those who know what happened behind those windows?'

'The living do not haunt, my dear.' Always she kept on the firm earth when he was flying high—she who, for her part, could so often fly out of sight in search of heroics and drama.

'There must still be many thousands who know,' he said, not heeding her. 'Or has the whole world forgotten?'

He stood again at her side in the summer-scented garden, and both gazed again at that house-front, he as silent as when he stood, hand on my shoulder, gazing at the Houses of Parliament.

'Well, it held all the best of my warm summer days,' he said at last, walking towards it. 'All the finest and best. And so God bless it. Not but what'— he turned, stood still and solemnly addressed her, with some old joke at play in his eyes—'there could be quarrels there sometimes. Ever and anon. She could be a petulant child at times.'

Auntie Flavia must have said some such words as 'No, no! Surely not?' for he answered, 'Oh, yes! She could be resentful and petulant if she had a mind to it. And then she'd insult me like any fishwife. Dear, dear, what a little spitfire. Eh?—What? What about me, did you say? *Me*? Nonsense. Nonsense. Come along.'

Against its western wall was a large conservatory with a long, shallow cupola which made it look as if it had been pupped by the Palm House at Kew. Beckoning her to follow him, he walked to the narrow path between conservatory and garden wall. 'Let's go and look at the stables. Perhaps we shall see Chancellor looking out for his master.

And Empress for her mistress. They at least are dead, and I'm sure Chancellor was an animal noble enough to haunt any loose box.'

'So silly you are!' she laughed; and followed him.

They passed out of sight, going towards the back garden, and Gael whispered, 'What on earth are they doing here? What are they up to now? Oh, but we must *know*!'

'Well, we can't ask them,' I said. 'We're not officially here. We're playing cricket.'

'Oh, but we *must* find out,' she objected. 'We can't *die* without knowing.'

'Assuredly we must find out.' I walked back to the piers of the carriage gate. 'Here's the name of the house. Inishowen.'

'What a soppy name. Something happened here; what do you suppose it was?'

'I can only gather that it was inhabited by someone with whom your Uncle Lucy was in love.'

'Oh, yes, that's obvious,' said Gael, always ready to discourage me from imagining I was clever. 'Probably his "poor lost Lottie".'

'Lottie for sure. He mentioned her at lunch.'

'Golly!' Gael stood staring at the house.

It was built of grey brick, stone and slate in a grimly Gothic mood. The porch was almost ecclesiastical with acanthus-leaf capitals to its columns. There were three stories, the third being high up in the steep gable, and every one of the windows sat within an ornamental pointed arch.

'Your kind auntie was wrong,' I said. 'It could well be haunted.'

Their steps crunched on the path by the conservatory, coming back; and we ran. Almost opposite the house there was a curving road which appeared to swing round to the Heath. We ran into this; and when we saw that they'd finished their strange visit, we raced back to the Heath and got to our cricket pitch before them.

When at last Uncle Lucy appeared, it was to summon us back to the fly. The driver was already on his box and Auntie Flavia in her back seat.

'Come on, chaps; get you in.'

But Gael, at the carriage step decided to divulge a personal secret and admit that in the carriage, somewhere near Hammersmith Bridge, she'd felt 'the beginnings of being sick.'

'Oh, dear,' deplored Uncle Lucy and then suggested that she should take the box-seat instead of me.

'But supposing I felt sick up there and can't get down before it happens?'

'It'll go over the horse. But you won't. It's steadier up there, and you'll have the wind in your face.'

'All right.' She clambered up to the box seat, but with palpable doubts about the outcome.

I felt glad that this time it was she, and not I, who felt sick and was therefore ridiculous.

I now sat in the body of the carriage, facing the adults; and inevitably, as we went jogging homeward down the flinty Roehampton Lane they began to talk as if I were no more than the upholstery of the opposite seat.

'I wonder how long it has stood empty,' Auntie Flavia said.

'Two years? Three years?' Uncle Lucy suggested, his gloved hands resting on his stick.

'I wonder why someone changed the name.'

'Probably they were ashamed of the old one. Too well known.'

'Inishowen . . . that's an Irish name, isn't it?'

'Inishowen is in Donegal. Probably they were Orangemen and rigid puritans.'

'Do you think it's empty now because of the notoriety?'

'Oh, no. That should only add to its value.'

'But it looks so abandoned. Could they be going to pull it down?'

'Impossible. It had a ninety-five year lease. It'll still be standing in the nineteen fifties.'

'Well,' she laughed, 'we shall have lost all interest in it then.'

'Do you know what I was seeing all the time?'

'No? What?'

'The hall and the wheeling staircase down which she used to come to greet him. She was very beautiful, I'd ask you to remember.'

'I never thought so. It seemed to me there were many girls far lovelier.'

'Not to me. She was a radiant creature, and I loved her.'

'Radiant? Would you really say that?'

'Of course I would. Everyone said so. She was not only a joy to look at but always so enchantingly gay.'

'*I* was looking at the window of her boudoir where she hid him. And at the conservatory down which he escaped. Why he didn't crash through the glass I never knew. Heaven knows he was big enough.'

'A comment which both judge and counsel were pleased to make. If I remember aright his lordship summed it up as a "minor miracle"; which was not very clever since glass houses have glazing bars and gutters and rain-water pipes; nor was it very funny, though it earned a jackal's laugh from the Colonel's counsel. They might have mentioned too that I've been a rock-climber most of my life, and therefore should have little difficulty in descending a conservatory.'

This memory appeared to sink him into a moody silence, which endured till we were across the common and getting back into the present, with that lonely, ugly grey house left far behind us in the past.

CHAPTER SEVEN

IT was easy to say 'we must get to work and find out' but
what could we do; where could we turn? We could not
persist in our questioning of Auntie Flavia because, if we
asked one more question than two, she was likely to become
a storm in the room, with stampings and slammings, and we,
at thirteen and fourteen, were still young enough to feel
frightened and just old enough to feel pity. If we questioned
Uncle Lucy he only treated us to evasive and teasing answers,
or to some picturesque story which, as he saw with relish,
we knew to be lies. Lizzie Blake, liking to see herself as a
rock of loyalty, and as secret as the heart of Gibraltar itself,
would never do more than hint at mysteries which she could
reveal, an she would. Sometimes she would shut the doors
of our mouths with savoury morsels from oven or pot. A
little later, and doubts, not untouched with shame, shut our
mouths even more effectively.

But the ages of thirteen and fourteen are big steps upward
from tutelage, and we asserted to each other our 'right to
know all'. I declared war—and few declarations have I
enjoyed more. 'If they're not going to play fair with us,'
I said, 'we needn't play fair with them.' We could adopt
any strategy, however Machiavellian. 'They can't be
allowed all the unscrupulousness. There must be fair
shares in everything.' Diamond must cut diamond; Greek
meet Greek. Gael was quite ready to be unscrupulous.
Indeed, prayers or not, Mr. Appledore or not, *Garden of the
Soul* or not, I think she would have been ready for any law-
less methods without my laboured justifications.

The war began. We crept into the deserted drawing-
room, and ransacked writing-table drawers for letters that
might touch on the hidden things. But Auntie Flavia was as
untidy in her emotions as sometimes in her dress, and her
heart would not allow her to destroy any letter that was the

least affectionate or kind or 'so interesting that it ought to be published.' The result was that every drawer was a refuse dump, pressed down and flowing over, of letters received by her from fifty different persons in the last thirty years. To try to find anything of help to us was like seeking for a single leaf in a forest after the autumn gales have littered the ground.

We listened at the drawing-room door when one or more of the aunts sat at tea, because we always felt certain that they must soon be talking about *him* or about us; but they never did while we waited at the keyhole. Never did the pot boil, never came the bus we wanted, never did a nightingale sing as we waited in the wood.

Soon I conceived a better plan, and a more restful one. There was a remarkable boy at school whose name was John Fenner Pryce, but who was known to everyone as 'Brains' because he knew all—or affected to know all—about mechanics, dynamics, ballistics, electro-magnetism and such matters, together with all the technical jargon that belonged to them. In my day at St. Paul's, if any boy was troubled by any problem, scientific, legal, musical, technological, theological, any problem about any event in the heavens, the earth, or the waters under the earth, the advice given him was 'Ask Brains.' To which might be added, 'Don't waste time looking it up with old Brains about. He'll know. And it's a kindness to ask him because he does so enjoy showing you where you are wrong. But don't argue with the lad because, you see, he just *knows*.'

Or perhaps a wit would say simply, 'You know what to do. God gave us our Brains to be used.'

Brains's father was a doctor in Chiswick with a large practice among the poor, most of whom he attended for nothing (or so Brains assured us). But a more remarkable fact about this unseen father was his great prominence (of which Brains was proud and talked at length) in the Liberal Party. He was nursing a West London constituency in the Liberal interest, so Brains knew all about politics too. Of course Brains was a Liberal like his father, and this invested him with an exotic, slightly weird, but wholly alluring aura, because we knew of no other Liberal among the six hundred boys at school. How his father could be a doctor, and so presumably a gentleman, and at the same time a Liberal we could not grasp. We mocked and jeered at old Brains, chanting, 'Liberals are cads, Conservatives are gentlemen,' but he had a tough hide and a damnable self-assurance, and he would shout back, 'You don't know what you're talking about, you idiots. Some of the greatest aristocrats are Liberals. What about Archibald Philip Primrose, fifth earl of Rosebery? What about the Most Honourable the old Marquess of Clunes? And what about Lord Elgin, the ninth smelly earl?'

'Never heard of 'em,' we sang. 'All Liberals are cads.'

St. Paul's in my time gave all its real devotion to Classical Scholarship, but it had also, somewhat shamefacedly, a Modern Side. I, like the great majority of boys, was on the Classical Side. Auntie Flavia had once put forward the faint suggestion that I should go on the Modern Side since I would have to earn my living, but Uncle Lucy had scotched the notion at birth. 'Oh no,' he had demurred, shocked. 'A fair smattering of the Classical Fathers is the natural dress of a gentleman. As is his membership, in England, of the Anglican Church. I'm not saying that either need be overdone. But really, my dear, to put him on the Modern Side is almost exactly analogous to making him a Methodist.' He could not have used a more effective illustration. It shot the notion out of Auntie Flavia's mind for ever. Uncle Lucy's view was certainly shared by me and all the other boys on the Classical Side. We could only bring ourselves to speak of our schoolfellows on the Modern Side as The Modern Cads. And as you will have guessed, Brains, son of his father, was a Modern cad. It was what one would have expected of a Liberal.

Well, one day Brains brought to school a Sansom's stethoscope of his father's so that he could sound the chests of us all and prophesy our early deaths. I was quite fascinated by this instrument, and in due time he allowed me to try it. I applied it, not to his lungs, but to his brains, to hear them throbbing. And suddenly—did I draw inspiration, tapping such exceptional matter?—suddenly I saw a distant light. And directly Brains had wearied of this toy, having brought to school instead a sphygmomanometer for testing our blood-pressures, I swapped a jelly-hectograph, empurpled with ink and pitted like the moon, for the stethoscope, and hurried home with it.

I had, I say, a plan; a fatigue-saving plan. The Playroom was over the drawing-room, and, with Gael watching, I drew back the carpet and chiselled up a piece of floor-board immediately over that part where the aunts' voices would go on and on like mountain streams when the snows are melting. (In my unoriginal way I was always liable to be pulling up floor-boards.) Beneath me now was the lath and-plaster of the ceiling, and with a bradawl I worked a hole no larger than a screw's head. I dared not make it larger lest a good plenty of the ceiling should descend to the furniture below. This hole pierced, I slipped downstairs to see what it looked like from below and was not quite pleased to see that it had developed a long hair-crack on either side of it. But I comforted myself with the thought that this made it look more natural. There was a powder of white plaster on the floor, and I kicked it around to spread it more fairly over the carpet. War was war.

Some afternoons later I came home from school to be told with delight by Gael that Gloria and Flavia were in the drawing-room, 'talking their heads off'. I dashed into the Playroom with the stethoscope, prised up the floor-board and, lying on my stomach, fixed the ear-pieces into my ears and the chest-piece over the hole in the plaster.

Gael stood watching and begging, 'Oh, let me, let me.'

But after a while I shook my head despairingly and removed the instrument because, in truth, I could hear better without it.

Gael then tried, enthusiastically; but at last agreed with me. Indeed she was rude enough to say that, whereas without the stethoscope she could at least hear voices, with it she could hear nothing (unless it was the sea).

So this attempt at eavesdropping in comfort proved abortive.

And then, while we didn't know where to turn for a clue, one came towards us; it was tossed before our feet on the pavement of Edith Road.

§

Sometimes on autumn days, when clouds or rain kept us imprisoned in the house, we would spend hours at the Playroom windows, our brows against the glass, our eyes watching the road. A wholly residential road, it was empty at most times and especially when its pavements were newly wet, or a cold grey sky hung over the roofs. Only at its far end, where the North End Road crossed it, did the buses and carts, the drays, vans and cabs, batter gently but steadily at its peace.

We were at the windows too on many a winter afternoon. I remember afternoons when the western sky was an apricot light above the towers of St. Paul's and a moon's pale quarter floated in a zenith of washed-out blue; or when the snow had come and the long roadway ran slate-coloured and purple between the white-carpeted silence of the pavements.

Usually we were playing a game, with our elbows on the sills. Each in turn must guess what tradesman would next come into our silence from around the corner of North End Road, and each guess earned marks, high or low, according to the likelihood of the visitor. An errand boy with a basket earned only ten marks, the van from the Army and Navy Stores earned twenty; but there were sixty for the peripatetic tinker with his song, 'Any knives to grind'; and fully a thousand for the lavender sellers coming up the crown of the road with their lovely cry, 'Lavender, sweet lavender, fifteen branches a penny.'

A thousand too for the old man selling groundsel, which he must have culled that morning in the wastegrounds of West Kensington or in the open fields, some of which were so much closer to us then.

The muffin man, I know not why, came only on Sundays. But he came always into the quiet Sunday tea-time, with his tray on his head, and shaking his mournful bell, which seemed to warn our wintry street that muffins, like Time and Sunday teas, passed all too quickly by. As indeed Time and the Sundays have.

Our house being almost in the middle of the north side, we might change the game and guess whether the next door to open would be on our right or on our left, and whether a male or a female would emerge. To get both side and sex right was a 'double'. On such a day, and at such an occupation, when the pavements were browned and greasy with rain and reflecting in patches the low mist-white sky, Gael cried suddenly, 'There he is again! At his window. Watching us.'

'Who?' I asked.

'Why, Beerbohm Tree, of course.'

Yes, there was a face at a first-floor window of a house nearly opposite, and it was looking steadily at us from behind the lace curtain. Not, of course, the face of that celebrated actor-manager but of a man whom Gael declared to be like Mr. Tree. If he was really like him, it was only as Mr. Tree had appeared when acting in *The Last of the Dandies*, a play to which Auntie Flavia had taken us some years before, and which was then illustrated all over London by a poster of Tree elegantly cloaked, with his silk hat at an angle and a hand resting gracefully on a tasselled cane. The man opposite certainly looked a dandy when he stepped from his house with his big wide-awake hat perched slightly to one side, his Inverness cape flying open to show his sheperd's-plaid trousers, and his long cigar pointing to the North End Road like a bowsprit. His walk was a stately strut with his polished toes turned out and his elegant frame so erect that it seemed to lean a few degrees backward. On softer days, instead of the long Inverness cape, he came forth in a cloak like a nurse's and carrying a black cane which he waved and rotated like a conjuror's wand over pavement flags, coal holes, and kerbs.

He had only recently come to live over yonder, and Auntie Flavia, Mrs. Willer, and Lizzie, all as inquisitive about the neighbours as we, had soon learned much about him. Despite his macaroni attire, he was no actor; he was a barrister, but one who had ceased to practise forty years before, and had devoted himself instead to popular journalism. We were all impressed when we learned that he 'wrote in the papers' because we had a simple notion that to be published in print was synonymous with fame and proof of intellectual quality. His name was Lynn Francis, but he was known to many as Don Francesco because as a young man in 1866 he had gone to Italy as a newspaper correspondent and marched with Garibaldi into the Trentino.

But the most astonishing thing about him, the sinister and accordingly fascinating thing, was that, in the teeth of his dandyish dress and his stately strut, he was something even worse than a Liberal, even more unsuitable for our ladylike road: a Socialist. A foundation member of the Social Democratic Federation, long a fellow-worker with William Morris in his Hammersmith outhouse, he was an enthusiastic prophet of Socialism and at one time edited a news-sheet, *Justice for All*. He had stood for Parliament in several elections, but never with success because, always liking to do things with an air (as witness cloak and cane), he must always contest impossible seats that none other would touch.

Needless to add, he had taken the side of the Boers in the recent war; but what perplexed us was that Auntie Flavia, so surprised at having a Socialist in the road, did not seem to mind his having been a pro-Boer. 'Many extremely intelligent people were pro-Boers,' she would explain quickly and then fly the subject.

'He does stare,' said Gael. 'I suppose he thinks we can't see what he's doing behind that curtain.'

'Perhaps he's writing an article on children,' I suggested, 'and studying two interesting specimens.'

'But I'm horribly afraid it's not only in us that he's interested,' sighed Gael. 'It's Auntie too. And Uncle Lucy.'

Yes, it was our house and its occupants as one corporation that interested him: constantly we caught his eyes resting on our windows from behind the curtain of that first-floor room. At the sound of our door opening or of voices on our threshold, he rose and stood behind the curtain, hands in his pockets, eyes on our porch. Eyes and posture said plainly,

'Now what is it that goes on in there?' If he passed us on the pavement he always turned to consider us, pondering, no doubt, 'Who are they, those two children? And who, pray, is the tall old gentleman with the silver moustaches and fur-lined coat? And the large fat spinster lady—she can hardly be his mistress because she's half-way to sixty, and he to eighty. Those children—look at them—how comes it they're apparently unrelated to him, to her, and to each other? Very queer.'

And the isolation of that household. . . .

Little doubt that the chief focus of Don Francesco's interest was 'Mr. Grenville'. His watching of our house had only begun when Uncle Lucy appeared in it. I remember an occasion when Uncle Lucy, after being given noisy fare-wells by us on the steps as he went off for the day, and several further shouts of 'Good-bye' from a window, waved to us generously and walked towards the North End Road. He had not gone twenty yards when Don Francesco, in wide hat and flying cape, stepped from *his* door and quietly fol-lowed him, but on the far side of the road. We were sure it was no coincidence: he was out to learn where Mr. Grenville went.

And then, at last, he actually spoke to us on the pave-ment. Gael and I, instructed to 'nip along to the baker's,' were walking towards the North End Road when we saw him coming out of it and walking towards us on our pave-ment. He stared at us, and Gael began to giggle fatuously. Having passed us, he turned to look back at us, at the very moment, unfortunately, when we turned to look back at him. This shot Gael's shoulders up to her ears in dismay, and her giggle up to her nose, where it did a trumpet voluntary—at which she giggled the more. Then she said, 'Let's go back. Let's pretend we've forgotten something and go the way he's going. The poor man looks as though he'd love to speak to us, but we don't give him the chance.'

'Right-ho,' I assented. 'But we shan't be exactly nipping to the baker's.'

'No, but—you see, I rather love him. I think he's fascinating.'

'He's a Socialist,' I reminded her.

'Yes, that's rather awful,' she agreed, 'but his hat's so sweet.'

'And he's sixty at least.'

'Seventy, more likely,' she amended, with the implication that age need be no impediment to love. Mr. Appledore was sixty.

He turned again, saw us returning, and deliberately stopped. We went on towards him, our hearts trembling. And just as we came abreast of him he raised the wide hat to Gael, as to a princess, and said, 'Excuse me, Miss de Brath . . .'

Gael stopped. 'I beg your pardon?'

'You are Miss de Brath, are you not?'

'De Brath?' she repeated.

'Yes, that is your charming name, isn't it?'

'Oh, no, my name is Harrington. Gael Harrington.'

'I am so sorry. I blush for my error. But I——'

'That was a French name, wasn't it? We are English.'

'Of course you are, but many English have French names. Half the nobility have French names; Norman names. Names they brought from Normandy nine hundred years ago.'

'Oh, I wish my name were Norman. But it's only Harrington. It is, really. So sorry.'

'Then you really must forgive me, Miss Harrington. I thought someone told me that your mother's name was Charlotte de Brath.'

'Oh, no. And my auntie's not my mother. That's our Auntie Flavia.'

'Who?'

'Auntie Flavia. Her name's Flavia Middian, and her father was a bishop.'

Middian. We saw an interest quicken in his eyes. As if this were a name of which he was remembering something. Something that he'd heard or read a long while ago. 'Middian? Is that so? Well now, really! And her name isn't Charlotte? No? Bless my soul, I got everything wrong, didn't I? It must be someone else whose name is de Brath. You'll be telling me next that you're not brother and sister?'

'Nor we are!' she cried triumphantly. 'Travers' name is Ilbraham. Travers Winfrith Ilbraham.'

'Well, well, well! Ilbraham!' He smiled very pleasantly. 'That's not the least like de Brath, is it? I couldn't have been more wrong. Then that exceedingly distinguished old gentleman with the . . .' His delicate tapered fingers indicated around his lips moustaches and an imperial.

'With an imperial,' Gael supplied, thinking that perhaps he didn't know what the ornament was called.

'With an imperial. Then the distinguished old gentleman is not your father?'

'Oh no, no, no.' Gael laughed gaily at the error. 'That's our Uncle Lucy.'

'Lucy? Lucy, did you say?'

'Yes. Short for Lucius. Which is short for Louis.'

'Indeed? Louis? And your uncle? He is lately married to our Auntie Flavia perhaps?'

'*No!*' So loud was Gael's denial of this mistake that her word seemed the ultimate expression of amusement and pity.

'No, of course not,' he obligingly agreed—but added, 'Though I don't see why not. Our Auntie Flavia is a fine comely girl.'

'Auntie Flavia is a miss,' said Gael, and, as if this required further elucidation, explained, 'She isn't married.'

'A miss. Quite. Ah then I have it! What a fool I've been all along. Why, he's her brother of course, and your uncle?'

Gael shook her head, grinning at his persistent bad guessing. 'We only call him Uncle. He's really only just a friend. He's been a friend of Auntie Flavia's for ever so long. But I love him just as much as if he was a relation.'

'You do?'

'Yes, and I only wish he'd come more often.'

'Come?'

'Yes. From Paris where he lives.'

'A Frenchman? Ah yes.' The elegant fingers outlined again the moustaches and imperial. 'He wears them in

96

loyal imitation of his late master, the Emperor.   Yes Louis, I see, Louis Napoleon.   *Vive l'Empereur.*'

Gael almost doubled up in her delighted despair of him as a guesser. 'Oh, gosh, no!   Uncle Lucy'd lie down and die if anyone thought him a Frenchman.'

'I apologise a thousand times.   Well, goodbye to you, my dear Miss Gael, my dear Master Travers.   *Addio.*' He raised his hat and swept it in a curve as he bowed.   '*Au revoir, peut-etre. . . .*'

We walked on, Gael trembling with her silent giggle. 'That *was* an excitement,' she declared with a little skip of delight.   'And isn't he adorable?   But where on earth did he get that outlandish name from?   De Brath, if you please!'

'If you ask me,' I submitted, 'he made it up.'

'Perhaps so,' said Gael.   'But at any rate it showed he thought we *looked* Norman.   And aristocratic.'

97

CHAPTER EIGHT

SINCE we shivered away in fear, and in pity, from Auntie Flavia's storming if she was 'pestered with questions,' we did not tell her of this strange accosting nor utter in her presence the name 'de Brath.' Once before we had rushed home with the news, 'A strange man came and asked us questions'; and instantly alarm had leapt into her eyes. 'Who was he? What did he ask?' As it happened, the questions were not such as perturbed her, but none the less she had stamped her foot and said, 'You're never to answer any stranger's questions. You're never to speak to anyone in the street. Do you *understand*?' So we now kept the whole matter of Don Francesco as a new secret mystery for discussion in the Playroom or in the cave under the stairs. In fact we did not attach much significance to it, accounting the name 'de Brath' a silly invention whereby he contrived to get into conversation with us. Uncle Lucy, loth to return into exile, was still in our house, but we dared not broach the subject with him, lest he should speak of it to Auntie Flavia.

This was the longest stay he ever made with us. It was also the least clandestine. In the past, if it was still daylight, he usually went from the house and returned to it, under cover of a cab; now, abandoning such extremes of discretion, he would often walk through the open street to West Kensington Station, allowing us to dance along noisily at his side. Happy days they were, with him no longer a fleeting guest, but dwelling like a father in the house. In the quiet evenings before dinner, if he was not playing cards or halma with us, he would entrance us with stories of great and famous people whom he had seen, or actually spoken to, in the 'terrible long stretch of life, seventy tedious and undistinguished years,' that lay behind him. He told the stories, leaning back in his deep arm-chair by the dining-room fire, while we two sat on ordinary chairs (since children do not ask comfort) with our elbows on the table and our eyes fixed, absorbed, on him.

The Iron Duke. He had seen the Duke at the Great Exhibition of '51 and he sadly shook our hero-worship by saying that, whatever he looked like at Waterloo, nearly forty years earlier, he was 'a skinny little cadaver' then. General Gordon he had met and had some talk with, after his return from the famous deeds which won him the title 'Chinese Gordon.' With Thackeray, 'a long leggy creature with spectacles and a flattened nose,' and later with Trollope, 'a big, banging, noisy, fox-hunting type' he had dined at their favourite club, the Garrick. He had attended more than one of George Eliot's celebrated receptions in her drawing-room at the Priory, Regent's Park, and he described with mischievous eyes how the great lady authoress would sit in her arm-chair by the fire, and all those who wanted to talk with her had to take it in turn to occupy the seat at her side, 'like a succession of penitents visiting their confessor in search of absolution and counsel.'

Not only of great and famous persons in Britain did he charm us with tales. In America he had met Emerson and Lowell and Wendell Holmes, of whom we had never heard, and Longfellow, of whom we had most certainly heard: 'Under the spreading chestnut tree . . .' Enjoying, and not without justice, his voice at its best, he would, upon mention of Longfellow, recite passages from his verse that lent themselves to a low, musical expression with accompanying flourishes of a hand, and that suited admirably these evening sessions. 'The day is done and the darkness Falls from the wings of night. . . .'

In Germany he had spoken with Bismarck, and in France, very often, with Gambetta, whom he called, 'my dear little squinting Gambetta.' In England he had seen much of Kossuth, the great Hungarian patriot and rebel who had raised an army to set his country free, but had been cruelly defeated at Temesvar and escaped to England, 'the natural refuge and sanctuary,' he said sadly, 'for all the outcasts of *other* countries.' I'll say that we first learned some modern history, sitting enthralled at his feet, for these were great names from Europe but so far they had cast no shadows into our rooms at school.

Occasionally, as the memories came back to him by the fireside, and he steeped himself in them till his heart grew soft at their touch, he would brag a little about banquets given in his honour in Paris, in Berlin and in other great capitals, and then Auntie Flavia, who sat there listening, would look up at him anxiously, as if wondering whether age were weakening his will and stripping discretion from him.

§

But all these happy days and nights, all these sessions of sweet thought when he summoned up remembrance of things past, were abruptly ended by an incident which shook the house and sent him from us again into his far Parisian mists.

It was a Sunday evening, of all unsuitable hours for a loud and scandalous disturbance in our well-conducted road. Sunday evening at half-past nine. Mrs. Willer was having her 'Sunday off'; Lizzie, after attending Evensong at church, sat alone in her kitchen plying her crochet needle as she rocked in her chair; Auntie Flavia and Uncle Lucy sat in the dining-room, he smoking a cigar, she talking on and on; Gael and I, supper done, had gone to our bedrooms to undress for bed.

I dawdled, as always, over this business of getting into bed. I removed my jacket and read a page of a book lying open on the chest of drawers. I slipped off my waistcoat and added some pencil shading to my study of artillery destroying the Boers. I undid my Eton collar, and went to the window for some interest while I undid—and then forgot to undo—my tie. At the window I enjoyed a long, thorough and unrebuked scratching of the head beneath my tumbled undisciplined hair. And while I comforted myself thus, I considered the gas lamp near our railings, because its flame, effervescing and jigging, seemed the only thing alive in the street.

It was a clear night, and still. Edith Road made a picture of Sunday's incorruptible peace. The only sound was the tempered Sabbatarian traffic in the North End Road. Over that highway a subdued brightness flushed the clean sky, because its public houses at least were open and their big pendent lanterns alight. I left the window to flay off my shirt; then returned to it for an interlude of refreshment and rest. And then it was that I saw Mrs. Willer.

She was coming home, and her line of advance was curious: it tacked from pavement kerb to area railing and back again. It varied its tempo, now slowing in sudden despondency, now tripping merrily, now coming to a halt while she stared at a house immediately across the road. Next another tripping on her toes, and another halt while she withdrew her fat chin into her neck to allow an expulsion of wind. I rushed down to Gael's room below and summoned her to this astonishing entertainment. And we watched together at her window.

Mrs. Willer was now trotting towards the railings, and these she stroked affectionately before travelling along a new diagonal to the kerb. Her hat, trimmed with cherries, was only held from tobogganing down her cheek by the network of her veil. Its cherries shook merrily as she wagged her head at an amusing thought. But now, after another internal adjustment, she was walking slowly and sadly, with jaw dropped, towards her home and rest. She came to our area, at which, while still six feet away, she stopped to stare, her head falling to one side as if, before taking any irretrievable step, she would make sure that it was the area she had in mind.

Satisfied that it was the way into her home, she chassé'd towards the gate, held on to it, and nodded at the steps before attempting the descent. She attempted the first two steps, but on the third abandoned her purpose, rolled the veil above her lips, and broke into song. The narrow step might have been her concert platform. Her song had a pleasing lilt, but was unsuitable for Sunday, even if it did mention 'church'; doubtless she had come from hearing it in a pub. 'There was I,' she sang, 'waiting at the church, Waiting at the church, When I found he'd left me in the lurch. . . .'

Another eructation, loud enough for us to hear and delight in; and Mrs. Willer, relieved, continued in a voice now happily cleansed, 'All at once he sent me round a note, Here's the very note, This is what he wrote. . . .'

Windows shot up in the houses opposite and people looked out. Doors opened and people came on to their thresholds. Some came down on to the pavement. Hearing their steps, Mrs. Willer turned on her narrow stage to sing to them. 'Can't get away To marry you today, My wife won't let me. . . .'

'Good Golly!' muttered Gael, never more pleased.

The chorus again: 'There was I, waiting at the church, Waiting——'

But now Lizzie appeared on the area steps and seized her hand.

''Evening, Liz,' greeted Mrs. Willer. 'Darling old Liz.'

'Come, Mabel. Come quickly.' Lizzie pulled at her hand.

'What?' Mrs. Willer desired more information. And, on second thoughts, some assurance that Lizzie had authority to address her like this. 'Wor'rat?'

'Come at once. Everybody's staring and listening.'

So Mrs. Willer turned to sing them some more. 'When I found he'd left me in the lurch, Law, how it did upset me.'

'No, no, *please* don't, Mabel dear. There'll be trouble. It's Sunday night. We don't want a row on a Sunday night.'

'No . . .' Mrs. Willer agreed; and hiccupped. 'We don't want—pardon me—no, 'strue—don't want no sun on a rowdy night.' She giggled at her mistake. 'Oh, what have I said? I do get things mixed up, don't I? We don't want—pardon me, all.'

'Come *along*,' begged Lizzie, pulling downwards.

'Now don't gemmy all hot and bothered,' begged Mrs. Willer, pulling upwards. 'All at once he sent me round a note, Here's the very note . . . Lead on, Liz.' And, singing quite softly, she accompanied Lizzie like a dog on its leash into the kitchen.

Auntie Flavia's and Uncle Lucy's voices in the hall. Auntie Flavia at the top of the basement stairs crying, 'Lizzie, Lizzie.' By this time Gael and I were down on the first-floor landing where we could see and hear all.

'Lizzie, Lizzie. Get her to bed at once. Tomorrow she shall leave this house.'

'No, no,' said Uncle Lucy, who had come behind her with his cigar in his hand. 'We are all sinners.'

'That may be, but——'

'I'm sure I've contravened most of the ten commandments. And committed all the seven deadly sins.'

'Oh, don't be ridiculous. This is terrible. I've never been so ashamed. What will the neighbours think?'

'She has never done it before.'

'How do I know she hasn't? She's probably been like this hundreds of times before, and I've known nothing about it.'

'Well, forgive her this once, in the name of all the times you've sinned and not been found out.' He replaced the cigar in his mouth. 'I shouldn't care to remember *my* successes in that direction.'

'Oh, I'll forgive her, but she shan't stay here. Not another day. I have my position in the neighbourhood to consider—more than most, as you know.'

'If you think I want to stay in your bloody house,' shouted Mrs. Willer, now at the foot of the basement stairs, 'you're mistaken.'

'Mabel! Mabel!' rebuked Lizzie, also at the stairs' foot.

'Oh dear, oh dear,' Uncle Lucy sighed. 'This is the language of the taproom.'

'I can go and stay wimmy sister in Eli Street.' Mrs. Willer began to come up the stairs, angrily and unsteadily. 'And I will. This very night. Oh, yes! Wi' Mah'rie.'

'Isn't it fun?' gloried Gael at my side.

'I'll go now. See if I don't. This is not a house I'm proud of, I'd have you know.'

'What do you mean by that?' demanded Auntie Flavia.

'Leave her. Leave her,' counselled Uncle Lucy, walking a few steps away.

But Mrs. Willer continued her furious climb. '*You* know what I mean. I should like to know what goes on here. And so would a lotta people. Liz never tells me nothing, but I gommy own ideas. I wasn't born yesterday.'

'Will you get out of my house?'

'I'm going, aren't I?' protested Mrs. Willer, though still climbing upwards. 'I'm going to my sister. My sister is respectable.'

'Lizzie, we can send her things after her?'

'Yes, ma'am.'

'I been wi' Mah'rie 's'evening,' Mrs. Willer volunteered. She was now at the top of the stairs and could say no more, because her breast was heaving.

'Is this Eli Street far?' asked Uncle Lucy from the dining-room door, against whose jamb he was resting a hand while he watched.

'No, it's only just across the North End Road.'

'Then let the poor creature go.'

'*Let* her go!' repeated Mrs. Willer, stepping into the hall. 'I don't go because I'm leggo. I go of my o'free will. Free will.' Suddenly something else became clear to her. 'And did you say "poor creature"? I'm not a creature. Creature yourself.'

'Lizzie, you know her sister's number in Eli Street?'

'Oh, yes, ma'am.'

'Very well. Mrs. Willer, will you please *go*?'

'Yes, you'd better go,' advised Uncle Lucy gently. 'There's a good woman.'

Just as on Lizzie's third invitation to 'Come along' she had gone passively, and only singing softly, so now on this word 'go' from Uncle Lucy she went towards the hall door passively and only muttering low, 'Creature—if you'll only believe!'

Uncle Lucy did what he would always do for a woman, in house or shop or church; he stepped ahead of her and opened the door for her with a small bow.

She gave him a bow in acknowledgment, and he returned it—automatically.

On the threshold she turned and said, 'Well, goo' bye, all.'

'Good-bye,' said Uncle Lucy, and bowed.

'Yes,' said Mrs. Willer.

Lizzie had now come up the stairs to see the end. 'Oh, ma'am,' she bewailed.

Mrs. Willer, after touching her hat into position, and fixing her veil under her chin, picked up the front of her skirt and went down the steps with her head high.

Not till she was on the pavement did Uncle Lucy shut the door, and then very quietly, so as not to offend her. But as the door clicked he said, 'Well, I hope the poor thing'll be all right. You don't think I ought to escort her?'

'There are police to escort her, if necessary,' said Auntie Flavia.

He shrugged; and they went back into the dining-room.

'Well, that's that,' said Gael.

But that was not the whole of it. Mrs. Willer, having arrived upon the pavement, began to wonder if she'd had all her rights. We had rushed to the Playroom windows and saw her standing there; and it was clear that she was asking herself if she'd said all the things that needed saying; if, perhaps, she'd been called things she oughtn't to have been called; if, in brief, justice had been done. She was nodding in meditation; and finally, decision arrived at, she turned and addressed the house, loud enough to be heard through its windows.

'Yes. Yes, indeed. And I'd like to know where *he* comes from. And I'm not the only one, neither. Coming and going like that! Here today and gone tomorrow. There's them that say you're none of you what you make out to be.'

Uncle Lucy appeared, hurrying down the steps. Magnanimity had given place to wrath. He gripped her elbow while she was still shouting at the dining-room windows, 'You can't look down your nose at me. You're not all that good, I dare say. Them poor little nippers, whose are they? That's something we'd quite like to know.'

'This is beyond all,' said Uncle Lucy.

She turned and saw him for the first time. ''Evening,' she said in greeting. Then recognized him. 'Oh, it's you, is it? Oh, I see.'

'Come, madam. Come away at once.' He tried to lead her away because the situation was desperate. Her shouting at ten o'clock, the bed-time hour, had brought the people back to their windows, their doorsteps, and the pavements. More and more were swelling her audience. Don Francesco's blind had gone up, and he stood in his study, flooded with gaslight, but veiled by the lace curtains, watching.

We heard Auntie Flavia in the hall below, deploring, 'Oh dear . . . oh, my God!'

'Come, Mrs. Willer,' commanded Uncle Lucy. 'Enough of this.'

But she dragged her elbow free and seized one of the twin lime trees behind the area wall. 'Oh, no! When I go, I go of my o'free will. I'm not the sort that's dragged. I never been dragged.'

'Are you coming? Or do I fetch a policeman?'

'I come when I choose. Nobby-fore. Certainly nobby —excuse me—fore.'

Without another word Uncle Lucy turned and went at his fastest speed towards the North End Road.

'Goo'bye,' she called after him. 'Send us a post card when you arrive.' This seemed to suggest a new idea to her, for after dropping her chin for a moment's deliberation, she yelled, 'Where you going? Paris? Yes, and I'd like to know what you get up to there. Eh?'

Uncle Lucy did not turn. Never before had he walked those three hundred yards to North End Road at such a speed. Now he was out of sight.

So Mrs. Willer addressed the people on the opposite pavement. 'He's gone to get a cop. He's bringing a cop. *Him* to fetch cops! I wouldn't say but what cops mightn't take a look at him. Calls himself Mr. Grenville, but I never been all that sure it's his real name. Lizzie knows something, but she's mum.' She compressed her lips and nodded knowingly. 'Liz don't say nothing. *Oh, no.*'

'Oh, take her away, take her away,' moaned Auntie Flavia.

Chance must have favoured Uncle Lucy in the North End Road because within a few seconds of turning its corner he came back with a policeman; a big policeman, as tall as himself and heavier in build. Together, coming with a slow, unhurrying dignity, they made an imposing pair, and Mrs. Willer stared at them.

'Goo'law!' she exclaimed, mainly in admiration of the policeman.

At my side Gael jumped up and down with delight. 'Coo! Isn't it fun?'

The people in the street seemed to think much the same.

'Well, I never!' continued Mrs. Willer, staring at the policeman. 'Where did he find him? You'd think cops were ten a penny on a barrer.'

Uncle Lucy and the policeman stopped opposite her. She looked at them both, and twice at the big policeman, and said, 'Well, now! Did you ever?'

'Come along, my dear,' said the policeman. 'Can't have you standing here and making trouble outside respectable houses.'

'Respectable!' She waved a knowing forefinger in front of his face. 'That's all you know, cock.'

'Tut, tut,' muttered Uncle Lucy.

'Well, never mind that, lady. Just come along. You don't want to be up before the beak in the morning. You can be fined forty bob for riotous and disorderly behaviour in a public place. Did you know that?' And he smiled at her.

We could see him well from our windows. He had a fat round face with a heavy black moustache and when he smiled his eyes folded up and a dimple formed in one of his cheeks.

Mrs. Willer, it was plain, 'took to him' at once. 'Now,

look here, mister. You're a gentleman and can understand. I'm a respectable woman. A widow, with a boy who's a soldier; and am I to be pushed and shoved about? This gentleman has tried to push me. Or to pull me—rather—let's be exact: pull. He spoke civilly enough, I admit, but not *her*; *she* didn't. She was rude, and am I to take that sor' o'thing, lying down? I mean, I ask you. I ask you fair and square. It's a problem, isn't it?'

'I'm not interested in your personal problems, lady.'

'Oh, but'—her palm flew from side to side in front of his face, like a distracted bird—'you should be interested. You should know all before you start taking steps. And telling me to come along is taking steps. You must admit that. And threatening me with beaks is steps. Ain't it? Listen; it may be that everything's all right in this house, but on the other hand it may not be. The Roman Catholic Church——'

'We can't deal with the Roman Catholic Church just now.'

'No, we can't, can we, love? No, you're right. Another time, eh, sweet?' Liking him so well, with his plump, smiling face, she leaned forward, winked, waved a finger before his nose and said, 'Cockledoodledo.'

'That'll do,' warned the policeman.

'That'll doodle do,' agreed Mrs. Willer, wagging her finger again and swaying her hips because these words reminded her of a sprightly duet and dance in *The Country Girl*.

'That's enough,' he said, but still smiling. Gently he pushed her finger away from before his nose. 'Now come along with me, love.' He laid a big fat friendly hand on her shoulder. 'I don't want no trouble.'

'I know you don't, but look, darling boy, look: I was p'raps a bit to blame, but not altogether, you see. I rather lommy temper; I admit that. I lommy temper a shade.'

'Yes, well, come along now. There's a girl.'

'I will say this,' Mrs. Willer deposed. 'I will say this, and take my Bible oath on it: I've always liked policemen, personally. I know there's many that don't—Mah'rie's

Fred isn't all that hot on them—but I've never had any trouble with 'em, meself. Always very nice to me. And if people are nice to me, I do what they ask.'

'That's right. And now shall we walk along?'

After nodding at her own thoughts twice and thrice, Mrs. Willer waved an invisible something away from between her and him. 'I'll say no more. Leave it at that. Leave it. Maybe I've been treated wrong, but, as you say, it's a problem. Or did I say it? I'll come along with you since you ask me nicely. But look, mate' —she lowered the waving palm on to his armlet, and her voice with it, as in a confidence—'when we get Nor' End Road, we part company. See?' She drew back her chin, and her head, and considered his face, to see whether he saw. 'It don't look good, walking with a policeman. People turn round and think things. They look. See what I mean? They look.'

'I see perfectly. That'll be all right, I think, sir.'

'Thank you, officer. Eleven, Eli Street.'

'Yes, sir. Good night, sir.'

'Good night.'

'Goo'night,' added Mrs. Willer, not to be left out of these farewells. She even turned towards the house and said, 'Goo'night, madam.' To the people across the road, both those to the right and those to the left, she waved and cried, 'Goo'bye. Gob'less you all.' Then walked away with the policeman, chatting to him merrily.

Don Francesco's blind went down; his light died.

§

I must allow that my Uncle Lucy, having been cruelly hurt some time in the past, liked, in these days when I knew him, to be hurt by Auntie Flavia or someone else— or should I say he liked to *feel* that he'd been hurt? 'Lord, he is touchy,' Auntie Flavia used to say; or 'He is difficult,' or 'He does like to have a grievance'; and there was truth in her complaint. In the morning, after this scene in the road, he announced angrily that he was going back to

Paris. He was angry enough to care little about the presence of us children at the breakfast table. He said, 'I bring nothing but trouble and scandal upon you—and so it has always been. From the first.'

'Oh, but you'll come back,' pleaded Auntie Flavia. 'Oh, what a shame it is. We were so happy.'

'I don't know that I shall ever come back,' he said, seeking, as he so often did, the dramatic and the tragic. 'It would be better to spare you my presence.'

'Lucius, don't talk like that!'

'Perhaps I do wrong even to trespass in my own country. You must forgive this trespass. But I should have thought a brief furlough now and then. . . .'

'Don't say such things! The children—think of the children. You know you're all the world to them.'

'Perhaps Win'll come and join me one day.' Oh, how my heart leapt at this word. 'I should like to see more oi him before the end. Which can't be long delayed now. And I have a feeling that when the time comes he will understand everything. I often dream, when I'm feeling alone over there, and very sensible of my age, that he might be with me one day as a support . . . and a solace. . . . In the loneliness.'

'Oh, but come back!' implored Auntie Flavia, with a little hammer of her fist on the table. And since this suggested that she was in danger of allowing herself a small storm of despair he said no more, and we two dared not speak.

Outside in the passage Gael demanded miserably, 'Oh, but why not me? Why not me? Why does he want you only? I'd be a perfect solace and support. A girl's always better at that sort of thing than a boy. Everyone knows it.'

'One of us, I suppose, will have to stay with Auntie Flavia,' I offered for her comfort, though really I was rejoicing in the thought that I'd been promoted above her.

'No, it's not that,' she bewailed, there in the dark passage. 'It's just that he loves you best. He's always loved you best. I've always known it. And it's a shame.'

So selfish was I that this assertion of hers only gave me a

sweet stab of joy. And when, the next evening between nine and ten, he went down our steps to the waiting cab, the darkness shielding him from the eyes of the road, I drove back the approaching sadness by thinking that one day I should follow him to Paris, and, leaving Auntie Flavia to Gael, live with him always. Auntie Flavia and Gael were both crying, so on the third step down he stopped and kissed them both and, humour having returned to him, said, 'The courteous Chinese teach that a guest should deliberately drag his footsteps when leaving the house of his host. I have no need to force myself to do that. I do it all too naturally. There, there! Perhaps after a while I shall be able to come again. Gael, be good, and take care of your kind auntie. Win, pursue your studies and in a year or two's time, perhaps, if I live so long . . . who knows? . . . you could pursue them in Paris. There is always the Sorbonne. . . . Good-bye. Good-bye, all. Think of me sometimes—an old, unhappy, far-off thing, and battle long ago.'

CHAPTER NINE

AFTER he had gone, and until understanding broke upon us with the first almond blossom of spring, the picture that comes most often to my mind is, once again, that of Gael and myself at the Playroom windows looking out into the street. It was full winter now and the fogs and rain had left the roadway below us grey-black with mud and glistening with damp. In winter a ragged crossing-sweeper came to his chosen pitch at the foot of the road and swept a crossing for the ladies' feet; a broad path with a dyke of mud on either side. He kept it clean and dry and free of horse-dung, with his birch-broom and, standing at its entry, invited pennies from those who profited by his handiwork. In the days when Uncle Lucy had been with us, and we walked with him to bus or station, he always gave 'the excellent man' a sixpence, asking of us, 'What nobler occupation than to spend one's life sweeping a path for civilization through the natural filth?' I can never smell wet horse-dung without seeing our Edith Road and the three of us, a tall old man in a topper and two children, walking along the sweeper's cleanly crossing, like representatives of what civilization had achieved so far. (We could have reached the North End Road much more easily by another and oblique crossing, but we all agreed that his feelings mustn't be hurt. 'An artist needs his public,' Uncle Lucy insisted; and we all walked, three abreast, along his pathway.)

Other artists came into the road to entertain us: the Italian with his barrel-organ slung before his paunch, a stick supporting it below, a monkey sitting on it above; the German band which played 'Are we to part like this, Bill' at the junction of Edith and Trevanion Roads so that it could delight with its pom-pom bass notes both streets at once; or the coal-heavers with the black sou-westers and the black sacks who plunged the Carboniferous Age through the holes in our pavements.

But after a time the most interesting figure to turn into the street, no matter from which distant end, would be some lady holding up her skirt behind, out of the grease and mud. Because we had now invented a new game: a light-hearted game; not in the least a pathetic one. The next 'real lady' to turn into our road would be, we declared, Gael's unknown mother—or mine—coming out of the mists in which hitherto they had dwelt—because we chose to believe that neither of them was really dead. Sometimes the woman would be elegant and pleasing, and then the lucky one of us would say, 'Yes, she'll do. I've no objection to her,' or she might be heavy and grim and formidable, and then the unfortunate one would protest, 'Crumbs, no! Not *that*.' But always, whether desirable or forbidding, they went into some other house, or just went by.

§

That other day of which I told you, when I went to gape at our house and street, I looked up it towards the towers of St. Paul's and down it towards the clatter of the North End Road, and suddenly *missed* something. Where were the murmuring pigeons that used to flutter down from the eaves and the sparrows that hopped and pecked in the gutters? There were so many of them in our day because (I suppose) of St. Paul's great red-walled playing-field and of the tall trees in the gardens behind us and of the horses that visited us. Perhaps, too, because of the quiet. But now, in the whole length of the road, not one pigeon; not one small fraternity of sparrows to dot and punctuate the long silence of Edith Road.

Is it that the internal combustion engines, which alone run up and down the road in these days, with their harsh, inharmonious breathing and pungent hostile smells have driven these fellow-lovers of London from round about our home?

§

Weeks passed with Uncle Lucy far away, and the drawing-room and his bedroom sheeted in death. The house seemed half empty to us children. It was like a body drained of vitality by a loss of its heart's blood, so that all its faculties were weakened. It would recover full animation, of course, but at present it was only in the first quiet phase of convalescence. Auntie Flavia, having no man in the house to dress for, stayed much of the day in her morning untidiness with her greying hair in long plaits down her back, and even, perhaps, in curling pins. Sometimes her blue or pink dressing-jacket, hanging in loose folds, showed that her large breasts and hips were joyously unbolted in corsets. Always capable of prolonged silences when none but ourselves and the servants were in the house, she would walk about its passages, or sit over her sewing, sunk deep in reverie. There seemed more than ever of these long silences now that Uncle Lucy was gone—gone with the cruel threat that this time it might be for ever. I conjecture that, in most of these reveries, her thoughts were absorbed by the past which would come no more.

But now it was Christmas, and she could be full of the present again, and happy and eager and unresting, because there was a party on the morrow. On Boxing Day the aunts would come for the usual family celebration, bringing, if possible, husbands and children too. And how Auntie Flavia rejoiced in the fuss of assembling the Clan around her on the second day of Christmas, even though she could get heated and worried and angry with me during the preparations! New leaves were screwed into the dining-room table till it was as long as a board-room table—a most satisfying mechanical task which I was always allowed to do—and this year we sat down nine to the symposium. A symposium in truth it was, since the aunts talked and talked, and still talked, over the food and the wine, and Uncle Arthur resolutely inserted his proper share into every discussion. The nine were Auntie Gloria and her two tall Hebraic-looking children, Brendaheim and Walterstein;

Evelyn and Arthur who had no children; Primrose the unmarried one; and our three selves.

As usual, Auntie Gloria arrived first, as a lesson in punctuality to the others. She arrived full of a throaty heartiness and the Christmas spirit. Behind her came Brenda like her lady-in-waiting, and Walter like her gentleman-at-arms. She gave Auntie Flavia her Kiss of Peace, resting both hands on her shoulders and hardly touching her cheek because she was talking all the time. She gave the 'Peace' likewise to Gael, still talking. Me she only wrung by the hand, but so heartily that her rings were a torment. 'Well, young man, you don't get any smaller, do you?' For me she always amplified her voice a little, conceiving a child of only fourteen to be something not far removed from an imbecile. 'Hope you're doing well at school. Attending to your studies properly? Good gracious, boy—why does he blush like that? Boys of fourteen shouldn't blush. You don't want to look like a girl.'

I could only reply to this idiocy with an economical smile, and damn the woman internally.

'Well, say good evening to your aunt like a proper little gentleman. You don't speak much, do you? He's no great talker, is he, Gael?'

Damn the idiot woman, and her mole sprouting hairs.

'Well, one can't draw blood out of a stone. Perhaps Gael has something to say. Gael dear, Christmas treating you well, I trust?'

Since she hardly ever stopped talking—not even when her sister was talking to her just as fluently—Brenda and Walter could say little. They were twenty-three and twenty respectively, but all their childhood they had been enjoined to sit upright and keep silent in the presence of their elders, and they were still inclined to do so. They were content, on the whole, to be 'seen and not heard.'

Next came Evelyn, bustling in, with Arthur following behind like a loyal and fussy little terrier. Always this rotund little woman bustled into a room leaving her Arturo somewhere behind, as if she were so happy and secure in this pleasing little possession that she could safely forget all about him. He would come through the door in time like a spaniel that has loitered. After kissing her hostess fervently, and Gloria formally, she cried to Gael, 'Come you here, Brenda, Margaret, Walter, Emily, Constance—*Gael*. Gael, I mean. Come and be kissed, my dear. And you, too, Travers. Arthur, kindly notice that I always get Travers's name right first time.' With a smile and a wave of her palm she swept all the previous inaccuracies aside.

Arthur, always neat, but at his very neatest in his satin-faced dinner-jacket and big winged collar, jerked up and down on his toes before Auntie Flavia as he gave her greeting, and bobbed hardly less as he spoke to Gael. With me he kept flat on his feet. It was only in front of the opposite sex that he went up and down.

So far all were deporting themselves as we expected them to do, but now came Primrose; and into the room with Primrose came a revelation. An astounding revelation. It was six months since we had seen her, and some time between that July and this December, on some great day, she had decided to be suppressed and silent no more. She had burst her strait-waistcoat, cast its strings from her and decided to be free. She had experienced Conversion.

This astounding conversion had been wrought by an odd little club off Piccadilly. As some other lonely spinster might seek company in a church and be won to sanctity by somebody loved there, so Primrose had joined this odd little club and there been wonderfully liberated from the sins of female submission by an extremely fascinating, good-looking, emancipated lady. She was now an effervescing spirit, charged—nay, overcharged—with gaiety, ribaldry and a readiness to shock all prudes. Did I liken her once to a dead city which the desert had conquered? Well, now the city had miraculously come alive, with all its palaces and fun-fairs gaily illuminated; a place devoted to pleasure and naughtiness.

'Well, children,' she shouted at her sisters, all older than she. 'How's the world? How are we all? Ready for some more Christmas fare? Hope you're all recovering from yesterday. No belly troubles anywhere.'

It was wonderful. We children gaped. But if it was a revelation to us, it was not so to the aunts. They, it seemed, had heard of Primrose's emancipation, but been too surprised by it, and doubtful of it, to mention it to children.

'Hallo, Gloria,' she continued. 'Hallo, Evelyn, and Arthur, ducks. My God, did I eat properly yesterday night? My dears, I did. I ate myself nearly sick. At my new club, the Taj Mahal. Why it's called the Taj Mahal, the Lord only knows. It's not in the least like the Taj Mahal because instead of going up it goes down; it's in a basement in Swallow Street. And there's nothing Indian about it except the decorations; but it's a cock-and-hen club, thank goodness. A club limited to females is quite unspeakable. Not that we can get up to any tricks because Vine Street police station is just opposite. But the grub is good. And the wines—what ho! I don't mind admitting they made me quite a little tight.'

Even though prepared for some such exhibition the sisters were staring. In silence.

'And how's our Gael? My God, she'll soon be a young woman. Darling, are the boys beginning to come around? They'll come all right, don't you worry. Travers—where is he? Where does he get to?' Always shy and uneasy at these adult parties, I had withdrawn, in my fashion, to a desert in a corner. I came forward, uncomfortably. 'My! Is this really our Travers? How he does shoot up!' She banged me heartily on the back and I jumped at the shock. 'Has your voice bust yet?'

'No,' I said; and the wretched syllable came from a voice obviously intact. But inwardly I wanted to say that, if she banged me like that, it wouldn't last two days more.

'How are you doing at your school? Not too badly—eh? Fine. But listen. Listen to me. Don't put up with too much back-chat from the masters. Keep 'em in their proper places.'

Since the others were still gazing at her in doubt and

disapproval, Auntie Flavia diverted the talk. 'Well, we're all here now. There was no getting Constance from Torquay. I think we can go down to the dining-room and eat.'

'Ah, thank God!' said Primrose.

'Really, Primrose,' Gloria chided as she rose. 'Need we have quite so much blasphemy?'

'You shut up, Gloria sweet,' laughed Primrose. 'Anyone may say thank God occasionally. That's nothing to what I can do sometimes.'

Gloria said, 'Tut, tut' behind her teeth.

'Now you be quiet, Gloria. I'm feeling jolly and don't intend to be made miserable by you. Walter, give me your arm and lead me down properly.'

'Certainly, Aunt Primrose,' said Walter, crooking his elbow before her.

'Such a gentleman!' said Primrose approvingly.

We went down to the dining-room, and all vented their admiration of Auntie Flavia's Christmas table. On her best white damask lay a centre-piece of holly, ivy, cotton-wool snow and glittering frost. Four tall candles in tall Sheffield candlesticks honoured it with their small, stately flames; and the crossed crackers lay all around it like printer's flowers around a title page. Elsewhere, on the shining cloth were basket-handled jars of preserved ginger and a dozen small dishes holding bonbons, chocolates, candied figs, glacé greengages, Carlsbad plums, dates, or almonds and raisins.

Arthur bobbed up and down before the table as if it were a beautiful woman. 'Quite lovely!' he said. 'There's nobody like Flavia for this sort of thing. There never was.' And he bobbed again. 'Perfect.'

Primrose said, 'Crikey! Looks promising. And is my mouth watering, girls?'

Auntie Flavia put Arthur on her right and Gloria on her left, and young Walter at the opposite end of the table. She put Evelyn between me and Gloria (thank God) and the sprightly Primrose on my other side. A jar of preserved ginger was in front of me, so on the whole I was content.

Arthur said Grace at his hostess's invitation, and it was hardly finished before Primrose said, 'We're sadly short of men. Three men to six females. Never mind, I've got Travers here, and he'll look after me.' From a dish she picked a raisin and an almond. 'Holy Matrimony,' she said, since this was what in those days we called the brown wrinkled raisins and the bridal-white almonds. 'This is about as far as I shall ever get to it.' And she shot raisin and almond into her mouth. 'Too long in the tooth now.'

The talk during the first course was a succession of loud and lively exchanges between the aunts, with Arthur resolutely forcing into every topic his rightful share, and being occasionally heard. But since this was the Christmas of 1905 the talk soon turned to the fall of the Conservative Government a few weeks before, and then the conversational ball dropped at Arthur's feet, and he was able to keep it there, dribbling it past any woman who tried to stop him. For he was the only well-informed politician at our board. He was an extremely keen politician; so much so that Evelyn would often say, 'My poor darling Arturo cares for nothing but his silly politics.' He was a fervent Radical, probably because he was small, and most of the men he met, bigger than he, were Tories. Never was he more completely the Radical than when he sat in the same room as Gloria, for she also was bigger than he and a Tory. And tonight—never had he such a chance to provoke her because he could prophesy an overwhelming victory for the Liberals and Radicals in the coming general election and aver with delight that Sir Henry Campbell-Bannerman, their leader, would command the strongest government the country had seen for years. Now at last the People's Cause would triumph in every field. Let the House of Lords, and Privilege and Wealth everywhere, look to their defences. (Uncle Arthur was ever the small man decrying, for his dignity's sake, the insolence of Privilege and Power.)

But I doubt if the aunts would have conceded him much silence for this manner of talk had he not said of a sudden, and in a mysterious tone, 'I can't help thinking of one name missing from Campbell-Bannerman's Government, and it was a name that, more than any other, would have helped to sweep the country.'

Silence. A silence as if the memory of us children in the room chilled the aunts. But young Walter, having no such reason to feel the cold, demanded, 'What name, Uncle?'

Arthur didn't answer him. Addressing the women as before, he declared, 'No man ever had the heart of the people as he did.'

They knew of whom he was speaking, and Auntie Flavia said softly, hoping perhaps that we should not listen and hear, 'Yes, but he would be too old now. He couldn't stump the country as he used to do. And he'd be too old for any great office.'

'Not a bit of it. Gladstone was prime minister at seventy-seven, and again at eighty-two. Palmerston was premier at seventy-one and practically remained so till his death ten years later.'

'Don't mention him in the same breath as Gladstone,' said Gloria. 'Gladstone, whatever his politics, was a great and good man.'

'I shall certainly mention him in the same breath,' Arthur announced, and I got the impression that the more Gloria disparaged this nameless Liberal, the more wildly Arthur would belaud him. 'Neither Gladstone nor Palmerston had his appeal to the masses. He had them in the hollow of his hand. And what was so utterly strange about this was that, if ever a man looked an aristocrat of the aristocrats, it was he.'

'But isn't that just what your precious People love?' snorted Gloria.

'Possibly, but did you ever see him on a platform? His manner was completely reserved and aloof. He wouldn't even smile at his jokes, even though the whole audience was laughing. You would have imagined that he thought all laughter and smiling a regrettable weakness of the common people.'

'A pose. Nothing but a pose, because he knew what

your People like. They like a gentleman for their leader. And the more of an aristocrat he seems, the more they love him.'

'Maybe, but not to the point of regarding him with veneration——'

'Veneration fiddlesticks!'

'They venerated him because, even though he belonged to one of the noblest families in the land, he was on their side always—even to the point of leading the agitation against the House of Lords.'

'Which was to be a traitor to his class. And I don't like traitors. I never did.'

'Oh, *but*——' began Arthur irritably, as if Gloria had made a remark worthy of a prep-school boy, as indeed she had.

'It was a mercy he never said to them what he once said to me,' laughed Auntie Flavia, having probably forgotten us by now.

'And that was?' prompted Evelyn.

'That he couldn't understand it, but he just felt it his duty to work for the people, however much he regretted their existence. Primrose, dear, a little more turkey?'

'Well, I'm full almost to bursting already, but there! I'll try a shade more. No one shall say I'm not sporty.'

'Maybe he said that.' Arthur had got the conversational ball back at his feet. 'Maybe he did, but he managed to win their hearts by his indignant speeches against any oppression anywhere. He fought for the oppressed and the exploited always, whether it was the Irish or the Boers or the Zulus or the Catholics——'

'Or us poor women,' put in Primrose. 'He supported votes for us poor girls. For single ones at any rate. And that's me. You married girls have got husbands to look after you.'

'He certainly never regretted the existence of women,' said Evelyn; which set the table laughing oddly. 'And now, Arthur, stop talking all your silly politics.'

'But who *is* this, Uncle?' persisted young Walter. 'What's his name? Who're you talking about?'

'I'm talking about one of the best-loved——'

But Gloria, who didn't listen to children, and least of all to her own, nor to her sister's husband if she considered he ought to be snubbed, interrupted, 'If he was one of the best-loved, he was also one of the most hated.'

'By the High Tories, yes. And I don't wonder. He———'

'The Queen objected strongly to him,' said Gloria, as if that settled the matter.

'Well, well, well; and what else would you expect? Good God, wasn't the lady a High Tory herself?'

'She asked Gladstone if there was no way he could be suppressed. And right up to the last she didn't want to have him in the Cabinet.' Gloria never listened to counter arguments, till she'd completed her own—if then.

'I don't care what she wanted. This country, thank the Lord, is no longer at the mercy of one old woman's will.'

'Now then, Arthur!' Evelyn admonished him. 'No getting hot now!'

But Arthur's arguments were not to be stopped any more than Gloria's. 'The old dear thought that to attack the House of Lords was a first step towards attacking the Throne.'

'And so it is,' muttered Gloria.

'So it *isn't*!' Arthur had spluttered over these words, and for the moment could utter no more. His lips moved, but no words came. He tossed his head in his indignation with Gloria.

So Evelyn, his wife, offered some words that might serve as reconciliation. 'But, Arthur dear, you've always told me that Herbert Gray, Herbert Cluffe, William Whiteley— oh, whatever was the man's name?—Oscar Wilde—*Herbert Asquith* told you that he was a sore trial, not only to the Tories, but to the Whips of his own party as well.'

'He certainly was! Naturally!' Arthur allowed this triumphantly. 'They were never quite sure that he wouldn't vote against them if he thought they were neglecting their responsibility to the poor or the friendless or the underdogs anywhere. And even after he'd been given high office he would make speeches that his less radical colleagues disliked. And since he had a pretty spice of venom on his tongue these speeches raised up enemies for him everywhere. Oh, yes! Mind you, I think he deserved it. His wit could sting. And those who suffered his ridicule enjoyed it not at all.'

'No.' Auntie Flavia, who had kept strangely quiet, now spoke softly and bitterly. 'And all of them watched for their chance of revenge, and they had it in the end. Evelyn, let me give you another slice. They got all they wanted in the end.'

'They did, they did,' Arthur sighed. 'And it was the whole country's loss.'

'I don't agree at all,' snapped Gloria. 'The man was proved in a court of law to be an out-and-out fraud.'

'*Never!*' cried Auntie Flavia, flinging down her carving knife, so that we jumped at the crash and then stared at her with interest. It looked as though she might stage one of her 'scenes', with tears flooding and breath pulsating. That word 'fraud' was a wind in the mountains, and the lake, calm a moment ago, might be swept up into turmoil. Her hands had gripped the table's edge as if she'd like to rise and give her sister such a cuff as would throw her off her chair. 'Fraud's a wicked word to use of him, and I won't hear it uttered in my presence. I just won't. Not from Gloria or anyone else. It's a lie. There, I've said it! Christmas or not, I've said it! I don't think it's kind to say such things in front of me.' A sob; a handkerchief touching her eyes. 'I don't. . . . None of you knew him in his great days. Only after he was broken. . . . He's said to me a thousand times that the one thing he was absolutely sincere about was his politics——'

'And you really believe that? Well, you always were ludicrously sentimental——'

'Of course I believe it. And I not only believe it, I know it. I know it as no one else in the world can know it. And in any case'—she calmed a little—'politics had nothing to do with it.'

'Oh, well. . . .' Gloria shrugged, as if remembering that Flavia had spread this handsome Christmas table;

perhaps, too, that this was a season of goodwill. 'Brenda, you've had enough wine.'

'Oh, let the child enjoy herself, lovey-duck,' begged Primrose. 'We can live but once.'

'Yes, you drink what you want, dear,' said Evelyn.

'Brenda, you will not have any more,' her mother announced.

Since it was obvious that Gloria had retreated a little, and was assaulting, for a change, a position which she could more easily overthrow, Arthur pressed after her with alacrity. 'You never saw him at a political meeting, Gloria. I did. It must have been all of thirty years ago; in '74, I think, because he was arguing in favour of the bill for extending the hours of polling, so that working men could have a fair chance; '74, and long before I knew I should be—well, in a way connected with him.' This confirmed our suspicion of whom they were talking, and our eyes swung, fascinated, from one to another. 'It was in the old Crispe Hall in Kensington, and the place was packed—largely with working men. First there was his voice. They used to say that his voice was worth thousands of votes to his party——'

'People will say anything,' scoffed Gloria.

'Yes, they used to say that.' Auntie Flavia spoke tearfully, to make amends for her outburst. Her storm had died at birth, quelled by a Christmas table. She didn't want her party spoilt. The lake was still again, or fairly so.

'Then he was a natural orator—though I've heard that his most eloquent passages were carefully prepared beforehand——'

'They were.' Auntie Flavia came in again, to show that she was behaving well now. 'No one knew the colossal pains he took with his speeches. Sometimes he worked on them right through the night.'

'And I doubt if any of that great effort was really necessary,' interrupted Arthur, anxious to get on with his story, 'because it hardly mattered what he said. It was a commonplace that audiences would listen to him if he only repeated the alphabet. And on this occasion he so charmed them that they were all standing and cheering and clapping after he'd sat down. And it was just then, just when the hall was shaking with their cheering and whistling and stamping, and he was looking at the ceiling, as if it all meant nothing to him, that some Tory roughs in the street below hurled bolts and iron bars through the windows, and the flying glass scattered on the floor. No one was hurt, and he just looked round at the noise, hardly condescending to raise his eyebrows at it. That kind of hooliganism was following him everywhere then, but it did him more good than harm; and I suspect that he knew this, and grimly enjoyed it—even saying things to provoke it. If you remember, the Liberals were thrown out in that election, and he was one of the few who easily survived the rout.'

'I've never denied he was a popular idol,' said Gloria with a sigh which suggested that she alone was keeping her head cool and arguing sensibly, 'but I suppose I may be allowed to say that in my humble view he was absurdly over-rated.'

'You may say it as much as you like, and not a statesman in Europe would have agreed with you.'

'I don't care about that. I form my own opinions.'

'And I have a fag at this stage,' said Primrose, lighting up a cigarette to shock them all. 'Go on, Arthur dear. Give Gloria what-for.'

'I quite agree with Arthur,' announced Evelyn, who was seldom silent if anyone was being rude to her Arturo. 'And I believe all the Tories think the same—all of them—and I'm not excepting Mr. Balmore, Beardmore, Birkenhead, Bobbadil—oh, *you* know—what's the silly man's name? Balfour. Mr. Balfour.' She rested on the name like a trawler that had come buffeting into its anchorage.

'Gambetta thought him the coming power in Britain,' Arthur pursued. 'Bismarck said something of the same sort, and everyone knows that Gladstone was looking towards him as his successor. It's pretty safe to say that, if his career hadn't been shattered by a shot from you-know-who's gun, the name of our present prime minister would not have been Campbell-Bannerman but de Brath.'

So that name dropped among the bon-bons and the fruits on that Christmas table. Gael's startled glance met mine. It was like the meeting of two wine glasses in a mutual toast. Each of us was seeing Don Francesco in his cape and wide-awake hat strutting along our pavements with feet out-turned.

'De Brath? Never heard of him,' said Walter.

'It was long before your time,' Gloria snubbed him.

'And he's quite forgotten now,' said Evelyn in a dropped voice, forgetting that she'd said the opposite at the party six months before.

'Quite,' agreed Gloria. 'And in any case it wasn't very interesting.'

Primrose hummed, 'Ta-ra-ra-boom-de-ay!' loudly, as one who would distract attention with music from a social gaffe.

But before they could flounder out from the morass into which Arthur's eager and self-justifying argumentativeness had dragged them, Evelyn had mumbled sentimentally, to no one in particular; to the table in general, perhaps, or merely to herself, 'There was a queer strain in all the de Braths. A wild, devil-may-care strain which could be attractive enough but brought more than one of them to disaster, and the great Lord Roland was a pretty good example of this.' Lord Roland! We were in possession of his full name. Lord Roland de Brath.

'But who *is* he? Who *was* he?' repeated young Walter.

Happily at this point they were extricated by a summons from the passage. The Christmas pudding was waiting in the hall, and Auntie Flavia, jumping up, begged Arthur to come and help her get it alight. Arthur, confident that this was something no woman would be able to do, and delighting to be the superior and efficient male, ran out after her like an eager little terrier. Evelyn said to his departing back, 'Yes, you go, Arturo. Arthur's wonderful at that sort of thing;' and in a few seconds she was proved right for Auntie Flavia entered bringing the dark dome of pudding with blue flames licking around it and the sprig of holly on its crown crackling and drooping in the fire like a martyr at Smithfield. A good smell of rum censed the table as she laid it down. Everyone cheered, Primrose hammered a spoon on the cloth, Evelyn said, 'Bravo, my Arthur!' and in those blue flames young Walter's question perished like the holly and the rum.

CHAPTER TEN

But unlike that sprig of holly our question remained brilliantly alight. It stayed burning like a flame inexhaustibly fed. Lord Roland de Brath. Our Uncle Lucy a lord! Really a lord. Great and thrilling news, since we were as snobbish as anyone else in our road. And once a statesman world-famous (we liked to exaggerate the fame)! And a Liberal. I who had supposed all Liberals to be cads became a Liberal in that hour. It must be possible now to find out all about him. But how? Into my head came the name 'Brains'. Who on earth was Brains, asked Gael. I explained: a Modern and Mathematical cad at St. Paul's; John Fenner Pryce, nicknamed Brains; Pryce, J. ('J' only, since no nonsense of double names was endured at St. Paul's unless they were securely hyphened). Was not old Brains's father standing as a Liberal candidate in the coming election, and would not Brains accordingly know all about, or be able to learn all about, the great Liberal statesmen of the past?

Yes, Brains, with his vast knowledge of the world, and of most other things too, could direct me to the truth.

Never mind if it was the Christmas holidays. Our school was a day school with boys converging upon it from all parts of London, and Pryce, J. did it honour by coming upon it, with his brains, from Chiswick. Nineteen hundred and six broke, Parliament was dissolved, the election campaign began, and I learned that Dr. Fenner Pryce was standing for the constituency he'd nursed so long; Chiswick and Acton. I went to Chiswick. I found one of his busy committee rooms in the High Road. It was full of women helpers, and I explained to one that I was a life-long Liberal and willing to distribute pamphlets and election addresses. I also mentioned casually my friendship with their candidate's son, and asked where to find him. He lived in

Sutton Court Road, they said, and there I found him in his father's large grey house whose long dining-room, left of the door, was now a littered committee room. Brains was in charge of it, and in glory. It was four weeks since I had seen him, and in those four weeks he seemed to have grown several inches. He was only fourteen but his voice had broken and his upper lip showed the first hints of a black moustache. I felt that this fine development must have something to do with his brains, and I was not a little annoyed to find myself of a sudden nervous in his presence. Nervous of old Brains? This was something I would not be. 'Brains, old son,' I said. 'I've come to help.'

'Come to help, man?' he echoed in his shocking deep voice. Its rasping masculinity made mine sound like Gael's. 'Hurray. We need all we can get. Not that we haven't got the enemy on the run everywhere, but we're determined to make it an absolute rout. Thank God they arranged this election in the hols when I could give my whole time to it.'

He might have been managing, here in Battle Head-quarters, the Liberal campaign all over the country.

High staff officer though he thought himself, he was glad, I saw, to have a friend of his own age to come into the streets with him and push the Liberal bills through people's doors and hammer joyously on their knockers. After we'd mini-stered thus to two or three streets I felt that I could tactfully open my researches, so I asked him between one letter-box and the next, and with an assumption of carelessness, 'Was there ever a Liberal M.P. of the name of de Brath?'

'De who, man?'

'De Brath. Lord Roland de Brath.'

'De Brath?' Brains didn't like not knowing the answer, so he pretended deep thought. 'Let's see . . . when would this have been?' he inquired, as if the whole recent history of the Liberal Party were stored in his head.

'He was going strong in '74.'

'Oh, but that's more than thirty years ago.' Clearly he was glad of this relief from the necessity of knowing. 'I

wasn't born then. But I'll ask the pater. He'll know for a
cert, you bet.'

Next day, in a spell of quiet between two streets, I asked
with the same appearance of carelessness, 'About that de
Brath chap: did you find out anything?'

But of course he'd forgotten all about the matter. 'Oh
no, I've been too damned busy. What was the name?'

'De Brath.'

'Gosh, what a foul name.'

'Lord Roland de Brath.'

'But why do you want to know all about him?'

'Because,' I said proudly, 'I may be a distant connection
of his.'

'Is that so? Good crikey! Then Debrett's Peerage
is your book. But if he was a peer, old cock, he
couldn't have been an M.P.' He was proud of this
piece of political knowledge. 'No wonder I hadn't heard
of him.'

'Oh!' I said, and was confused. Uncle Lucy had certainly been 'in Parliament for a little.' 'Golly,' I muttered.

'He could have been in the House of Lords, of course.'

'Is that "Parliament"?'

'Of course it is, you consummate cow.'

'Well, perhaps that was it.' Perhaps it was; and that
evening when we parted I reminded him, 'Don't forget
about my distant but noble connection.'

He did not forget. So little had he forgotten that next
morning he ran out of the crowded committee room in the
High Road, where we were to meet and saluted me on the
pavement with 'What ho for Lord Roland de Bath Soap!'
(His brains might be above the average for his age but his
humour was not. Personally I thought it retarded.) 'I
can tell you all about him, my son.'

'Good.'

I said 'good', but my heart rocked like a half-inflated
balloon. Fear was inflating it.

'It's a story and half, man. *Whooo!* It certainly is.
Dad knew all about it.'

My heart rocked further. 'Then he was in Parliament?'

'Not half he wasn't! He was a younger son of a marquess, so it was all right for him to be an M.P. You didn't tell me that. You should have told me that.' He implied that he could have explained everything if he'd known that, but I felt sure he'd only known it since last night. 'Lord Roland Louis Grenville Caen de Brath——'

'*Louis*, did you say?'

'Louis Grenville Caen de Brath.'

'Grenville?'

'Yes, he was called that after one of his godfathers, Lord Grenville, Dad says. He was a terrific figure in his day. Dad says his speeches in the House were wonderful and all the members used to crowd in to hear him. They were so witty and so deadly to his enemies, that all the other chaps in the House who weren't getting shot to pieces simply loved listening to him. Dad says they'd rather hear him than anyone else, never mind whether he was on their side or not. If he was all that clever, you can't take after him. I doubt the connection, myself.'

I saw him standing outside the Houses of Parliament that evening, with his eyes upon them and his hand on my shoulder, pressing it.

'But the trouble was'—Brains's next words scattered this dream—'he got into terrible disgrace.'

A bullet in my heart. 'Yes?' I said wretchedly.

'There was a case of some sort, a trial, and it was one hell of a sensation in half the newspapers of the world.'

'What sort of case?' I asked, feeling a little sick, and trembling, but anxious to hear. 'Come on. Tell us.'

'No, don't go in there, man. It's not something I can talk about before all those women. It's not a subject for women. Have some sense, my dear man. Come for a stroll.'

We strolled along the noisy High Road, winding our way through hurrying people; and Brains told me stories of long ago, while the general election of 1906 waited. 'I'm not quite clear about the case because Dad was too busy to talk much, but it was a pretty ghastly affair, I imagine.

Mum said it was "something one doesn't talk about", but Dad who always says you must answer children's questions at once and fearlessly, told me it was all about a woman. A woman called Lottie Morris who seems to have been a real stunner——'

('My poor lost Lottie.' 'She was with me there once upon a time.')

'Mum agrees that she was a knock-out for beauty. Gosh, I'd like to have seen her. A really saucy piece of goods; really swish.' He smacked his lips, as one who'd had experience of women who were swish. 'At any rate your Lord Roland thought so, and he and Lottie got up to games together, meeting in secret and even sharing a lonely house in secret, though she was married, just as he was. He was separated from his wife, but she wasn't, and after a time her husband, a colonel, and quite a famous old boy in his way, found out all about it and really opened fire. Then hell broke loose with a vengeance, because Lord R. was a cabinet minister at the time, and some truly meaty episodes came out in evidence at the trial.'

'Trial?'

'Oh yes, it was a trial all right,' said Brains cocksurely. 'Of him and her. And he a cabinet minister in old Gladstone's government, mark you. And the G.O.M., so Dad says——'

'The who?'

'The Grand Old Man, as they called old Gladstone—didn't you know that?—the G.O.M. had just been thundering from Midlothian against unrighteousness everywhere. No wonder the Tories were cock-a-hoop, and the Liberals down in the depths, because we Liberals, you see, are just about sunk if we upset our Nonconformist supporters who're more than half our party. Dad says that, with the admirable purpose of keeping the Nonconformist vote, your Lord Roland used to pretend to enormous godliness. He always went to church and often read the lessons much better than the Vicar. He's said to have told them that he never made an important decision in his ministry, or a big speech in Parliament, without first saying his prayers. So when the old colonel really opened up with all the ammunition he could find—or when, as you might say, he sounded the Charge and came galloping down the hill waving his sword like Richard Coeur-de-Lion or someone—well, you can see it made a very sweet story for the newspapers all over the world.'

'I suppose it did.'

'But Mum says it wasn't altogether fair to call him a hypocrite, because he really did love the Church and its services and the words of the Bible. He used to say he was glad he did so, because it was really the only way to get anywhere with Mr. Gladstone and the Bon Dieu.'

'What happened to him?' I asked, not smiling because still trembling. 'Was he put in prison?'

'Good gracious no, you ox. You don't go to prison for that sort of thing. But everything was blasted to high smithereens for him. He had to resign his office and his seat, and soon afterwards he disappeared. And Dad says an enormous number of big-wigs from the Queen downwards were quite glad to have seen the last of him.'

'The people were sorry, weren't they?' I said—or, rather, begged.

'No. They sang comic songs about him in the streets, though he'd worked for them all his life. A bit thick I call that.'

'What sort of songs?'

'Well, one went, "The sweet little Lottie sends everyone potty" and another said something like "The noble Lord Roley wasn't so holy". And dirty songs too, which Dad wouldn't tell me. Not even Dad. So they must have been pretty awful.'

I sighed. 'Perhaps it was their fun, because they used to love him a lot. I know that. When was all this?'

'Oh, twenty-five years ago, about. Mum just remembers it. She remembers hearing the songs as a girl. But of course that sort of popular excitement is very quickly over. Something else comes along and it's forgotten. Dad says he hasn't heard his name mentioned in a dozen years and he wonders what became of him. He doubts if he's still alive.'

§

I ran home to Gael. I leapt up the stairs. I found her in the Playroom, sitting at the table before a story book and weeping at its climax. Her tears flopped on to it last pages. Published by the Sunday School Prize Association and entitled 'Odd-Girl-Out', it told of a schoolgirl, Susan Rosie, who was the most unpopular girl in the school because she would take no part in unChristian practices and persisted in saying her prayers in the dormitory at night. Everyone baited her, but she behaved in the most Christian way, rescuing her chief tormentor from drowning in a pond. For this the crowds on the bank cheered her; the whole school, after a speech by the Headmistress, acclaimed her; and the Royal Humane Society sent her a medal. But in the midst of her triumph a little dog, Timothy, who'd been her only friend in the loveless days, died in its basket. Her tears fell into the basket (Gael's tears following) but 'suffering is a great teacher', said this elevating book, and she learned that Life was inevitably a mixture of joy and sorrow, gain and loss, and, taking comfort in the text, 'Whom the Lord loveth He chasteneth', she was able to look down on the little still body in the basket and say, 'The Lord gave, the Lord hath taken away; blessed be the name of the Lord.'

An unprepossessing child, but Gael didn't seem to be thinking so.

My grim statement, 'I've found out everything,' lifted her instantly from her vicarious grief. It stanched her tears better than adrenalin halts a flow of blood. She sat in her chair and stared, while I, still standing near the door, rehearsed all that Brains had told me. Her reception of it caused me surprise because, whereas I had been immersed in sadness by it, almost as if I'd heard of Uncle Lucy's death, she showed no distress but only a consuming and inextinguishable interest in the beautiful Lottie Morris. In

134

Lottie Morris who was surely nothing to us, while the whole of my mind was occupied with Uncle Lucy and his disgrace!

'Oh, I love little Lottie,' she cried. 'She sounds adorable to me. We must find out all about her. I feel sure she was heart-breakingly lovely. How can we find out more? When did all this happen? Did you ask the Brains boy?'

'He said about twenty-five years ago.'

'Yes, but what year, what month? When was the trial?'

'I didn't ask him that.'

'Oh, you ass. Ask him tomorrow.'

This I met with silence. Always timid in my talk with anyone except the family, always dreading a rebuff, I recoiled from asking the extremely busy Brains any more. 'He'd have to ask his old man,' I submitted, 'and his old man's far too busy electioneering.'

'But we must *know*. If we could know the date of the trial we could find out everything.'

'Where? How?'

'In the back files of *The Times*. At the Reference Library. I know we could because Winnie Clynes did something like that once. She went to the new Library in Brook Green Road, and she says they dragged up for her an enormous bound volume of *The Times*, all dusty and smelly, from the bowels of the earth. It was *The Times* of 1889. She wanted to read about her father's death. He was a lieutenant in the Navy and died in an accident at sea, doing something brave; and she wanted to read all the nice things said about him. She thinks she takes after him.'

Gael was now fifteen, and whereas a boy of that age is still but a coltish child, she seemed already a plump young woman. And whereas a boy of only fifteen can hardly associate with tall lads of seventeen she had friends of seventeen and eighteen and longed to 'put her hair up' like them. Winnie Clynes was seventeen and more and she and Gael were as devoted to each other as if they were coevals. Their mutual love was partly rooted in a common adoration of Mr. Appledore and a common addiction to piety and prayers.

They exchanged their autograph albums, and Winnie wrote in Gael's:

> Contemplate when the sun goes down
> Thy death with deep reflection,
> And, when again he, rising, shines,
> Thy resurrection.

And Gael in Winnie's:

> This life is but a pang and all is over,
> But in the life to come which fades not away
> Every love shall abide and every lover.
> Christina Rosetti.
> Gael Harrington.

I made fun of this mutual 'pash' and, since my humour at fourteen was still coprophilous, would always refer to Winnie Clynes by her initials. Conversely I always spoke of the privy on the landing as the Winifred Clynes. I acted thus vulgarly now: I suggested that Gael must go to the W.C. without fail tomorrow. She agreed enthusiastically to do so.

'I'll go immediately after breakfast when she's sure to be there. Winnie'll get it all out of her mother. If it was all that scandalous Mrs. Clynes'll know the last thing about it and be ready to discuss it by the hour. Can I say we're kind of related to it? No, I suppose not. Winnie says that if there's any gossip going, her mother'll chatter about it with her all day and all night. She had no one else to talk to, poor sweet. We must have the exact date and then hey for the Ref. Library and the back files of *The Times*.'

'But will they let anyone as young as us see them?'

'I shall be seventeen,' said Gael. 'Seventeen and a half, to be exact.'

There was no more we could do that day, so, Gael having finished 'Odd-Girl-Out', I read it all that evening and wept no less bitterly than she.

§

But by the time I was in bed I was sunk again in my memories of all that Brains had told me. Ideas for questions to be put to Winnie Clynes sprouted in my head, and some of them seemed so good that they jumped me out of the bedclothes and drove me down to Gael's room. I opened the door quietly and saw that she was still kneeling at her bedside, deep in prayer. So I crept upstairs again and lay for a little longer in my warm bed. But here the ideas sprang and sprang, and so swelled within me that I was taut with them, and must run down to her door again. I opened the door reverently but she was still on her knees, with her face in the quilt. I shut the door gently but stayed in the passage, confident that her devotions couldn't be protracted much further. Perhaps a minute later or perhaps thirty seconds, for a minute is a long time in a dark passage and the cold of a January night, I opened the door a third time and looked in. There she was, still on her knees, so I grumbled aloud, 'Oh, hell,' and compressed my shivering shoulders; while she, without lifting her face, spat out, 'Oh *go* away, can't you? Go *away*!'

Then I noticed that her little black manual, *The Garden of the Soul*, lay open on the quilt before her, so, knowing that all the Hours of Prayer were in this book, including Vespers, Compline, Nocturn, and Lauds (I knew, because she had once—and only once—invited me to take my part in Compline) I mumbled, 'Oh, blast!' and left her to her gardening.

§

In the morning I begged a blessing from so holy a child, but received instead some heavy abuse, being likened to a hog and a skunk; after which we got back to the question of Winnie Clynes. I gave Gael all my new suggestions, and she ran with them to Winnie directly breakfast was done.

And two afternoons later she came rushing home—knowledge, great knowledge, a driving and pulsing engine in her breast. 'Oh, it's too wonderful. He was the co-respondent in—' she sank her voice to a whisper—'a simply terrible divorce suit. We haven't the date yet, but Winnie's going to get it somehow. Her mother says she remembers it because she was at school at the time, and all the girls were thrilled to bits about it. They went about telling each other all the spiciest parts. She was about sixteen, she thinks, so it must have happened in about 1880. She says that Lottie Morris had been famous as one of the loveliest débutantes of her year and was still very beautiful when the huge storm broke, being still only about twenty-nine. She says *her* mother used to say that all the conversation in a room stopped when Lottie Morris entered, and in half a twinkling all the men were around her. Oh I wish I were more beautiful. I wish everybody turned to look at me as I went by.'

'No danger of that,' I said; and she, after admitting sadly, 'I know. I'm afraid not,' burst on, '*He* was quite terrific too. His hair was brown and curly then, and so were his moustaches and his funny little imperial. He was more than twenty-one years older than my beloved Lottie when they first met—about forty-eight—and in 1880, when it all blew up, he must have been about fifty-one. So nice. Just right. I shall never marry anyone less than twenty years older than me. Her husband was a colonel—Colonel Giscourt Morris—and he was a lot older too, and very rich, and a tremendous Low Churchman—I hate Low Church—he was treasurer of his Diocesan Conference and chairman of his Diocesan Fund, and something big in the Church's Council for Moral Welfare; and Mrs. Clynes suggests that Lottie, who was the gayest of the gay, probably had a fancy for rather less prudery and rather more passion.'

'Golly!' I mumbled, thinking this an indecent remark.

But Gael said only, 'I bet she did! And why not; what else, if, as Mrs. Clynes says, she was the most bewitching creature ever? Of course I know she and my beloved Uncle Lucy oughtn't to have done what they did, but I can't help feeling on their side, somehow. I'm sure the Colonel was a horrible old prig. Gosh, isn't it thrilling?'

It was weeks before she and Winnie got the date of the divorce suit. Having none of my recoil from importuning, or my fear of a rebuff, she kept plaguing Winnie to harass her mother into finding out, but nothing came of this infestation. In the end they got it by writing to the journal, 'M.A.P.' (Mainly About People) which always had a page of 'Reader's

Questions and Answers.' They wrote (I was there in the Playroom as they composed the letter): 'We have been asked to compile a brief history of Liberal and Radical Politics during the latter half of the last century. It will be designed chiefly for foreign students in this country—' this was a contribution of mine—'and we should be most grateful if you could give us the exact dates of the celebrated divorce suit which brought about the fall of Lord Roland de Brath.' The letter was signed, 'Frederick Leonard Whitby' (Winnie having spent a holiday that summer at Whitby) and 'Oswald Tollemache' (which Gael thought sounded like an historical author's name).

The answer appeared three weeks later. The case had been heard on two days of July, 1880.

CHAPTER ELEVEN

By now it was February, and we had long been back at school, so it was only on a bright Saturday morning that we could hurry off to the Public Library in Brook Green Road, having first assured the household that we were going to enjoy the sun in Kensington Gardens. We went towards it in a great eagerness, and I in some fear. Besides this fear of what we might read, there was guilt in my heart lest we were committing some serious offence by wilfully deceiving a Public Library; my heart shook within me as we turned into Brook Green Road and saw the red-brick-and-white-stone building in all its shop-newness; it thumped in protest as we climbed the cold stairs to the Reference Library.

This was a fine rectangular room with a vaulted white ceiling arching over it and a stained glass window at either end. The east window was particularly brilliant and caught my eye at once because it portrayed a life-size figure of the founder of my school, Dean Colet, in his coloured robes. The arms of the school were blazoned beside him, and the instant gift to me from this resplendent window was a fear of expulsion. I turned from it uneasily and saw that the west window glowed with the arms of the borough. Then I began to feel between the devil and the deep blue sea, the devil being Dr. Hillard, my High Master at St. Paul's, and the deep blue sea the policemen in the borough. My sense of guilt was not lessened by the sight of several probably straightforward and truthful students at the long oak tables, including two coloured men with wide noses, pale lips, and watching, flashing black eyes. Their skins might be dark but their souls, I felt, were whiter than mine this morning.

Perhaps because she was older, or perhaps because she was female, Gael seemed troubled by none of my guilt; she went straight up to the assistant behind the counter, a girl of about twenty in a blue overall, and, throwing her head to one side so as to look charming and establish happy public relations, said, 'I wonder if I might see the file of *The Times* for July 1880. It's to find out something for my father, and he needs it rather urgently because he's a journalist.'

'Why, certainly,' agreed the assistant, who, still young, was inclined to believe that all people who came to do research in a reference library must be persons of probity.

'He says,' continued Gael, 'that he knows you have the files because he came and consulted them only a little while ago.' Her readiness to lie in the daytime after praying for twenty minutes at night was always a perplexity to me. But even she rather over-did it today, as everyone is apt to do when he knows he is lying. She stressed her innocence too wordily, like an arrested man in a charge-room. 'Daddy says he's sure you'll let me see it because I'm seventeen now. And he's so dreadfully busy.'

'Oh, that's quite all right,' said this innocent behind the counter, with a helpful smile.

'And my brother here can help me? I rather wanted him to take down some notes.'

'Why, of course!' And with a further smile she disappeared through a door at her side, while Gael turned and grimaced triumphantly at me.

She returned, smiling, and said, 'It'll be here in a minute.' But we had to wait longer than that before an ancient grey porter in a dusty boiler suit, as if he'd just come up from a mine gallery beneath the Hammersmith earth—or up from the buried past—entered bearing a huge black bound volume laced with dust and cobwebs and smelling of both. He laid it on the counter and rubbed it clean with a cloth. The dust flew, and the girl assistant shied back like a pony to avoid the cloud, wrinkling her nose and smiling. He brought the volume through the counter-flap and laid it on a table for us; then grinned and nodded and went. I noticed Gael's fingers quivering as she turned the pages to July 1880; they shook so much that she actually tore the rotting edge of two pages. We came upon it at last. It had not been easy to find because, though there were columns of it, it was given no unusual prominence but merely treated as the first of other such cases, under the heading:

HIGH COURT OF JUSTICE
Probate Divorce and Admiralty Division
(Before Mr. Justice Cornwell)
Morris v. Morris and de Brath

Gael rested her quivering arms upon the table and began to read. I pressed up against her shoulder and read too. Sometimes she drew impatiently away from me as I pressed too hard, bending forward to read a piece of print that was already fading. The low winter sun, piercing through the jewelled window, threw patterns of bright colour on oak tables and book cases; outside in Brook Green Road the tram bells rang and the cart wheels drummed incessantly; the carters whistled at their horses, and the children on the pavements shouted in their Saturday morning play; the patterns of bright colour lifted with the earth's eastward turning and slid away through the window whence they had come; but all this had gradually died for us, as we went back together, side by side, and completely silent, twenty-five years into the past.

CHAPTER TWELVE

I WENT quite alone up Roehampton Lane to that mysterious house on the edge of Putney Heath. Mysterious? No; it was a house of mystery no longer, but it was haunted now as never before. Quite alone I went because I did not feel that Gael felt the same need to gaze upon a place where sad, exciting, haunting things had happened. Gael, I felt, would talk too much, and want to come away too soon. I wanted to be alone before it. To stand and stand . . . and stand.

It was easy to evade the household and take the bus to Roehampton (though it cost me all my pocket money). There was a Rugger match that afternoon between St. Paul's and Dulwich; I told Auntie Flavia that I wanted to watch it; and, for all she knew, a Rugger match, like a cricket match, lasted from noon till sunset.

I enjoyed my long drive on a front seat of the bus top, where a warm February breeze combed and raked my hair all the way. The sun had the winter sky all to itself and, in companionship with the ash-blue haze, had created a world of pastel tints and opalescent air. On all the upper faces of the westerly houses it laid a wash of pale light; and it so flood-lit the endless roofs of London that all high distant things, even chimney stacks and factory windows, rose sunlit and beautiful above reservoirs of watery mist.

Over Hammersmith Bridge and along the cosy stretch of Castlenau, and across Barnes Common—all the way I was engaged with an idea which had seized upon my heart in the Library and had filled it with excitement—with more than excitement; with a kind of breathless exultation. Long before this I had asked Auntie Flavia 'Is Uncle Lucy by any chance my father?' and she had answered, '*What? . . .* No! No, of course not. Who put that notion into your head?' I had gone on, 'But he could be, I suppose. It's just possible——' but at this point she stopped me angrily. 'Once and for all I tell you No! *No!*—do you hear? Now that's enough.'

I believed her, because I didn't think it possible she could lie so emphatically as that. But in that court—the lies, the perfidy, with which, as the evidence showed, Uncle Lucy and Lottie Morris had tried to screen their meeting and their times together from the Colonel, and from all the world! I wasn't blaming them (because I seemed incapable of blaming Uncle Lucy for anything) but I was asking myself whether Auntie Flavia was as ready to lie in his interest as Lottie Morris had been, and whether, perhaps, I really was his son. With Lottie Morris perhaps as my mother. Of course I hadn't been born till ten years after the trial, but so far Gael and I knew nothing of what had driven Uncle Lucy from the sight of his countrymen. Oh, was it really possible that I was their son? *His* son? Solemnly, on the top of that bus I looked for likenesses between myself and him. In my face I could find nothing, but of course its bones were still unformed. My tall slight figure might be the beginning of his. But it was from my character that I dredged up something that gave me hope and joy: our common melancholy. In public we both liked to jest gravely, but we both fell easily into melancholy, and, wandering off into solitude, could be moody and silent for hours on end. I was very happy about our melancholy.

The bus carried me up between the grey garden walls and the leafless trees of Roehampton Lane; it dropped me at the Earl Spencer Inn, and I was walking in Roehampton again, that hill-top village among the green landscapes. Six months had passed since we drove here in the fly, and I prayed that the house might still be empty, so that I could walk in its abandoned garden and, standing close to its windows, peep into empty rooms between the slats of broken blinds. I hurried towards it, along its curving side-road, with a mixture of pleasure, since the satisfying of an eager interest is pleasure, and sadness, since the story I had read told of shame and disaster to the only person in the world whom I loved. As its steep slate roofs showed above the trees, my heart trembled more than when I had approached the Library. It held more now.

Inishowen. The sun slanted down on its southern face as if mischievously lighting up its Gothic pomposities for me.

Yes, it was empty still and looking much the same as six months ago, except that the leaves were off the limes and one of the gates to the sweeping drive was adrift and askew. Not a doubt that behind each of those closed and blinded windows lay a dusty emptiness where I could make the ghosts of the past walk as I wished.

So I came to the house as, some thirty years before, Uncle Lucy and his beautiful mistress must have come, carefully to consider it. And, considering it, staring at it, my feet ankle-deep in the old greying grass of the lawn, I saw in imagination the Solicitor-General rising to speak in that crowded court, now tranced to stillness and rapt to hear.

§

'Long before the opening of the court,' *The Times* had said, 'a dense crowd of barristers and general public had assembled in the corridors outside, and at a few minutes past ten, when the doors were opened there was a rush and a scramble to secure seats. Some seats had been reserved for special orders of admission, and among the many distinguished persons who went to these places a notable figure was the co-respondent's brother, the Marquess of Hayle and Ensor. Colonel Giscourt Morris sat near his counsel, but neither Mrs. Morris nor Lord Roland de Brath were present in court.'

My eyes lost all knowledge of the house before me, as my imagination created this scene.

'The Solicitor-General, opening the case, said that he must occupy some time of the court in relating the many material facts which had forced the petitioner, a distinguished officer and a man of stainless honour, to take this extremely distasteful step of a suit for the dissolution of his marriage. "The petitioner," he said, "a man much older than his wife, being over sixty at the relevant time, occupied a house in the

Close at Selby St. Albans, under the shadow of the Cathedral——" '

'Ah!' Gael had whispered in the Library. 'Selby St.
Albans! Then *that* was how the Middian Girls came to
know him and my darling little Lottie. You remember
Auntie Flavia saying she had tried to comfort him when he
was cast out. Oh, gosh, why wasn't I there to comfort him!'

'Yes, yes,' I had whispered, and 'Golly!' and read quickly
on.

'Apart from the many honourable and honorary services
which Colonel Morris gave to the Cathedral and the
diocese, his chief interests were his books and his home,
and it was of course natural that his young wife should
crave those social occasions in the county or in town, few
of which appealed to him any more. In 1877 the co-
respondent, then an exceedingly famous politician, having
been a minister in the last Liberal government, came to
Selby St. Albans to address a great Liberal meeting in the
city's Corn Exchange. Now, as is not seldom the case,
this cathedral city was overwhelmingly hostile to the
Liberals (laughter) and no one in the Close was prepared
to entertain a Liberal so notorious for his Radicalism as
Lord Roland, and one, moreover, whose caustic wit on the
platforms of the country had so often wounded them or
their friends. Colonel Morris, however, though himself a
strong Conservative, refused to subscribe to this policy of
exclusion and entertained him to dinner at his house
in the Close, an example of fair play and magnanimity on
which many remarked. But never, surely, was a piece of
Christian magnanimity more disastrously repaid, because
this first meeting of Colonel and Mrs. Morris and Lord
Roland de Brath around the Colonel's hospitable board
was, if I may so put it, Fate's malefic assembling of the
characters for a drama whose terrible and tragic issue will
now unfold itself before you. It would seem that the co-
respondent, though nearing fifty, fell instantly in love with
this young woman in her twenties, and within a matter of
weeks a furtive intrigue was in being between them. The
picture is not made the more attractive by the fact that

they would meet for misconduct while the Colonel was away on Church affairs. Lord Roland, I should perhaps tell you, has long been separated from his wife, who now lives in Ireland, and whom he has not seen for many years.

'Alas! I have now to uncover some very dark secrets of Lord Roland's life. Evidence will be before you that a man whom we can establish without question was Lord Roland, but who called himself Mr. John Knox—a strange name, you may think, unless it was a specimen of Lord Roland's humour—hired a room in Rufus Street, Somers Town, a squalid neighbourhood sufficiently remote from Piccadilly where he lived and from Westminster where he was playing so conspicuous a part.'

Oh, I had rushed last evening to Rufus Street, Somers Town, and stood and stared at No. 7. It was a street of narrow, stucco-fronted houses, now scrofulous with decay. Some, but not all, of its ground floors were shop premises mainly given over to dealers in old clothes or second-hand furniture. The ground floor of No. 7 was an old furniture shop, stacked with the relics of dead or ruined homes. It breathed out a smell of old dust. As I stood before it, unable to draw myself away, three coloured men came from a house three doors distant, and I realized that this was a part of London much favoured by dark lodgers from Africa or the West Indies. Did poor Uncle Lucy come this way, with a joke on his lips, believing he'd be unrecognized here?

'To this back room in No. 7 Rufus Street came this strange new tenant, dressed almost like a working man, and with his cap pulled over his eyes. He would come of an afternoon, to be joined by a slight young woman who kept her veil down. Further evidence will be given that this young woman would come in a hansom as far as the main entrance of Euston Station and, there leaving it, would pass through the station so as to come by its side entrance at the Somers Town streets.

'Apparently they found this method of meeting as unsatisfactory as it was unsavoury, or it may be that Lord Roland learned that he had been recognized and his identity was being noised abroad. This is more than possible because his face must have been familiar to most readers of papers which include pictures of celebrities and political cartoons. Accordingly a plot was now conceived whereby Mrs. Morris, who loved society, should have a second house in London where she could often stay during the Season, but to which her home-keeping husband would be unlikely to come. Together, according to the evidence of a house agent, Lord Roland and she found a house in the village of Roehampton, over the river, and sufficiently far distant from Westminster. This was a large villa then known as Borden House, but now, I understand, given a different name. The Colonel, in his generosity and his desire to make his young wife happy, willingly provided this ample residence as a *pied-à-terre* near town, and you may think that, in accepting for their immoral purposes this kindly provision, they played an unspeakably cruel trick upon an ageing husband whose long life of honour and service had completely disabled him from suspecting perfidy in a great servant of the state.

'Mrs. Morris came to the house with a housekeeper, a parlourmaid, and her own personal maid, Olivia Haley, from all of whom you will hear.'

Olivia . . . Haley . . . somewhere I had heard this name before. Had Lizzie once spoken it in her kitchen?

'There was also a coachman and a stable boy who will tell you their stories.'

Yes, the servants' evidence. From my place in the knee-high, bleaching grass of the lawn I walked to the window of the drawing-room and peered into it through the broken Venetian blind. A large room with its wall-paper peeling and hanging. An ornate fireplace of white marble framing a red-rusted grate. There, years ago, when that grate was not this poor dead skeleton but a thing most brightly alive, with a heart of fire that sang and chattered to the quiet room, she would sit beside it, her crochet in her hands, sometimes till three in the morning, waiting for the sound of a horse's hoofs or of his steps approaching. For, as the servants avouched, her brougham would fetch him from the little station on Barnes Common, or he would come all the way from the House in a hansom cab, or if it was very late he would walk the whole four or five miles from Westminster through the darkness and quiet of midnight. They knew him at first as Mr. Grenville, an old friend of her father's, and were ready to believe this story until the coachman, taking a walk on the Heath, one bright Sunday in June, saw them folded together in the bracken.

I stayed before the window till I saw Lottie Morris sitting by the fire. Then, keeping very still, I forced my imagination to give me a horse's hoofs coming up Roehampton Hill; and very slowly I turned and saw a younger Uncle Lucy coming through that gate now torn from its hinges and lurching. After watching him without blame, but only with forgiveness and love, for, whether or not he was my father, I could feel only a passionate loyalty to him that wouldn't, or couldn't, listen to these savage attacks, but would fight for him with a deaf, dumb, head-down, unreasoning furious defence—after considering him thus, with a sad, bitter love, and imagining him entering the house, I turned and strolled past the big conservatory towards the stables at the back.

Here he had kept the two horses, Chancellor and Empress, on which he and she would go riding together over the Heath. I tried to imagine the ghosts of Chancellor and Empress in their loose boxes. 'Chancellor was an animal noble enough to haunt any loose box,' he had said. As I remembered these words, standing before the stable door, my heart plunged and nearly died, because I heard a horse pawing and champing inside. Fearfully I pushed at the top half of the stable door and saw a noble bay mare nodding her head at the wall and rustling her straw litter with a hoof. My heart settled. Evidently the stables, if not the house, were let.

Those rides out together to the quiet places of Putney Heath or Richmond Park in the coloured summer days. I was fourteen and knew enough of life now to wonder if the splendid beasts, tethered to trees, had been the companions and witnesses of their guilt. Was there a wild love then in the tall summer grass? One of the servants had given her brutal witness, that 'sometimes when the mistress returned from these rides, her appearance was anything but that of a respectable woman.'

When the mare turned and looked at me with her great eyes, I felt as shy of her as of an adult, and walked quickly away. Returning to the front of the house, I went on to its threshold under the pillared porch, and tried to see through the leaded and coloured glass of the front door. I could discern little and after making sure that no one was near, I cracked a diamond of blue glass and forced a piece of it away. It fell with a clink on the tiles within. Then I saw clearly the elegant staircase wheeling round towards me. Usually, the servants had said, she would wait for him by the drawing-room fire, but sometimes, if it was two or three in the morning, she would come down from her bedroom to open to him. I saw her, like some romantic heroine in a story book, coming round the curved sweep of that staircase in frilled nightdress and silken bed-chamber robe, with her long fair hair reaching down to her waist.

Now, remembering something else, I stepped back to look up at her bedroom windows. That time the Colonel came. In his Cathedral Close he had suspected nothing till he saw in a popular weekly an impish paragraph about 'Lord Roland's hill-top retreat to which he repairs at week-ends for refreshment after the cares of office, and whence he issues for long riding exercises with his fair hostess, the beautiful wife of Colonel Giscourt Morris, C.B.' Any suspicions this paragraph may have stirred were completely allayed, said the Solicitor-General, when his wife assured him, with laughter and a loving embrace, that it was just a wicked piece of scandalmongering, unworthy of their notice: Lord Roland had come to see her perhaps two or three times, and she couldn't remember riding out with him more than once.

'Such suspicions, however, are never quite as dead as they seem, and when, at a later date, the Colonel saw in one of his servants' Sunday papers an occult allusion to

"Lord Roland's weekly consolation in his haven at Roe-hampton," he awoke from what you may think his calm summer slumbers in the Cathedral Close and, hurrying up to London the same day, arrived on the threshold of Borden House.' (That threshold there, on which I had just stood.) 'One can imagine the consternation in the house. It was Sunday, and there was only one servant at home, Miss Olivia Haley. On going to answer the knocking at the door she must have recognized through its glass panels the shadow of her master, and with great discretion she hastened upstairs to her mistress's bedroom before opening to this visitor. Through a locked door she told her that the Colonel stood on the threshold. Since the door was locked, and she heard voices within, she could have no doubt that Lord Roland was there with her mistress. You will be interested to know what happened then. Another maid and the coachman will tell you that the unseemly incident was a joke in the kitchen for ever afterwards. In a very brief time Mrs. Morris came down to open the door to her husband and stood in the hall laughing gaily with him. Meanwhile, Lord Roland sped higher upstairs. High up in Borden House there was a cistern room with a very small window which looked down upon the side wall and the conservatory roof. Lord Roland went through that window and down some stout ivy on to the conservatory; he clambered over its glass roof and by means of the rainwater pipes slid down to the back garden. Why he didn't crash through the glass on to the ferns and flowers below passes my comprehension, since he is anything but a small man. Had this happened, one is certainly tempted to imagine what would have been the consternation in the hall—and, to be sure, in the conservatory.'

'Swine!' I thought unfairly—and yet perhaps not too unfairly, because he was seeking to get a laugh out of another man's public agony.

I gazed at the little window and the conservatory roof (there was no ivy now on the side wall, but only its late footprints) and I could not come away till I had recalled the Solicitor-General's last words: 'I don't know if you are familiar with the old mediæval legend, *Le Roman de Tristan et Iseult*, which tells of King Mark of Cornwall, Iseult, his wife, and Tristan, her secret lover. I find myself thinking of it again and again as I put this story before you. King Mark was a gentle, kindly, notoriously unsuspecting man, and for a long time his wife and her paramour were able to deceive him by their lies and treacheries and subterfuges. They had a secret cabin in the forest where they led an idyllic existence till a day when King Mark came upon them sleeping there and laid his sword between them. This, I respectfully submit, is what my client, Colonel Morris, has been compelled to do. He has laid his sword between them; and in this tragic case, gentlemen, that sword is the symbol of the Law. None of his alleged facts appear to be disputed, and I must submit, therefore, that the co-respondent allows judgment to go against him by default. He admits his guilt by not coming into court to deny it. To deny it would very possibly be to add a criminal offence to faithlessness and falsehood; and for some people the criminal law may have terrors which the moral law has not.'

'Swine, swine! Dirty filthy swine!' It was long before I could leave that garden. Over and over again I recalled these stories told in evidence and gazed at the scenes of them. At last the dusk fell about me and I came away.

§

The bus in which I came home was so crowded with people returning from a Saturday on the Heath that I found myself packed against the wall on an inside seat; and here, with an elbow on the window-ledge and my chin in my hand, I was remembering the even harsher words of the Judge's Charge: 'One would imagine that every motive of pride and decency must prompt him to enter the witness-box and rebut the shocking stories which we have heard in this court today and yesterday and which will inevitably be broadcast by the Press to the whole watching world. But no: there has been no defence or denial, and one can only assume, as counsel has said, that to deny them in a witness-box might render likely a successful prosecution for perjury. If this is so, and all these terrible facts are not susceptible of denial, then I can only suggest that the co-respondent's behaviour has shown a total lack of all moral values, and that counsel's words were hardly too strong when he characterized all these shameless deeds and wretched evasions as those of a betrayer, liar, coward, and cheat. . . .'

I seemed to have grown older and wiser in these last few days, for I remember wondering, as I looked out of the bus window, if the old Judge had never in his life sinned furtively, and been afraid, and told a lie.

I knew also, dreaming in that bus, why in the past Uncle Lucy had come so rarely to England and had gone so quickly. One avoids, or averts one's eyes from places where one has been proclaimed a malefactor, sneak, and coward, and turned into a dirty jest for the streets; because there is no smart quite so everlastingly painful as the memory of a public shame.

The shorn trees of Roehampton Lane swept past as the heavy bus rollicked me homeward, but my eyes were not seeing the road; they were seeing instead much of the leading article in *The Times* to which Gael, with a gasp, had drawn my notice.

'But for the circumstances that the case of Morris *v.* Morris and de Brath affects the character of one of the most prominent of public men we should have passed over in silence the very disagreeable evidence which has been heard in court these last two days. . . . No statesman, however great the offices he has held, could hope to survive the blow of having such charges proved against him in open court. It is widely believed that he has aspired to lead his party, and this was an ambition fully justified by his great position in the country, his great name, and his undoubted gifts. But now, how can this be? He has forfeited the moral ascendancy which should be possessed by a political leader, and must be possessed by a party professing to be peculiarly the party of moral purity. What will the serried ranks of Puritanism and Nonconformity say now? The answer is plain: we have witnessed the fall, irretrievable and complete, of one of the greatest figures in our public scene. On another page will be found the letter he has written to his constituents. In this he says, "As far as public life goes I have no choice but to accept the verdict, and I respectfully, and very gratefully, bid you all farewell." That is to say he bows to the stern canons of public life; and now, in the natural course of things, his name will be struck off the list of Privy Councillors, and he will pass for ever out of sight of the world in which he has played so noteworthy a part. To sentimentalists this may seem a tragedy, but we make bold to say that we accept as an admirable thing the social judgment which, when a man has been proven guilty of gross domestic treachery, when it has been shown that he strove to cover the same treachery with a whole squalid apparatus of disguises, assumed names, lying letters, and falsehood piled upon falsehood, excludes him from the company of ordinary decent men.'

'Dirty, horrible, Tory paper!' I said to the passing walls of Roehampton Lane, my eyes on the window lest anyone should see in them a child's furious tears. 'Dirty, beastly, caddish swine.' And as with the Judge, so with this leader-writer, I thought that probably the only difference between him and my dear Uncle Lucy was that he had never had his stealthy little sins exposed.

CHAPTER THIRTEEN

I DID not tell Gael, or anyone else, of my visit to that house. When she chatted about Lottie Morris, as she so often did now, I would hide my real thoughts beneath pompous facetiæ such as 'Lottie was not a good girl. One mustn't go indulging one's illicit passions.'

This secretiveness now infected most of my detective work: when I could I hunted alone. This was partly because my feelings had now a poignance of which I was half ashamed; but there was another and more childish reason for it: I had an ambition to arrive at the truth before Gael and to display it in triumph before her; just as, if I left the house a minute after Gael to go with her to the shops, I would race, unseen, round by Trevanion and Gunterstone Roads, so as to arrive at the mouth of our Edith Road before her and there stand grinning.

Then, again, some of my methods touched me with shame, but I think now that a little of this stain can be wiped off them because, after all, I was preferring these sly little hole-and-corner methods to giving pain to Auntie Flavia. The shame must remain, I suppose, on the undeniable fact that one of my reasons for wanting to prove myself Uncle Lucy's son was my strong desire, as a true child of Edith Road, West Kensington, to be the son of a lord and the grandson of a marquess.

I was seeking now, quite alone, my proof of this.

And one evening, coming home from school, I found myself alone in the house. At that time, since Auntie Flavia quarrelled easily with her servants, we had no maid but Lizzie, and it was her 'afternoon out'; Auntie Flavia had taken Gael to the Kensington stores to buy clothes; and so the whole house was at my mercy. I rushed up to her bedroom and, opening that bottom drawer which was so crammed with old letters, sat myself on the carpet beside it and began to rake among the jumbled miscellany and read.

I probed for a silent hour and was wearily unsuccessful, except for two curious finds. One was a letter in Uncle Lucy's hand. To whom it was written I could not know, for some of Auntie Flavia's *omnium gatherum* of letters had belonged to her father and mother and a few (I can't imagine why) to her sisters Gloria and Evelyn; but it began, 'My loveliest and liveliest and sweetest.' It looked very old, but it had no date, and its substance was a record of adventurous climbing in the Swiss Alps. I became so interested in these vertiginous climbs on precipitous slopes with ropes and slings and ice-axes that I forgot for a while the purpose of my scrutiny. Indeed I have always regarded my lifelong love of mountains and climbing as a by-product of this evening's work on Auntie Flavia's floor.

'My loveliest and liveliest.' Addressed to Auntie Flavia? If so, I must believe that Uncle Lucy with the passing of time had transferred his love for Lottie to no less a person than Auntie Flavia. This I didn't at all want to believe because my soul was romantic and I wanted to think him loyal always to the lovely Lottie. Further, I found it difficult to believe, because I couldn't imagine anybody loving Auntie Flavia like that. But of course it might account for her irritable, her passionate refusal ever to answer our questions. She unmarried, and once his mistress! And perhaps jealous of Lottie Morris and his past. But hold: didn't this idea lead to a most unwelcome thought: that I might be her son? When I perceived this possibility I said, 'But this is death.' And in truth it was so lethal to my dreams that I shrank from the touch of it.

The other find was an envelope of that lightweight paper in which letters came from abroad. Its postmark said 'Firenze 1891'; it was addressed in Uncle Lucy's hand to 'Miss Flavia Middian'; and across one corner Auntie Flavia had scrawled in an obvious passion of misery, 'Oh, my dear, my dear, that you should have done this to me.'

It was typical of her untidiness that the envelope was empty. But there seemed to be so much grief in that scribbled cry, 'Oh, my dear, my dear . . . done this to me,' that I felt a sharp pity for her, and the words stayed written across the emptiness of my searching mind, as across that empty envelope, which must once have held the answer, but was long ago laid by to gather dust and fade.

§

Then in April he returned. A telegram in the morning —excitement in the house—much work by mistress and maid on his room—then evening, and we sat listening for cab wheels in the road—as Lottie used to listen by her fire. At last the purr of wheels, the clopping of hooves, and the cab was outside the door. All three of us hurried to the door, and there on the pavement, standing by the four-wheeler, was Uncle Lucy, tall and lordly in his fur-lined coat, but—the first time I'd noticed this—a little bowed and worn and, as it were, ascetic. Gael and I, standing on the steps, might shout, 'Hurray,' but we were looking at that tall figure with a new interest, and our heads were theatres in which scenes were enacted from an old dusty volume of *The Times*.

He lifted a hand to his hostess. 'I am sorry for this sudden and unseemly irruption, but I am utterly weary of the whole Seizième Arrondissement de Passy. Yesterday I decided that I'd lain buried too long in my cemetery, the Avenue d'Iéna, and it was time for a joyful resurrection. This is it. Rather sudden, I fear, but I imagine all resur-rections are like that. Also, I am sick.'

'Sick?'

'Yes, and needing care. And affection. Gael, my dear, how good to see you. And Win, *sacré nom*, how you grow! Ah . . . let me come in. Children, when next you are sick, remember that there's nobody who'll fuss over you like your kind auntie. Her house is my Maison de Re-traite, when I—yes, thank you, sir, just put the bags on the top step. I thank you. In Paris there are Maisons de Santé for the sick and infirm, but I so much prefer this kindly house in grey old London.'

'But, Mark—Marcus, my dear!—what is the sickness?'

'Heart. Heart. The blockhead of a French doctor not only hears abnormal goings-on in my decrepit heart, but must needs tell me about them. Imbecile that he is! He says I must avoid shock and then gives me a shock like that. And he must needs be funny about it when I'm feeling abject; he says, "No more running along the Champs Élysées for a *fiacre*, or the day'll come when you won't catch it." What an idiot remark to someone with a heart. I've felt a wreck ever since. My dear, can you pay this excellent man his fare? From Victoria. I came away in such a hurry that I've only French money. It is like that when one rises from a grave. No, here's a half-sovereign. Win, hand it to him with my compliments and tell him that he drove excellently. Gael, is your Auntie Gloria, that uncouth woman, dead yet? No, alas! still too young. Ah . . . heigh-ho . . . yes, I desire nothing so much as my bed and your auntie's kind solicitude. I was feeling thoroughly unsound this morning—seedy in the extreme—and the passage on the steam-packet was anything but alleviating. It may be that my time has come to die.'

'Don't talk about death! Lucius!'

'Why not? I am seventy-seven and in my dotage. The kindest thing really would be to send me to the knacker's.'

'What is a knacker?' asked Gael with more interest than sympathy.

'A dealer in old horses who quietly extinguishes them. He then turns them into dog's meat.'

'Don't!' cried Auntie Flavia. 'I hate that sort of talk. I don't think it's at all amusing.'

'It is not, you say? Not witty? All right. My mistake. What is that? No, sir, I don't want any change. What? Not at all; don't mention it. Good-bye to you and thank you. Ah, Lizzie, it is good to see you. No, no, Lizzie, let me help you. That bag is far too heavy.'

'Don't touch it!' cried Auntie Flavia. 'You say you have a heart!'

'Oh, yes. . . .' He remembered his heart and rose most promptly from stooping over the bulging gladstone bag.

He left it there on the step like a stove red-hot—or like the Ark of the Covenant, to touch which was to die.

I seized upon the bag to show my strength and quickly wished I hadn't. But I struggled in with it. Uncle Lucy followed me. He looked round our narrow and featureless hall, now dingy with time, and said, 'Ah, it's like coming home.' And he kissed Auntie Flavia on the cheek in gratitude for this home.

§

Of dinner that night she had made, as usual, a celebration. Silver, glass, and linen all shone in his honour, and four ferns in four china swans swam on the white damask round a centre-piece of narcissi and daffodils. In his absence we would often meal untidily on a soiled cloth in the little breakfast-room, or even down in the kitchen without a cloth, if no one but the faithful Lizzie was there; but always our table and our rooms were cleaned and dressed as for a party when he returned; and so was the mistress of the rooms.

Over the first of the dishes he spoke of the recent general election, and I, remembering the Christmas talk at this same table, thought I detected bitterness in his tone about the new Prime Minister. 'Why does England always allow herself to be ruled by her junior partner? The English feel themselves born to command, but they almost invariably choose a Scot to govern them. Win, I'll tell you why. It's because that school of yours up the road, and all the public schools of England, believe that the purpose of education is not intelligence but character, while the Scots, a canny people, have the notion that education has to do with brains; and it's a law of nature that the animal with brains will always rule the animal without them. These ridiculous schools, Win, were founded to give the poor some scholarship, but now the rich have purloined them all and turned them into mills for hatching out character. By which they generally mean heavy-witted conformity.' He turned from the subject in some sadness, I thought, and smiled at Gael. 'Why, Gael, I can hardly believe that that young woman sitting there is our Gael. How old are you now? Eighteen?'

'Don't be absurd. You know I'm only fifteen.'

'Fifteen? Is that all? Then I take it you're still at school.'

'Of course I am. You know I am. Worse luck.'

'But it'll soon be time for you to go to some finishing academy. Perhaps we might find you some such place in Paris, so that you could be near your old and fast-perishing Uncle Lucy.'

'Oh, *yes*! Yes!'

'There's an excellent Mlle Binard in the Faubourg St. Honoré who receives a select number of young ladies."

'Oh, *please*, yes—when can I go? Next term?'

'The Faubourg St. Honoré is near the Champs Élysées, and no doubt you and the other young ladies would be sometimes taken for a safe walk there—it is, after all, a fashionable promenade—and then you might see under the trees a lonely figure sitting on an iron chair for which he's disbursed his three sous——'

'Oh, yes! And I'd come and stay with you. Where do you live in Paris?'

'I do not live there, my child. I merely have an apartment in which I do not die.'

'Yes, but where—where?'

'A humble lodging in the Avenue d'Iéna. But I have an idea of moving farther up the avenue into the Rue Galilée. It would be a hundred yards nearer to you all; and there are some quite nice morgues there.'

'Humble lodging indeed!' laughed Auntie Flavia. 'I should call it a palatial place.'

He shrugged. 'Yes . . . well . . . it is not small, but that only means that it provides ample space to be miserable in. How greatly I prefer this small home.'

'Then, Mark, come back. Come back for good.'

'Oh, yes, yes,' endorsed Gael, and then remembered that perhaps this would prevent her going to Paris, and so stopped.

'No, no,' he sighed. 'A poor old remittance man is not expected to come back.'

'A remittance man in the Sixteenth Arrondissement!' scoffed Auntie Flavia. 'That's good.'

'There are more of us in the Sixth, I admit, but wherever we are, we are brothers.'

'What's a remittance man?' demanded Gael.

'Someone, dear child, who's never wanted back again.'

'But that's not you. We all want you to come back. Terribly. For ever.'

'Too kind. Too kind. . . . But no. I trifle with the idea sometimes, but I have too many roots in Paris now. There are times when I am not wholly miserable there. I have to thank my Creator that He has granted me, along with my great gift for melancholy, a tendency to suffer from sharp attacks of gaiety ever and anon. They recur with a certain frequency and so enable me to endure.'

'But you could have them here,' suggested Auntie Flavia.

'Yes, to be sure; that is so. And I do. I do. But you must remember, my love, that Paris offers kindlier opportunities for social intercourse to us poor outcasts than any other capital. Which reminds me'—and here, unaware that we had knowledge wherewith to perceive the association of ideas, he spoke another name that had been publicly disgraced—a name that had troubled a far larger world than his—'whom do you think I met the other day at the Minister's soirée? I had but a word with him because at these crowded assemblies it is not *bon ton*, as you know, to talk at length with anyone. A passing bow, a few sentences here, a fatuous smile there—these are the utmost that politeness allows. But the name of this guest was called at the door of the salon——'

'Oh, can I go to soirées if I come to Paris?' Gael interrupted.

'What?—No, I doubt that. The number of ladies that figure at Ministerial soirées is lamentably small. The Minister's lady, his daughters, perhaps——'

'Oh, don't *interrupt*, Gael! The name at the door? Please.'

'It was a name to stop all talk everywhere. We turned to it, and saw this new guest make his salutation to the Minister and then begin to circulate self-consciously among the people. I manœuvred to come near him——'

'But who was it? Don't keep me waiting. Who, *who*?'

'Who? Captain Alfred Dreyfus.'

'Dreyfus! But, goodness gracious, is he received in places like that?'

'Most surely. All Paris knows that he is to be completely exonerated. That shocking judgment of the Court at Rennes is to be quashed by the Court of Cassation, and he is to be made a Chevalier of Honour on the very spot where he was disgraced before all his comrades—where the braid was torn off his uniform and his sword snapped in two and thrown down before him.'

'Oh, but how wonderful! Oh, I'm glad. You always said he was innocent. And you actually spoke to him? My poor dear Dreyfus? What did he say?'

'I asked him what he would do after this amends, and he looked at me with his haunted eyes and said, "I shall go quietly out of sight, monsieur, because, all said and done, Dreyfus remains a name that is best forgotten."'

This touched at once Auntie Flavia's exceedingly low melting-point. Her mouth, tight shut, twitched and quivered as she kept back the tears.

'Best forgotten,' repeated Uncle Lucy, who loved pathos at any time, but most especially when he could employ it on the easy task of piercing a leak in her vat of tears. 'And,' he reminded her after a long, sad gaze at the narcissi, '*he* was innocent.'

Instantaneously she arrested that trembling of her mouth and glanced our way, as if warning him that we were there.

§

That night when I was newly abed, he came up to my room three staircases high. He came rather slowly and heavily, as if careful of his heart. And he sat on the bed's foot and tried to cover with tired jesting his obvious sadness.

This depression was caused, I felt, by the sag of his heart at the thought of death.

'Well, good night, Sir Travers. Sleep well. Still only fourteen, are you? That is a pity. That means you'll have to be four more years at that foolish school. Four years before you can come and live with me in Paris.'

'I could come in the holidays,' I said, not very helpfully.

'Yes . . . that is true. You should have come this Easter. We would have gone together to Grand 'Messe at the Madeleine and Benediction at Notre Dame. I love these services. I don't know that I even believe in the faith that inspires them, but I get something—I don't quite know what—from the music and the incense and the lovely Latin words echoing far away. I say my prayers to the Unknown God. I ask His pardon for all my despicable sins. And all sinners like me, if there are any as bad. A week or two ago I was walking down a long hill towards the famous valley of Port Royal; and oh, how quiet and peaceful and secluded it looked. Have you ever heard of Pascal?'

'Pascal's fruit drops?' I offered, trying to be helpful.

'No, no. Blaise Pascal, the great writer of the seventeenth century, who had the style of an angel and the vision of a saint. Weariness and disgust with the ways of men, coupled, I fancy, with some baffled dreams, drove him to seek a retirement from the world among the solitaries of Port Royal. Port Royal des Champs. He was no monk, just a layman like you and me, but he practised all the austerities of a religious in an effort to set his soul free, as a man should. Much of his life he gave to writing down, in exquisite fragments, his thoughts about God. Pascal's Pensées. Many of them haunt me . . . haunt me. . . .'

He began to recite French words, and beautiful their syllables sounded when spoken softly on his splendid low voice. '*Quand je considère la petite durée de ma vie, absorbée dans l'éternité . . . le petit espace que je remplis, abimé dans l'infinie immensité des espaces que j'ignore et que m'ignorent*—' but the French they teach you in that silly school doesn't run to that, I fear. No. "When I consider my life's little span, absorbed in eternity before and after, engulfed in the infinite immensity of spaces that I know not, and that know not me. . . .'" But the temptation to hear his voice again in the noble French was too great, and he sighed out like an actor, '"*Je ne vois que des infinités de toutes partes qui m'enferment comme un atome et comme une ombre.* . . . I see nothing but infinities on every side, closing me in as if I were an atom or a shadow which lasts but an instant and returns no more. . . ." Yes, yes, there's much in me that would have liked to be a solitary—and indeed a saint. Next Easter perhaps you and I will walk together down the hill into that grey marshy valley and look at the site of Port Royal, and remember these good men. Remember Blaise Pascal and the other solitaries who prayed and laboured there.'

'I could come next hols,' I suggested.

'It is hot in Paris in August. But we'll see. We'll see. And now good night. Think kindly of all your friends and relatives—except perhaps your Auntie Gloria—no, try to think kindly even of that hag. We are all sinners, but some of us know it. The peculiar disgustingness of that woman is that she doesn't know it.'

'Don't go,' I pleaded.

'Yes, I must go, because you must sleep. Children need sleep if they're to grow big and strong. Good night. August in Paris, perhaps. In December certainly—though I generally go to Monte in the winter—south into the sun. But I'll wait for you there this time, and we'll go together to Midnight Mass at the Madeleine. Like the poor Madeleine herself, we need the Master's forgiveness, I am sure.' A last smile at the door, and he turned his head and was gone.

§

In the morning we were all still seated at the dining-room table when we heard many footsteps and some voices on our front-door steps. Then a strong knock and a ringing of the bell. Who could these callers be, so many and so early? Lizzie opened to them and, unmistakably, we heard the deep-throated voice of Auntie Gloria.

'Oh, my God!' exclaimed Uncle Lucy.

We sat transfixed.

With relief we heard the discreet Lizzie taking all the people past our dining-room door and up to the drawing-room. She returned and announced Gloria, Evelyn, and Primrose.

'Oh, my God!' said Uncle Lucy.

'At *this* hour of the day? Not ten o'clock?' Auntie Flavia rose quickly. 'What can it mean?'

'You go to them. I am not here. I am sitting under the trees in the Champs Élysées, before the gingerbread stall. Where I usually sit. Though I admit,' he added, 'I'd like to see Primrose since the devil breathed on her and she became a living soul. It must have been a powerful gust if it could turn that deflated little Artemis into a gay little Aphrodite. My own view is that he pinched the little lady hard and forced the real soul out of her as you force the kernel out of a monkey nut. I must see her performance one day.'

To these pleasantries Auntie Flavia did not listen. 'But what can have happened?' were her last words as, happily excited, she hurried from the room.

Uncle Lucy looked at us in mock alarm. 'Gloria, Evelyn, Primrose,' he murmured.

'And no Arthur,' I said. 'Evelyn has come without her appendage.'

'Hush,' he adjured, with a finger up. 'This is serious.' And he kept his seat till sure that the drawing-room door was shut. Then, on tip-toe, he crept out of the room and up the stairs and into his bedroom. I watched from the stair's foot. Soon—but only after a careful peering round the bedroom door—he came tip-toeing down the stairs, holding his black hat before him like a beggar's bowl, because in no circumstances would he put on his hat in a house—not even in so grave an emergency as this. He did not go out by the hall door but crept towards the back kitchen parts and, by favour of Lizzie, escaped through her scullery into the garden.

Lizzie understood the situation perfectly and grinned with her thin lips as she stood watching him travel more quietly than a low wind through her scullery door. And stalk on feet softer than the wind's up the tradesmen's passage at the side of the house.

Not till we all sat at the dinner table again did Auntie Flavia tell us, with much vivacity, and to Uncle Lucy's chortling joy, the whole story. No, not quite all of it because, as you will see, parts of it were ill-adapted to his hearing. These parts she only told us children some years afterwards when we were old enough to understand.

Gloria had received by the morning's post an urgent summons from Evelyn; and, since Gloria held herself to be the one member of the family competent to handle disaster or disease—and was, in fact nearly as competent as she thought herself—she forthwith shot out of her chair, uplifted by a super-charge of self-confidence and said to Primrose who was staying with her, 'I go to poor Evelyn at once.' Primrose, uplifted also, but less by a Samaritan helpfulness than by her new thirst for life and excitement, insisted on going too, that she might enjoy the worst. They were at Evelyn's flat near Brook Green by half-past nine. There Gloria, having heard the top of the news, said with her throaty guffaw, 'Well, as we're so near to Edith Road, let's make it a foursome; a real family gathering while we're about it;' and brought them round to our door. In our drawing-room, the door being shut they explained their coming—or, rather Gloria did before anyone else could. 'Arthur,' she said, 'has been misbehaving himself.'

'Yes, naughty little man,' said Primrose.

'It's no joking matter,' Gloria snapped at her.

'But it *is* frightfully funny, you must admit. Arthur, of all people! Dear little man!'

'Is it funny for Evelyn?' Gloria looked towards Evelyn who was quietly weeping. 'Is it, pray?'

'Well, I don't really think she should take it to heart so much. Men: you know what they are. Flavia knows, if you don't.'

'Yes, and bitterly she suffered.'

'Well, I'm damned if I'd lose a moment's sleep for any man.'

'You have never been married. I thank God that my Robin was a good man, and honourable; and I trust that young Walter will be the same. And if ever Brenda marries I hope it will be to some good man.'

'But, Gloria, what are you talking about?' demanded Flavia, beating an eager toe. 'Misbehaving? What do you mean?'

Primrose answered. It was one of the joys of her emancipation that she could now despise all timidity of utterance and call things by their jolliest names. 'She means, my dear, that he's keeping a tart in Bloomsbury.'

'Primrose!' exclaimed Gloria, in shock, while Flavia exclaimed, '*Arthur?*' in amazement.

'Yes.' Gloria was in command again. 'Evelyn found some of the creature's love-letters yesterday and charged him with them. He admitted it all and, what was worse, chose to be rude about it.'

'Rude? But Evelyn, dear, what did he say?'

'He said he wasn't going to apologize for it,' sobbed Evelyn. 'And if I didn't like it, I could lump it.'

'Good gracious.'

'He said not one wife in a hundred, once she was fifty or so, knew what a husband's needs were, or cared tuppence about them.'

'And he may be in the right about that,' suggested Primrose.

'He said he craved beauty and—and—' Evelyn got the sobs into control—'and I once had a lovely face, but I hadn't got it now.'

'No! Arthur said *that*?'

'Yes, he did.' Evelyn made a ball of her handkerchief and pressed it against her mouth. 'He did.'

'He certainly wants his bottom slapped,' said Primrose.

'What did you do, Evelyn?'

But Gloria supplied the answer before Evelyn issued from the handkerchief. 'She hasn't spoken to him since. She has her meals in the dining-room and gives him his in that little room off the drawing-room.'

'But what on earth does Miss Coleridge say?' (Evelyn

was as likely as Flavia to lose her temper and a servant at the same time; and just now she had only a 'lady-help', Miss Coleridge.)

'Oh, she knows all about it and is wholly on Evelyn's side.'

'Yes, and between them,' declared Primrose, 'they feed him like a convict in a cell. Evelyn or Miss Coleridge plumps the rations down in front of him without a word, and he bows most gratefully, and grins, but without a word either. No one's speaking to any one. Sometimes he holds open the door for whichever of the girls it is and bows her out. But never a word said.'

'Oh, he is behaving badly,' sobbed Evelyn.

'And when he's had his meals', continued Primrose, delighted, 'he goes whistling about the flat, as if to show them that he's quite happy, whatever they are.'

'He's utterly cruel.' Evelyn rearranged the handkerchief. 'And I'll never forgive him.'

'And I think he *is* quite happy in his little condemned cell. He's pulled the most comfortable chair into it from the drawing-room and he sits there and smokes and reads. It's awkward, of course, if he wants to emerge and Evelyn's sitting there in the drawing-room but he manages to walk past her whistling, and when he's done whatever he wants to do, he goes whistling back into his cosy little retreat.'

'Whistling? Whistling what, Primrose?'

'Generally it's "Let me like a soldier fall", isn't it, Evelyn?'

Evelyn nodded miserably, and Flavia commented, 'Which is meant to be insolent, I suppose?'

'Oh, yes, I think it is,' said Primrose. 'Yes, pretty sure of that. Because, you see, when he goes into his little prison and leaves her sitting alone he varies it with, "E'en the bravest heart may swell in the moment of farewell."'

'Gracious goodness! Oh dear, oh dear, and this is our little Arthur! Oh no, but he can't really mean it. He doesn't know what he's whistling.'

'Oh yes, he does. He delights in it, awful little man. It's obvious he does, because if she walks out looking particularly furious, he changes it to "Are we to part like this, Bill." '

'Has he gone mad?'

'Oh, no.' Primrose wouldn't hear of this. 'He's just being a dreadful little man.'

'But they can't go on like this. What's going to happen?'

'That's what we want to discuss,' put in Gloria, 'if Primrose would let me speak. What do *you* feel ought to be done?'

'She can separate from him——'

'Oh, no, no, *no*,' cried Evelyn. 'He did say he was still very fond of me. He said that he loved this creature in Bloomsbury but after twenty-five years together I inevitably meant more to him than she did. He did say that—he did really—just before he lost his temper and suggested that I was ugly. Hideous.'

'I have always maintained,' Gloria reminded them, 'that it was a pity the little man had just enough money to live on. If only he'd got some honest work to do, instead of hanging round his home and his wife all day. . . .'

'I guess you're right there, ducks,' Primrose nodded. 'He sees too much of his home and Evelyn, and begins to want a little variety. You can understand it, in a way.'

'Oh, what am I to do?' wailed Evelyn.

According to Auntie Flavia's story it was she who brought them all to a decision. She said 'Evelyn dear, he meant it when he said you were the only woman that really mattered to him. Most men know in the end that there's only one woman for them, and if they can be made to know it before it's too late, they always come back to her . . . always. I know what I'm talking about, because . . . well, you know what I mean. You know too well——' here, I can guess, she stopped, overcome by the pathos of her own words. She had to control the quivering of a tight-closed mouth.

When the tears were mastered, and the lips could part again, she said, 'So what I advise is, Tell him that if he does not at once break with this creature, you'll take steps about a separation. Let him think you really mean it, and if I know Arthur, he'll come to heel like a good little dog. Because he couldn't really bear the thought of a parting for ever——'

'That may be,' snorted Gloria, displaying her superiority to Flavia's sentimentality, 'but I can't help thinking a stronger reason will be that he hasn't very much money and he loves the comfort of his home, which he'd have to forgo if he was forced to pay a separation allowance. Forgive my sordid intrusion among all these sentimentalities, but I believe in speaking the simplest truth.'

'What the hell does it matter if it's sordid,' asked Primrose, 'so long as it'll bring him to his silly little senses? If you ask me, Evelyn, my pet, you've got him by the short hairs.'

Evelyn nodded over her handkerchief more happily.

The three sisters, this strong action unanimously decided upon, went down our steps, and we followed them, saying good-bye. As I halted on the fourth step down, I saw Don Francesco peering from behind his curtains at this considerable and rather noisy exodus. Needless to say, our three visitors remained on the pavement gossiping with Auntie Flavia for another ten minutes, and it was as Gael and I were waving them a second good-bye that Don Francesco came walking slowly towards us. How he got himself on to our side of the road I do not know, but I observed that he hadn't stayed to gather cape or cloak. He wore only his black wide-awake hat. He smiled at Gael, raised the hat with an ample and gracious gesture, and asked, 'What has been toward? A deputation of political ladies? A sewing party? A spelling bee?'

'No,' said Gael. 'It's our aunties.'

'Not ladies of the Primrose League to wait on our Uncle Lucy? He is, I take it, a distinguished pillar of the Conservative Party?'

This was so mistaken as to be unbearable. I interposed, 'Oh, *no*! Uncle Lucy's a Liberal. A life-long Liberal. So'm I.'

'Really? You don't say so! To look at him you'd say a high Tory of the old school. The *ancien régime*; no? Then obviously they were not Primrose dames who came to see him.'

'They didn't come to see him at all. He was terrified at the sight of them and did a guy.'

'Did a . . .?'

'Did a bunk.'

'Oh, yes. I see. Slung his hook. I get your drift. Exactly.'

'I told you they were our aunties,' repeated Gael.

'Ohhh . . .!' He let forth a long jocular sigh. 'It was aunties, was it? Like your Auntie Flavia. You have four aunties then? God's plenty indeed.'

'No, five,' corrected Gael, not to be denied any distinction that came with numbers. 'But we never see much of Auntie Constance. She lives in Torquay.'

'Five! Well I hope you have love to spare for them all.'

'I like Auntie Evelyn and Auntie Primrose, but I don't like Auntie Gloria much.'

'Evelyn, Gloria, Primrose. Such elegant names.'

'Do you think so? I don't. But I'm afraid I must go in now. Good-bye.' And in her turn Gael smiled pleasantly—even coyly. Good public relations with the other side of the road.

'Good-bye, dear madam.' He swept off the hat and waved it through a large arc over kerb and gutter. 'My dear sir, good-bye.' He bowed to me and passed on.

'Isn't he sweet?' said Gael, as we went back into the house. 'And doesn't he just love us?'

'Only to the extent of finding out people's names,' I said.

CHAPTER FOURTEEN

How Uncle Lucy gloried in this story of Arthur's insubordination, when Auntie Flavia at the dinner table told him as much as she could of it. 'Such disobedience!' he said, and straightway began to quote, 'Of Man's first disobedience, and the fruit . . .' but decided that, after all, the words weren't as apt as he had thought them. 'To think that that neat and tidy little man, instead of springing up and down on his toes, has jumped over the traces and resolved to be his real self for a change! I can't help feeling glad. He's quietly escaped from the possessiveness of that plump little cushion of a wife. Excellent. Good for Arturo! He's tired of being her nice little, neat little, well-behaved toy. But he'll never stay the course, my dear, if all you Amazons are after him. I doubt, Gael, if the Iron Duke himself would have stood much chance against your Auntie Gloria in a domestic campaign. I managed to defeat her myself once, but as the Duke said of Waterloo, it was a dam near thing.'

Oh, yes, he was enjoying it all immensely, Arthur's peccability, Primrose's indecorums, Evelyn's shock, Gloria's heat—'the whole chorus of aunties, Win, dancing their corybantic measure around the latest family disaster'—all of it till Auntie Flavia, infected by his liveliness, and laughing no less merrily, said a wrong thing. Or reported a wrong thing said by the chorus. She reported in a light-hearted moment, when her chatter was running too fast for control or caution or memory, that Gloria had tried to crush Primrose's too easy tolerance of Arthur's depravity with the words, 'We've had enough of that sort of thing in our family. One dreadful scandal is enough.' Then there was a silence.

Uncle Lucy had gone into a silence which, we all knew, would last for hours and hours, if not for days; a silence as total as that which must dwell in those deep-sea fissures which have known no movement in a million years.

She tried to pierce the dykes of his silence with a few artificially gay remarks, but they drew no replies. A hunch of the shoulders perhaps; no more. And at length she gave up the attempt; and now she too was silent, and Gael was silent, and I was silent, and though none of us was speaking, Uncle Lucy was certainly the most silent of all.

Dinner over, we all rose from the table with sighs.

Uncle Lucy went slowly and sadly up to his room and after slowly and sadly pottering about there, came down with his top hat in his hand. He went out of the front door with a sigh. We watched his beloved figure walking towards the North End Road, with his stick held in both hands behind his back and swinging there like a pendulum which is continuing in normal business but has lost all heart in it.

§

He was done with the story of Arthur; but let me here report its issue, before I return to the current disaster. Evelyn walked out of her Brook Green flat, and Auntie Gloria took her most willingly into her home where she held her, so to say, in dry dock; Miss Coleridge remained for a little to wait upon the accused, who might be said to be on remand—or perhaps on probation; but she gave notice that she was only doing it to oblige and couldn't stay forever; Gloria's solicitors acted for Evelyn, and Arthur received a most disturbing letter on his breakfast plate one morning; he dwelt in angry gloom with this communication for a few days, not wishing to admit defeat; but at last conceded victory to the women. In a peace conference with Evelyn on neutral ground he reaffirmed, with tears, and with much tramping about the room, that she was the only woman he really loved, and he promised that, if it really caused her such distress, he would not see the Bloomsbury lady again.

I dare say he kept his promise.

§

Uncle Lucy had still not returned from the dark streets

173

to the place of his hurt, when we children went to bed. And that night Auntie Flavia did not wait up for him but, in a wretchedness that equalled his, went to bed too. I could not sleep but lay listening for his return. Ever and again steps approached the house, but always they passed by. A clock struck eleven . . . and the quarter . . . and the half-hour, and then steps came along the pavement, which did not pass but mounted to our door. His key turning in the lock was more to me than happy bells in the night. He closed the door very quietly because he believed in being considerate to those who had wounded him; then came up the stairs step by step, very slowly, as if needing the banister's support because weighted with care. I pictured his head down as he came. Once he halted on a tread as if to cope with a memory or a fear. Whether this dejection on a single stair sprang from his memory of the quarrel or from a pain in his heart and thoughts of death I do not know. He reached his bedroom and went in with his heaviness; and his door shut me out from it all, latching very quietly.

§

It was exceedingly grim at breakfast next morning, which was Sunday morning. We did not have Family Prayers because Auntie Flavia didn't know if he was ready yet to speak aloud, either to her or to God. She didn't dare ask him how he felt about this, because she was always a little afraid of him; and, on his part, though I'm sure he longed to talk with us all, he was quite disabled from doing so. Nor did any of us say Grace, since we were all shy of saying anything at all. Nor did Gael, in a climate so unfavourable, like to remind him of this duty. Thus we all sat down to our oatmeal and eggs with our souls unshriven and our food unblessed.

After breakfast we all prepared for church, but none dared ask him if he was coming too, and, as for him, his voice, imprisoned within a stony cell of sadness, couldn't even open a window to make this small announcement. In the end Auntie Flavia, Gael and I went off with our prayer books, our gloves, and our silence. Summer was at hand, but Auntie Flavia still wore her tailed brown fur and muff; and once or twice she seemed to shrink into them, as from the cold. But it was the cold breeze that came from Uncle Lucy in his distant chair, not from Siberian wastes or the calm skies of an April day. We must walk along Glazbury Road to come at the distant St. Margaret's Church, and again and again, because my heart ached for Uncle Lucy in his prison, I turned my head to see if by any chance he was coming too. And just as we were about to turn from Glazbury Road into Talgarth Road I saw him. There he was, a furlong behind us, in flying frock-coat and a vest slip like the King's; in grey gloves, grey plaid trousers, and, I think, in tears.

With a prayer book in his hand, he came desperately and at a distance behind us, rather like a dog which is in disgrace but follows the family nevertheless.

A lump like a young melon blocked my throat in Talgarth Road.

In the church he sat far behind us, in the back pew of all, like the least of the congregation of God. And in our forward pew Auntie Flavia prayed long and deep, with her head in her hands. I am certain they were some of the sincerest prayers spoken that day in that church. How Auntie Flavia contrived to match her laxity of behaviour with her devoted churchgoing I did not understand for many a day. She could lie to Uncle Lucy about Mr. Herbert Cluffe and even impose the need for lying upon us children; she could cheat in small ways in buses and trains; coming out of church, she could shed all godliness in the sunlight and talk shocking scandal with a fellow-worshipper walking home—and yet her prayers were sincere and she worked ardently for God's Church upon Earth, and especially for that branch of it called St. Margaret's, West Kensington. Extraordinary, even to a fourteen-year-old boy. Not till I was ten years older did it break upon me that she was the truly religious person because she saw intuitively that religion was one thing and morality something else. Religion, the sense of a Living and Aweful God, was something primary; its effects on behaviour something quite apart and secondary, though admittedly desirable. To perceive this, however unconsciously, was to be magnificently religious, though not necessarily magnificently good. Auntie Flavia, a bishop's daughter, swam in a sea of religion as in a native element. It was a sea with a high running swell so that sometimes she was on the crest of a religious wave and full of prayer and contrition and hope of good works, and at other times she was in a trough, still religious, but lower down from Heaven and less interested in morality. It was her periods of deep, leaden dolour which lifted her on to the crests, and she was in such a period today. The Lord God of her father, the bishop, was driving her into prayer and self-correction and firm purpose of good deeds.

Since she was far more often cheerful than cheerless, the troughs were much longer than the crests.

§

Uncle Lucy being so far behind us in church on this day, it followed that, at the end of the service he was out in the street long before us, and when at last we emerged he was out of sight. In the house we saw that he was back in his deep chair and in his even deeper silence.

That late April day of fifty years ago was as sunny and smiling beyond our walls as, within doors, it was clouded and damp and unhappy, and at about three o'clock, our heavy Sunday dinner having long since been consumed—in silence—Uncle Lucy spoke his first words. Opening the Playroom door where I sat alone, Gael having gone off to take her Infants' Class in the Sunday School—a religious employment to which she had invited me and which I had resolutely refused to undertake—he said, 'Win, why not come for a walk?'

'Oh, I'd love to,' I said, flinging down my book and feeling that one sunray at least had riven the cloud-banks.

'Well, come along, then,' he said, and sighed. The sunray was not yet very bright.

We two went from the house—in silence—and only after six steps along the pavement did he speak again. 'Where to?'

To this question, in our parts, there could be but one answer. 'Kensington Gardens, I suppose.'

'Very well.'

And to Kensington Gardens we went on the top of a bus, he still in his silk hat, I in my school straw, though still in my Sunday Etons.

In the Gardens we sat on two green chairs right in the heart of the trees, as if for privacy. The sky above the crowns of the trees was a blue so full that it bore a hint of purple in its depths. The sun, falling aslant of us, striped the long green vistas with the blue shadows and, flooding the farthest hazes with its golden glow, seemed to set their every mote alight. The great planes dappled the grass beneath them with broken shadows to match their dappled trunks. And for a long time Uncle Lucy, his large gloved hands resting on his stick, gazed into these flecked and sun-windowed vistas, and was silent. I could feel that it was a pregnant silence, heavy with something that must come to birth.

'You have not,' he said of a sudden, 'read Montaigne.'

'Who?'

He sighed, and drawing his cigar-case from a breast-pocket, abstracted a cigar. 'No. I rather thought not. Montaigne; a gentleman of Gascony. And a gossip of genius.'

'Never heard of him.'

He clipped the cigar, lit it, passed it thrice beneath his nostrils to savour it; then, taking it into his lips, laid his hands upon his stick again. 'You must read him one day. Very different from Pascal, but wonderful, too. His Essays . . . *De la tristesse*. . . .' He paused for a sorrowful moment to brood on his own *tristesse*. '*De l'amitié*. . . . I read him first when I was about sixteen and some of his sentences have stayed in my memory for ever because they helped to determine the course of my life. One of his wise sayings made a particularly deep impression on me, Win: it was to the effect that one should strive to know oneself and then enjoy being completely loyal to that lonely self. He said the same thing again in a very famous phrase: "One must cultivate one's own authenticity." That simply means that one must dare to be one's essential self. Do you understand?'

'I think so.'

'Yes . . . yes . . . one should seek one's own enlargement as naturally as a rose does, and despite the obloquy of fools. If one accepted too much the values of the people around one, and feared too much their censures, one would just wither on one's stalk, because the world is mostly composed of fools. And yet that, my dear Win, is just what your typical English Gentleman thinks it right to do, and just what I'm sure your ridiculous school strives to inculcate in you. Don't let them do it, Win; don't let them cramp and bind up your free soul like that. The English Gentleman, bless his heart, dare not do anything that is not done by his class; his ideal is to be in no way different from his peers. Consequently the excellent fellow walks about in a stiff mask because he must always be looking like what he is not—before others certainly, and when possible, before himself. Well, that's just mummery and hocus, isn't it?'

'I suppose so.'

'It is. Soul-destroying hocus-pocus, because it means that the strawberries on the top of his basket are very different from the slightly unsound ones below. And the poor man knows this. He may even know that those underneath are not strawberries at all. Poor fellow. Though, mind you'—he turned in his chair towards me—'I'm not saying, Win, that he isn't rather splendid in some ways. Because of his terrible repressions there is a contemplative charm about him as about many people in a costive condition. Certain excellent qualities, moreover, spring from this appalling repression: a reliability, a reserve, an outward modesty at least, and a great skill in climbing precipices. And a quiet voice, thank God. His manners are charming, but only, I think to his own class and those above. Those below are apt to take a different view. His palpable sense of class-superiority, with which he's been saturated like a sponge all his life, seems considerably less than charming to them. A really perfect breeding, like Win's, would cover with its infinitely careful consideration every living creature, even the most degraded and disgraced. . . . Perhaps, especially the disgraced. . . . You are listening, are you?'

'Yes. Rather!'

'Good. God forbid that I should be a bore and a burden to any young thing. You must tell me the moment my talk becomes a continuing and grievous affliction. Why most men of great age become garrulous bores I have never understood, but I walk in dread of joining their totally unlovable company. Even so, I often listen and hear my voice maundering on and on like a ship's engine on a voyage from Devonport to Sidney and the Antipodes. Yes, I have met many charming types of the English gentleman wandering repressed and forlorn along the tops of the mountains or quietly scaling the very steepest of their precipices. Climbing out of their emotional frustrations, I conceive, and into God's free air. Delightful creatures, but to a large degree unreal and therefore lacking in functional perfection and its corresponding value. No . . . I prefer Montaigne's ideal, but then, of course, he lived, not in Eton, but Bordeaux.'

'Oh, he was a froggy, was he?'

'A what? Oh, yes: a froggy.' He drew forth his cigar to savour its aroma again. 'But, Win, you must understand that if you dare to be yourself you are apt to make enemies at every turn.' The cigar went back between his lips. 'People dislike and fear those who won't conform. If they can, they throw them out like refuse. In the old days they burnt this refuse; now—well, they just do what they can to destroy it. And that reminds me, Win, of the other thing I learned from Montaigne: to suspend judgment. *Que sçais-je?* was his motto; "What know I?" And if we can't be certain of anything on earth, Win, how can we persecute anyone for his faith or punish him too cruelly for his sins? *Que sçais-je? . . . Que sçais-je?*'

He sat dreaming with his hands upon his stick; then inquired, 'How's your French at school?'

'Pretty foul.'

179

'Well, let's see. Can you translate this?' He enunciated the words very slowly. '"*La passion ne peut etre belle sans excès. Quand on n'aime pas trop, on n'aime pas assez.*"'

I got the second sentence right. 'When one doesn't love too much, one doesn't love enough.'

'Exactly. Exactly. Go to the top of the class. That was Pascal again. One of the wisest men who ever lived. . . . *Quand on n'aime pas trop. . . .*'

It was as he said this that I guessed what was happening in the chequered sunlight beneath our branching elm. With my new knowledge of his past story and my new suspicion of his relationship to me, I saw that he was preparing me, as I grew older, to think the best of him and, if possible, be on his side. And, however I judged him in later years, I know that, sitting there with him in the park, I kept my eyes upon the ground because I could feel the pity of it, that an old man, who had once been great, should be obliged to appeal, not without attempts at joking, for the gentle judgment of a child.

§

Perhaps because his words had reminded him that he, too, must be gentle with offenders, perhaps because as we strolled homeward along the Flower Walk, the tulips flung the seeds of a happy idea into his head, he fell into a meditative silence until we stood opposite a florist's shop in Kensington High Street (it is there still). He stood and studied it. Its face was as shut as that of someone asleep on a Sunday afternoon, but its breath as it slept smelt of hothouse flowers and funerals and cold green standing water. He looked at the windows above: one was open to the balmy April air.

'We can but try,' he said, and put a finger on the bell of a side door.

'Oh, no!' I begged, having a schoolboy's dislike of anything abnormal.

To Uncle Lucy, however, anything abnormal had its own attractiveness; and he pressed the bell.

A large, fat, pink-jacketed woman, herself a bright but rather overblown flower, opened to us. Her eyes were as friendly and astir as her shop was asleep and dismissive, but before she could speak a word, Uncle Lucy, raising his hat (I was too slow to lift mine) had begun. 'I am so exceedingly sorry to trouble you, madam, on a Sunday afternoon—it is unforgivable—but you will understand, I am sure. My young nephew here and I have just heard that a very dear friend is seriously ill—she may even be at the point of death, because she is a very old lady. Eighty and more. We are hurrying to see her and as we passed your excellent shop we got the idea of taking her a few flowers. Actually it was my nephew's idea. He thought perhaps you—of your great kindness——'

The word death will open the heart of any woman, and it flung wide the doors of this good lady's heart and of her shop. And not that dark word only. Uncle Lucy may have been seventy-six but his appearance was fine and his apologies were charming; she may have been no more than fifty, but when did a difference of twenty-odd years disable a woman's heart from swelling with admiration—especially a bosomy creature like this? Palpably she was 'smitten' with Uncle Lucy and loved at first sight.

'Why, of course, of course! Come in. I'm so glad—so delighted that you called me down. I wasn't asleep; I'd just had some tea. If we can't all help one another in trouble, what's the good of us? Do have all the flowers you want. And the young gentleman too.'

'It's most extremely kind of you.' We walked in. 'Most kind.'

'Don't mention it. What I say is, If there's illness next door, it's all hands to the pump. What may the poor lady's illness be?'

Uncle Lucy shrugged. Shrugged while he considered what to say. 'Old age chiefly. With fever. Much fever. She's eighty-four. Or is it five, Win? And at that age, their resistance is low.'

'I know. I know.' Sympathy breathed in a gush from the good woman. 'Does she live near here?'

'She lives in . . .' Uncle Lucy bent over a noble array of tulips while he considered where she lived. 'In Edwardes Square. Now which is it to be, Win? These carnations? These tulips? Was ever so much beauty assembled in one place. To live always amid such beauty must be very good for your soul, madam.'

'My soul?' She laughed roguishly. 'It'd take more than a few flowers to make much of that old dustpan. It's past praying for.'

'Ah no, madam. That we refuse to believe, do we not, Win?'

I grunted assent, and she, hearing this sound, laughed shrilly and said 'Bless the child,' which embarrassed me not slightly, so that I turned away.

But he and she stayed on the happiest terms of chaff and gallantry, he complimenting her on her blooms, and she saying flattering things about his taste.

In the end he bought an assembly of tulips, carnations and hyacinths and then, noticing a display of imported apples, labelled with prices that defied belief, asked if she would be so exceedingly kind—'but really it is unforgivable to ask you'—as to arrange some of these splendid fruits in a basket—'though I doubt if our poor old friend will be able to eat the apples,' he said. 'The grapes, yes.'

She built up a comely basket, and our thanks were profuse, I tagging mine on to his, but she demurred, 'Not at all. I'm so glad you rang, and I do hope your friend will recover. I'm sure she will. Eighty is no great age with some women.'

But Uncle Lucy shook his head as one who feared the worst, and she enjoined him, 'No, don't lose heart,' as, lifting our hats (I quicker on the draw this time) we went to the door.

She followed us to the door, loth to see the last of us— or the last of him. 'I *am* so glad you rang my bell and got me down. I am, really.'

'It was unpardonable of us to disturb your well-earned rest on a Sunday. It was only because we were *in extremis*. Extremis.'

'Don't give another thought to it. What I say is, The better the day, the better the deed. Have you far to go?'

'Far. No; no. Just—just to Edwardes Square.'

'Well . . . good-bye . . . good-bye. . . .' Her smile was quite sad at losing us. She shut her door, as if unwillingly.

'A perfect woman, nobly planned,' murmured Uncle Lucy, brandishing his stick at a bus. 'May she live for ever. We did her a great kindness because she obviously delights in helping the sick. And she'd have been just as glad to give these to me if she'd known what I really wanted them for. So all is well and fair. Home now, I think. Yes . . . yes . . . *on n'aime pas assez.*'

Arrived home, he took the basket of fruits from me, and with the flowers in one hand and the fruit in the other, opened the door of the dining-room where he rightly surmised that Auntie Flavia would be sitting alone with her misery.

'A few flowers and some fruit,' he said. 'Nothing much. Practically nothing,' and, laying them quickly on the table, hastened out of the room. He hastened up the stairs before she could open her mouth. I had never seen him ascend our stairs so fast. For once he had forgotten his brittle and endangered heart, or was taking a risk with it. I rushed up to Gael to tell her to 'come and see the harvest festival downstairs,' and as we hurried down together we met Auntie Flavia hurrying up. She could not speak as she passed us, because her mouth was twisting and her head shaking, in an effort to hold back the crowding tears, as she climbed out of misery towards the sweetness of reconciliation.

CHAPTER FIFTEEN

Now all was happy in our house again, with Uncle Lucy seated like the glowing flame in a lamp, and Auntie Flavia ministering to, and when necessary fussing over, the slightly agitated flame.

For my part I was now so nearly sure of one relationship among the apparently unrelated inhabitants of our house, and so happy in the thought of it that, craving certainty, I was driven to a deed which nothing could persuade me was less than shameful. Shame played tunes on my heart as I performed it, and I still feel a faint shame as I write of it.

Uncle Lucy had brought on that four-wheeler a black strong-box such as one sees in lawyer's offices. It held all his important deeds and documents, and Auntie Flavia had said to us, 'Poor darling, he was so frightened by that French doctor that he now takes it about with him everywhere in case he dies. I dread every day his remembering that silly man's words because, when he does, he sits living the day as if it were his last.' A black, inexorable, heartless coffer it looked, thrust far beneath his great brass bed. And I, forever searching, delving, probing, for some answer to my questions, began to believe desperately that revelation might wait in that box.

Sometimes when the upper landings were quiet I peeped at it and touched its lid; but to what good: it was closed as tight as a coffin. Only this good: that the sterner its resistance to my visiting fingers, the stronger grew my desire to open it.

Then came a day when Uncle Lucy rose feeling ill. He had a new pain at his heart, he said; and he sat in his place sagging like a half-emptied sack. Auntie Flavia, condoling with him and fussing over him, as her manner was, begged him to come there and then to her favourite doctor ('no one like him') in Wimpole Street. He consented most willingly and in his alarm and general disablement left on his dressing-table all the contents of his trouser pockets: money, silk handkerchief, ring of keys.

The house being silent, I began my customary feline prowl about the landings, and, stepping velvet-padded into his bedroom, saw those keys.

Back to the landing. Not a sound anywhere, save in the kitchen far below. Gael out. Lizzie and Hilda, the new maid, done with their bedroom and staircase work. I rushed to the vast bed and dived under it. I dragged forth the box, sat beside it on the carpet, fumbled for the right key—my heart hammering its reprobation all the while—found it, and lifted a lid on the past. Wills, agreements, leases, shares, receipts, his marriage certificate, his deed of separation, and a stack of thick foolscap manuscript books, tied with a white tape. I undid the tape and opened the topmost. A diary, dating back to 1857 when he must have been twenty-nine. All but fifty years ago, and the paper had grown brown at the edges and cracked; the ink had faded into a pale sepia. Nothing in those distant years could meet my need, so I discarded book after book till I came to 1880, the year of the divorce case. Eighteen-eighty was in the last book, and only in its first half, as if he'd had no wish to continue the diary, now that his life among famous men, and his share in great events, were ended. I turned to July, but the only allusion to the divorce was a single passage covering two pages in his small neat hand.

I read it, sitting on the floor by the box.

'The *cause célèbre* is over. Well, I accept his pure lordship's words, that I am unfit for decent society. Also those of the Solicitor-General, no less pure in public, and the plain endorsement of the crowd who, being likewise men of spotless morality, were free to hiss me as I came away. I will go lest I contaminate any of their white souls. God forbid that I should infect with my corruption those who have never told a lie, never done an immoral thing, never been guilty of subterfuge or deceit, never in all their lives taken furtive steps to avoid exposure. I have done all these things, weakly and feebly; I confess it, and acknowledge therefore the right of Judge and Counsel, since they are men without sin and without a trace of weakness, worldliness or social fear, to pronounce me liar, cheat, and coward.

'"There are no words strong enough to condemn him," said his lordship. What, my lord? Not in the Bible? Not in all the Law and the Prophets? Not in Shakespeare? No words black enough in *Lear*, *Othello*, or *Macbeth*? So? Have I then sinned as no man ever before me?

'I have done great harm to a few, let it be granted, but it also seems to me that in my twenty odd years of service to my country, even if my motives were partly selfish (as whose are not?), I have done some good to many. Somehow or other—I don't know why—the needs of the poor and the oppressed got into my heart and stuck there for ever. And not only in my own country have I done a little good. I have always championed—sometimes against my own interest—the oppressed and the exploited and the enslaved; and these, strangely enough in our world of sinless men, are the majority everywhere. Loving so greatly the idea of England, I have longed that she should lead the world in demanding justice for such as these. But now she has spewed me forth as a filthy mouthful, and I will go.

'Or perhaps it is not England that has done this, but her present governing class; for my kindly-hearted England is once again under the Rule of the Saints.

'But let me not pretend to myself that I go only in a mood of haughty contempt. I go in great pain. A pain that lacks all grandeur, for it is but the sick anguish of one who has passionately desired fame and striven for it during thirty years and achieved it in a measure beyond all his dreams, and then, overnight, sees it turned into obloquy, scorn and ridicule. A man who has suddenly become a lewd joke to the people; a source of loud laughter in club-rooms and taprooms and of arch and naughty sniggering in the drawing-rooms of the ladies.

'No, as his pure lordship stated, I am a coward. I can live no longer among people who cannot see me without remembering those words, liar, betrayer, coward and cheat, and without speaking afterwards, with little grins of relish, about a cistern-room window, a conservatory roof, and a drainpipe.

'I agree, my lord, I am a coward, so I bid you good-bye. Be happy in your white sanctity, and your assurance that Heaven must delight in you.

'But one moment more, my lord—and you too, my learned friend—before we part. What do we not know, you and I, about life as it is lived in, let us say, Devoncourt House, Watermouth House, and another great mansion that stands between Pall Mall and The Mall? Can it be that your public piety and indignation, your shock and upraised hands, are paraded before the people because certain acts of mine have unhappily burst through the barrier of mere scandal into the public press? How eagerly—and how politely—you would accept the hospitality of any of these great houses whose lords have kept their lives safely outside a courtroom's walls.

'But why do I write all this? Because, I suppose, it is some relief to do so. Let the pus pour out of the sore. And there is almost a creative joy in it, as when one used to prepare a speech to slay the enemy in the days now gone.

'Will anyone ever read it? No. No one ever, if only I remember to destroy it before I die.'

§

Shame pierced me, but it was drowned in the compassion that surrounded it. There was a deep gap between this and the next passage, and I took advantage of it to touch my eyes.

Unlike any other parts of the diary, this next passage had a heading in capitals, and a strange heading, too.

PISA CRAG

It could have been the heading of an epilogue, for there were only three brief entries after this one.

I read it eagerly, shamefully.

'We made our great expedition to Pisa Crag today, and how shall I ever forget it? Something happened on old Pisa's top that will hardly abide forgetting. Let me write of it all while my memories are fresh.

'After a month here at Thorswater, Lottie is no longer overawed by the mountains and she is fast getting used to the dizziest heights. She has learned with joy the truth of what every climber knows, that the weakest head can, with time, get used to any exposure at any height. We are both in good shape after our walks and climbs in the mountain air, or after our long days of rest in this silent valley, sitting by a wood fire in our hill-farm room, and seeing nothing outside but the rain, rain, rain. Then, sometimes, I have read poems to her, as in the old days, and we have recovered some of our delight in them—but, alas! not all. Nothing like all. We are too self-centred to lose for long the pain in our hearts.

'There are other climbers in the valley, but as none of them turn their heads when we pass, I can't think they know who we are. So, feeling well out of the world, and trying to believe we are already forgotten, we manage to laugh together often, even though the scorching fires of the Divorce Court are less than two months behind us— even though we know only too well that the smoke of that fire has dropped its reeking soots all over the world. There have been days on the mountains and days by the fire when Lottie has been the enchantingly gay creature she always was before the skies fell.

'It's a long walk from Thorswater to the base of Pisa. One must plod up and up to Sunder Great Slabs, then climb over Strawn Gap, which may be called a col, but is as high as many mountains, then, alas! lose nearly all this height by dropping down into Emberdale. In the past I have always approached the Crag from Garthwaite, but they know me too well in the farms there, and Lottie and I want rest from following eyes.

'Today we woke to see the sun high above Comber Fell and blazing a benediction on our venture, so we set out early, but, all the same, it was midday before we were down in Emberdale and climbing up through Bottom Wood towards the foot of Pisa.

'It was lovely in the wood this September day, and each of us at the same moment said almost the same thing: that the world still had much of beauty and pleasure to give us if only we could forget mankind. The stubborn old lichened oaks rose from a floor of rusty leaves; and as for the rowans by the sides of the waterfall, they were on fire with coral berries. The waterfall, as we both noticed, was a white mass where it came roaring over the rocks, but a moss-green where it spread into pools that were still as tarns. Strange that the same force should produce both uproar and a quiet peace.

'Climbing through the still, green-painted twilights of the wood, we came at last upon the empty fell-breast, and there five hundred feet above us was my noble, my most royal, Pisa Crag. It outcrops from the mountain's side and towers up haughtily to within a hundred feet of its summit. This is the point from which to see why the first climbers called it Pisa Crag. The great dark pinnacle seems to lean to the west.

'The face of Pisa was first climbed by Ashley Ewer fifty years back (I met the old man before he died. Peace to a great climber's soul; I'm sure he climbed into Heaven). I myself have climbed it several times since, led by, or leading, Tom Locke with Scotty Atholl behind; but no woman had ever climbed it till ten years ago. Since then, save the mark, you can see the comely creatures rushing to its foot with their ropes and climbing it like wood-peckers up a tree-bole. I declare you can sometimes see them sitting on its few grassy ledges like kittiwakes alighted on a cliff.

'This I told to Lottie, but she would not come up with a rope, so we toiled to its top by what the rock-climbers have the insolence to call the Walkers' Route; that is, up through the herbage and boulders at its side. If this is not climbing, I know not what is: the slope goes on and on forever and seems next door to vertical, so that the walkers have a different name for it from the climbers; they call it the Grass Wall. And other names which I may not write here.

'We did an hour and more of this breathless work, Lottie pausing often to come alive again and ask, "Why do people do this sort of thing when it isn't really necessary?" or perhaps to pick one or two of the flowers that came climbing with us—and praise to the tiny yellow tormentil that climbed more bravely than they all. An hour or more of it, I say, and then we stepped, aglow with the glory of achievement, on to Pisa's summit. And here a most gracious arrangement by the god of the mountain: the summit is not only level like the platform of a belvedere, but furnished with cushions of moss for your comfort and rest. Did the harsh winds plane it down, and the soft winds furnish it?

'We sat together, Lottie quite untroubled by the height, even though the precipice edge was not twelve feet away.

'She showed me the flowers she had picked and asked me to name them.

'"Hawkweed," I answered promptly and proudly (though guessing at this one). "Scabious and harebell. And corn sowthistle, I fancy. But they're all very common—just the common people, Princess."

'Of late I have been calling her Princess in the fashion of the old French ballades which we've been reading together, and I have felt more than ever ready to give her this title since the Judge and the people flung their filth at her, and at her love for me.

'"Never mind," she said, "I shall keep them in memory of this day. I shall press them and put them in my Bible."

'"*Fleurs du Mal*," I suggested.

'But she shook her head and murmured, "*Fleurs de joie*."

'For a while we sat, or lazily reclined, on that moss-cushioned mountain shelf, high above the habitations of our unforgiving kind, and we delighted together in the vast prospect spread below. In the long hull-bottom of Emberdale a glistening silver beck fed the Ember Mere, and the lake itself was a sheet of slate blue, just ribbed by a breeze.

All round it rose the mountain slopes, fledged with a gold and green feathering where the dead bracken met the quick. Down there among the bracken we could see two men scything it down, to make bedding for their beasts, or bridges for wet pastures, now that winter was near. Men undisgraced. Then, suddenly, the ridges of the opposite mountains changed into one dark blue silhouette, as a cloud crossed the sun.

'"There are times among great mountains," I said to her, "when one can almost forget one's self and one's passing pain. Up here one feels so small and temporary— and one's detractors, too."

'"But our little temporary time is all we've got," she objected.

'And I agreed, "Yes, for us it's forever."

'Above us, in a world of pure light, two crows were mobbing a buzzard, their harsh cries competing with his low, mournful hiss.

'You can be sure I attempted a parallel here, but I added, "No doubt the old buzzard deserves it all."

'"No, no," she declared in a low voice; but then you can't get the truth from a passionately loyal woman, and, upon my soul, I think that Lottie has clung to me so passionately in these last weeks far more for my comfort than for hers. In the old days she was easily angered by me and very ready to give me the whole of her tongue if she held I deserved it, which no doubt I sometimes did; but since the disaster never one angry word; nothing but the old ministering and cherishing. And yet she must have suffered at least as much as I.

'Let me not forget this.

'I don't remember just when it was that I rose and walked towards that brink of the precipice where, did Pisa really lean, the edge should be an overhang. Actually the huge outcrop does not lean, and the cliff here is no more than an irresolute perpendicular. To an eye above, however, it looks to fall straight as a plumb-line for hundreds of feet.

'"Come and look," I called to Lottie.

'"Dare I?"

'"Yes, you are a mountaineer now, fully professed."

'She came towards me very heedfully and prudently, and I put my arm round her and held her tight that she might not sicken as she looked down.

'We stood there silent. I know not what she was thinking, but I was thinking that death could well end it all. And that death with her would be a perfect peace.

'Thinking this, and clasping her tight, I turned her face up to mine and asked, "What do you say? Shall we make an end of everything? Here and now?"

'I suppose I was hardly serious, but I think she thought I was, and her eyes filled with terror as they stared into mine. Nevertheless, she said, "As you wish, my only love."

'I glanced down at the tumble of rocks beneath the far base of the cliff. "It would be quickly over," I said. "There'd be no surviving those rocks—hardly for a second."

'Holding tight to me, she turned her eyes quickly down to them, and brought them yet more quickly away. Her face was white, her lips pressed hard together, and she trembled in my tight embrace, but she said again, "As you wish, my dear."

'Maybe for a nightmare minute she wondered whether I would take her down with me, but I drew her back and paid for her words with a kiss. Looking round upon the outspread pageantry of mountain and dale, pinewood and beck, I said, "No. The world can be so beautiful, and it must have plenty to give you yet, Princess, because you're still so young, and you haven't fallen anything like as far as I."

'"I want nothing that you can't have," she answered.

'I accepted this from her without reply, though knowing that the world is not made that way.'

§

After that there were only three stray entries in the diary, all written in Paris. None of them mentioned Lottie. Then nothing more: only a thickness of clean, blank, feint-ruled pages.

CHAPTER SIXTEEN

For days that story of Pisa Crag moved in my mind like a film in vivid green colours, and yet I could share it with none because I was so ashamed of the way I had come by it. It was almost a burden to me, to have this possession in my mind and to be unable even to hint at it—to Gael, to Auntie Flavia, to Uncle Lucy himself. Uncle Lucy, to be sure, was not long available. Very soon after this he went back to Paris. That doctor in Wimpole Street had so mended his spirits, telling him that with care he could live to ninety-two, that Uncle Lucy had joined Auntie Flavia in maintaining 'there was no one like him.' We gathered from her that the talk in the doctor's consulting-room went something like this. (She had told us the story with her usual relish and gusto.) Having finished his examination, the doctor put a comforting hand on Uncle Lucy's shoulder and said, 'Nothing seriously wrong that I can find. With reasonable care you could live to a great age.'

'But I *am* a great age,' said Uncle Lucy indignantly.

'Nonsense, my dear sir. Seventy-seven? That's to be in your prime.'

'Prime? Alas! no, doctor. Over-ripe. Unpleasantly over-ripe and slowly rotting.'

'Well, we've all been slowly rotting since we were about twenty-five.' The bland hand now rested on his shoulder blades. 'No, you come back in ten years' time, and we'll have another look at you.'

'Survive ten years?'

'Certainly. With care. You should survive all of that and more. Fifteen, let us say.'

'Till ninety-two?'

'Till ninety-two. And beyond.'

'In a state of general debility, perhaps, and ever increasing imbecility. But, still. . . .'

'Forget the mathematics of it, my dear sir. A man is as old as he feels.'

'Then I'm about ninety-eight,' sighed Uncle Lucy.

'Not a bit of it. That's only because you feel you ought to feel old. There's no reason why you shouldn't feel about fifty.'

'*Fifty?*'

'Well, say fifty-five. And a bit,' laughed the doctor.

Uncle Lucy shook his head, but less in rejection of this pleasing diagnosis than in loyalty to his previous despair.

'Too kind. Too kind,' he said. 'But still. . . .'

But still, he agreed to do his best, and went back to Paris.

But he didn't lift any of the bags on the doorstep when the four-wheeler came. The doctor had said 'with care.'

§

Thinking over that scene on Pisa's summit, I could not tell whether those last words, 'The world can be so beautiful, and it must have plenty to give you yet,' meant that he and Lottie had soon parted. The absence of her name from the brief notes in Paris might suggest this. But if not, if they had lived together for another eleven years, then I could be their son. I remembered him saying to the Frenchman in the teashop that Madame Ilbraham, the boy's mother, was 'young, quite young,' and that she had died. 'Yes . . . yes . . . she is dead.' And he had quoted something about queens who had died young and fair.

Charmed by this new idea that Lottie Morris might have been my mother and have died while I was a baby, I took it one day to Gael in the Playroom and went into conference about it. It was May, 1906, and I was on the verge of becoming fifteen, and Gael was half-way to being sixteen. In the wisdom of our teens we had both decided that Uncle Lucy was our father, there being no one else in sight, and no candidate so desirable as he, a lord and a Marquess's son.

Some time before this I had gone to Gael and uncovered before her my suspicions that he might be *my* father, and smartly she snubbed me. She just quenched me like a smoking candle-wick. 'Oh, I thought of that long ago,' she said. 'You're rather like him, only not half so handsome, of course.' To which I replied 'Well, I'm delighted to be his son, but it's all very aristocratic and shameful. And what precisely do we do now?'

'And I'm beginning to suspect,' she went on, not heeding my question, 'that my dear Uncle Lucy bore me, too. Oh, I do hope so.'

'Gentlemen do not bear children,' I reminded her, and added, 'I never had much faith in Mr. Ilbraham, nor any great affection for him, and I'm not all that sorry to lose him. Nor, if you'll forgive me, have I ever had much faith in Colonel Harrington.'

'Oh, but I was rather fond of him,' Gael insisted. 'I thought he was brave, and rather a poppet. I'm sorry to lose him in some ways, but I'll cheerfully sacrifice him any day for Uncle Lucy. Gosh, isn't it all thrilling?'

I met with no such merry reception when I went to her with the suggestion that Lottie might be my mother. I was surprised at the instant anger with which she resisted this. She was playing bagatelle alone on our miniature bagatelle board as I entered; I offered my suggestion, and instantly she flung down her cue on to the table. 'Oh, no! That's just bilge. *I've* pinched little Lottie for my mother.'

'Since when?' I asked, in a curious sudden jealousy.

'Oh, for ages. So don't you start butting in. I think Lottie was adorable. As adorable as Uncle Lucy, and that's saying a lot.' She was now sitting on the table with her back to the bagatelle board. 'I know she committed a lot of sins, but I've decided that, if we knew the whole truth, we'd see that it wasn't really her fault: she was driven to it, as it were, and so to say. Absolutely driven to it.'

'She was incredibly brave,' I began, forgetting. . . .

'Brave? Why do you say that?'

'Oh . . . I just meant that she seemed to be ready for anything. But he couldn't have married her. His old wife was still alive, and still is.'

'They lived in sin,' Gael announced.

'Where?'

'In Paris. You can, in Paris.'

I mused on this, and Gael proceeded: 'And don't forget I was born in Paris. That much I've always been told.'

'Perhaps I was born there, too.'

'Not with Lottie for your mother. You're less than eight months younger that I am. I've been into the question carefully, and it's practically impossible. I made Winnie Clynes ask her mother if——'

'You've never been and told Winnie Clynes all about it?'

'Of course not. I'm not quite mad. I pretended it was for a play I wanted to write, about two people who got engaged and discovered just before the wedding that they were brother and sister.'

'What a rotten play.'

'And Winnie Clynes's mother told her that it was practically impossible, unless you were a seven-months' child——'

'Me?'

'Yes, you; and even then, she said, it wouldn't be quite nice. It would mean—well, you can see what it would mean. She's told Winnie tons more about Lottie Morris. She says that she was quite lovely and ever so popular everywhere, but after the terrible scandal she disappeared and was never heard of again. She says that awful shocking songs were sung about her in the streets——'

'Yes, I knew that.'

'She saw them selling them in pamphlets along the gutters of Victoria Street—things like "I love a Lottie, Love her quite a lottie"—and they made jokes about her in the music-hall that fairly brought the house down. Dirty beasts. Someone referred to her in Parliament as a "convicted adulteress".'

'Well,' I submitted with a shrug, 'that is, unfortunately, just about the truth.'

'Yes, but they needn't have said so.'

'It was rude,' I allowed.

'So she went off. Obviously to Paris, where Uncle Lucy was. And there the delightful Gael was born, an adorable baby whom they both worshipped. You're not asking me to believe that you appeared eight months later, a premature baby and rather revolting?'

'Perhaps they lied about the date of my birth.'

'Oh, my God,' said Gael, 'I never thought of that!'

§

This new but simple idea was so oddly uncomfortable, so little made to the measure of our dreams, because we'd never thought of ourselves as full brother and sister, that it cried to be put an end to. Gael had now a girl's passionate love for her dream-figure of Lottie Morris and recoiled violently from sharing her with anyone. She pictured her always as beautiful as a morning in June; slender as a fawn beneath the elms, and as graceful; a bewitching person who fascinated all with her glee, high spirits, and wit. 'An enchantingly gay creature'—I could have given her Uncle Lucy's own words, had I dared to tell her the Pisa story. And the nearer she came to sixteen the higher rose her sense of her rights, while mine grew hardly less tall, and at last we decided that it was unfair to expect us to spare Auntie Flavia for ever. 'We've been very decent in keeping quiet so long,' we said. And we resolved to go soon . . . fairly soon . . . and challenge her point-blank to give us the truth.

'There's some risk of an appalling scene,' I said.

'Can't help that,' answered Gael. 'I shall tell her that we can't be expected to wait any more and that, for my part, I shan't leave the room till she's told me all. Absolutely everything.'

'All right,' I said. 'I'm with you. When?'

'Well . . .' she temporized, '. . . soon . . . as soon as possible, but . . . but we must be careful to choose a suitable moment.'

Brave talk, but not for a long time did we decide finally on a suitable moment. Then we went slowly down to her, determined to be Children of the Mist no more.

CHAPTER SEVENTEEN

Iᴛ was four months later when we chose the moment. A September evening; Auntie Flavia sitting alone in the breakfast-room with her sewing; quiet in the kitchen down-stairs; quiet in the street outside; a rather menacing quiet everywhere; and Gael said, 'Shall we go?' not really wanting the answer Yes. But I gave it her, saying impatiently, 'Oh, yes. We must do something some time. Let's get it over.'

'All right,' she agreed, but less than happily. 'Come on.'

And she led me down from the Playroom; down through the dusk and quiet of the ill-lit stairs, both our hearts throbbing; down to a cold and heartless hall; and so to the closed door of the room where Auntie Flavia sat.

I tried to conceal my nervousness by saying behind her in the dark hall, 'This is the Great Moment,' but the nervousness tripped up the voice, and I had to clear my throat to set it free. 'This, my child, is It,' I said.

Gael said nothing, but I noticed that her hand hesitated and halted, before she could grasp the handle of the door.

Nothing to do, however, but to turn it. And enter.

We did so, and Auntie Flavia, sitting by her evening fire, looked up from her sewing with a startled question in her eyes, so like a serious embassy did our entry seem.

'What is it?' she asked.

'Look, Auntie,' Gael began. 'I'm nearly sixteen and Travers is fifteen, and we want to know the truth about who our parents were. We do really. You must see that we have a right to know.'

'Yes,' I said, supporting her, but from half a pace behind.

Auntie Flavia only stared at us. She had turned pale—white—as if an hour long dreaded was come. Her right hand, holding her needle and thread, with a thimble on its middle finger had dropped to her lap. The other had fallen on to the table with the white garment whose hem she'd been sewing. In my nervousness I apprehended all things in sharp detail so that they have stayed incised upon my memory ever since: her small work-basket housing carelessly the cotton reels, darning wools, and tarnished scissors: the dirty little pincushion at the basket's side, its hump pierced with needles still holding their broken threads; her handkerchief resting nearby; and above everything else her eyes with the terror in them—a terror of this moment—a terror fulfilled at last, and, because fulfilled, speechless, impotent.

This was not a day when she had made herself resplendent for a party, or even tidy. She was in her old pink dressing-jacket; her hair was disarranged after some scratching of her head with a knitting needle; and if ever there'd been powder on her reddened face, her handkerchief had wiped it away.

'You see,' Gael continued, trying hard to soften this pistol-point demand, 'it's ridiculous being kept in the dark at sixteen. It is, really.' But, as if frightened at what she'd said, she walked towards the window, looked out at it, then turned and leaned back against its sill. I remained where I was—near the door, with my hands behind my back, one stroking the other.

Auntie Flavia's lips moved up and down, waiting for words; she found words at last. 'Will you leave me alone? Coming in and attacking me like this! Will you kindly go?'

'No,' said Gael.

'Go at once, when I tell you!' Perhaps to her relief, that 'No' had set her temper alight so that her head was now ablaze with words. 'How dare you answer me like that? Go when you're told. I'm in no mood to answer any questions just now.'

'I am not leaving this room till I know who my father and mother were.'

'Nor I.' I said this because I must act up to our brave talk, but it was all I could say. Gael was very much the leader of this embassy; I her echo.

'I'm not going to be talked to like this. By the pair of you! I never heard anything like it.' She saw a way of evasion, picked up her sewing, and made for the door. 'Leave me alone, can't you?'

But Gael had come from her window sill and stood across the door. 'No, don't go. Please. Do be sensible. You can't keep us in the dark for ever like this. We're just not going to stay in the dark. After all, it's been rather decent of us not to have worried you before. We've tried not to, but there comes a time. . . . Uncle Lucy was my father, wasn't he?'

'And mine?'

Auntie Flavia stopped dead. She stared, amazed. And her amazement annoyed me. Was it possible that she imagined we'd reached our present years without guessing this much? Imagined it because she wanted to, needed to?

'Uncle Lucy your father?'

'Yes.'

'Yes,' I echoed.

She turned and went back to her chair. She dropped on to it like one whom a blow had made sick. Then her head began to shake, and her mouth to shake, as the tears over-threw all government; but after a while she saw, and seized upon, another means of evasion. 'I won't betray secrets. Ask *him*. He is your guardian.'

'How can we ask him? He is not here.' Gael had gone to her side and laid an arm along her shoulder. 'We don't want to be beastly. But you must see we can't go on like this. Why should we?'

'Do you *know* who my father was?' I asked.

'Of course I know.'

'Please tell me then.'

Silence. Which irritated me. So I said with a sigh, and looking away, 'Will you be so very good as to tell me.'

'Don't adopt that tone with me. You're no one to talk to me in sarcastic tones. Oh, how like your father you are! But you of all people have no right to try being sarcastic with me.' She stamped her fist on the table. 'Don't bully me, I say! *You* to talk to me like this! Haven't I done everything for you? Haven't I given up my life to you? To you as well as to Gael? One day you'll know what I did for you.'

'I wasn't trying to be sarcastic,' I said, lying perhaps, because I now wanted to spare her all I could. 'I only want to——'

'One shouldn't expect gratitude in this world.' She addressed this to the air about her, preferring drama and self-pity to listening to me. 'One is foolish to look for it.'

'I only want to know this: can you say Uncle Lucy *wasn't* my father?'

She said no such thing, preferring to wipe her eyes.

'Then he was?'

No answer. Only the handkerchief applied to cheek and nose.

Gael stooped and kissed her forehead. 'Don't cry,' she begged. 'Honestly, we don't want to be beastly.'

'Please,' I persisted. 'Was he?'

'Oh, yes, yes, *yes*!' A loud admission. 'Of course he was your father.'

'Oh, I'm so glad! So glad!'

'And mine too?' demanded Gael eagerly.

'Yes. Yes. Of course.'

'Oh, I'm so glad. Oh, good . . . good!'

'You are glad? But why?'

'Because I love him.'

'But you must understand what this means. Gael, it means . . . it means that he was never married to your mother.'

'Oh, I can't worry about that. I don't care about that so long as he was my father.'

'We've really known this for ages,' I said, feeling it was time she learned that children were awake and aware much sooner than adults supposed. 'And we've known too that his real name isn't Grenville. At least that's only one of his names.' I was not guiltless of cruelty in triumph, as I added, 'His name is Lord Roland Louis Grenville Caen de Brath, and he's the son of the Marquess of Hayle and Ensor.'

'In the name of Heaven how long have you known that?'

'How long, Gael? Oh, for ages.'

'Did someone tell you this?' The fright was back in her eyes.

'No. It was not difficult to find out. Did Uncle Arthur really think we didn't guess who he was talking about at your Christmas dinner?'

'He's silly enough to think so,' put in Gael.

'He went on and on about how marvellous Uncle Lucy was when he was making political speeches, and he ended by letting out the name "de Brath." I went straight to a chap at school whose father is a Liberal M.P. to find out all about a de Brath who'd been a Liberal statesman. And, Auntie, do please tell me: was Lottie Morris my mother?'

'*Lottie Morris!*' The fright in her eyes was now terror. 'What on earth do you know about Lottie Morris? Your mother? Good gracious, no.'

'Was she mine?' asked Gael.

'Who has told you anything about Lottie Morris?'

'We've read all about the divorce case in the papers.'

Auntie Flavia plunged her face into her hands; then threw arms and face on to the table among the wrecks of her sewing. 'Yes,' she sobbed. 'Lottie Morris was your mother. But not Travers's. Not his. Oh, my God, this was bound to come.'

We could do no more to a suffering woman, save that I asked very gently, 'May *I* know who my mother was?'

'No, no; I'm not telling you. She was no connection of mine. It's no business of mine.'

'It's very much business of mine,' I submitted.

'Ask *him*,' she sobbed from her arms. 'Ask *him*.'

'But he isn't here, Auntie.'

'Oh, well . . . oh, well . . . I suppose you may as well know. He would have to tell you. Your mother was. . . .' She stopped, reluctant, on this side of the name.

'Yes?' And again, 'Yes?'

'Your mother was a Peggy Waybon. Lady Peggy Waybon. She is dead.'

I gasped. '*Who* did you say?'

'Peggy Waybon,' but before she could add more, Gael asked, her hand, like a mother's, stroking the weeping woman's back, 'And is my darling mother still alive?'

Now Auntie Flavia looked up from her arms. 'What did you say?'

Gael repeated her question, adding, 'I'm so terribly pleased to think that Lottie Morris was my mother. She was beautiful, wasn't she? And sweet and utterly charming . . . even if . . . but I don't believe half the wicked things they said about her, and I'm sure that most of it wasn't her fault. I'm proud that she was my mother.'

At this Auntie Flavia gave a little cry and threw her face back on to her arms, sobbing more violently than we'd ever seen her sob before.

Gael's hand still stroked her. 'Is she—is she still alive? I so want to know.'

Without lifting her face, Auntie Flavia said, 'Leave me, oh, leave me now. I'll tell you more some time. I promise I will. Leave me, please. I can't speak now. I want to think.'

§

We could not hurt her any more, so we went from the room and, both shaken, climbed the stairs again. 'Peggy Waybon. Lady Peggy Waybon.' I could only repeat the name behind knitted brows, as we mounted in silence to the Playroom.

'Well, we know now,' said Gael, when we were safely in that room.

'We know *some*,' I corrected, thinking it was like Gael to have forgotten that my portion was still incomplete.

'We know that Lottie Morris was my mother.'

'But who between Earth and Heaven was Lady Peggy Waybon?'

'Don't ask *me*.'

'I'm glad she was a lady, at any rate. Even if it *is* all very aristocratic and shameful. I must say I'm glad she wasn't a parlour maid. You can never be sure what these aristocrats get up to.'

We continued discussing these matters, I sitting on the table with hands in trouser pockets, Gael roaming the carpet, and neither of us troubling to light the gas, even though the September darkness was slowly extinguishing our Playroom. Abruptly we stopped. We had heard steps coming up the stairs and knew them for Auntie Flavia's. We looked at the door-handle, waiting for it to turn. It turned, and she stood in the frame of the doorway. Her face was dry-eyed but set in sadness, like the white marble portrait of a Niobe who would weep no more. Eyes and nose were reddened with weeping; her hair was yet more dishevelled by that rocking of her head on her arms; but it seems to me now that her figure, straightened unconsciously by self-mastery and a resolution, had draped itself, despite the old pink dressing jacket, in something like grandeur.

'Come, children,' she said, 'and I'll tell you all.'

CHAPTER EIGHTEEN

THE three of us descended the stairs in silent procession, she leading. Back in the breakfast-room, she walked straight to the chair by her discarded sewing. Sitting in it, she picked up the crumpled handkerchief from the table and pushed it into her belt. The action was a little like someone sheathing a sword whose use was over.

'Sit down, Gaelie,' she said gently; and to me with more affection than I'd ever heard in her words to me, 'Sit down, Travers dear.'

Gael sat on her favourite seat, the window sill; I sat humped on a stiff chair against the wall, like a client in a waiting-room.

She could not begin at once; and when at last she spoke, it was to say, 'How much do you really know?'

To comfort her Gael said, 'Not much,' and I murmured the same.

'I must try to tell you everything. You are right. You have a right to know. Perhaps I ought to have told you long ago. But one puts it off and puts it off.'

'Of course,' Gael said; and I said, 'Of course.'

She felt for the handkerchief, but abandoned it courageously.

We waited.

'Gael darling, I am your mother. I was Lottie Morris.'

In all my long life no moment of surprise has equalled this. Gael says the same, and I remember her gasp. It may be you think this answer should long before have stared us in the eyes; but there was so much dust in our eyes. '*Miss* Middian', 'Flavia', her heavy figure and Lottie's slender grace; her occasional loose sluttishness and Lottie's legendary beauty; her swift irascibility and sometimes soured temper, and Lottie's enchanting witcheries. And if it is true that grown-ups are blind to children's acumen, so also is it true that children with elders of fifty do not easily imagine them young and slim and surcharged with animal spirits. Anyhow, blind or not, this revelation was a shock of bewildering surprise to us both; and to Gael—though she hid this—a shock of heart-slaying disappointment. She was white—white as Auntie Flavia had been when we first put our question.

From my humped position I was looking at Auntie Flavia and thinking of Pisa Crag.

'You see,' she went on, 'I was always known as Lottie as a child. My name was Charlotte Gertrude Flavia Middian before I married and became Charlotte Morris, but after . . . after the disaster, which really did echo round the world . . . or, rather, after I came back from Paris eleven years later—bringing you, Gaelie, I returned to my maiden name, hoping that hardly anyone would know who I was. I was forty then, so I pretended I was an unmarried and lonely woman who had adopted a child. You were the sweetest baby.'

We stayed silent.

'Colonel Morris and I had no children, though I was married to him eight years. You were the first. It sometimes happens like that with another man, and when you are getting older. The first and the only one, of course—you were the child of a great love. We loved you, and——'

But here these fine-sounding, sentimental, words set her wrestling with her tears and striving to stay them, so Gael lied for her comfort. 'I'm so awfully pleased. I couldn't be happier. Do tell me more. It's all so wonderful.'

'It's sweet of you to take it like that, Gaelie,' she said, feeling again for the handkerchief, and again abandoning it. With a sigh she turned her chair away from the table and towards the fire. And gazing into the heart of it, as if the memories lay in its glowing caverns, she told us of that first meeting with Lord Roland de Brath when he came to Selby St. Albans to address the Liberal Rally and her husband and she entertained him. 'Colonel Morris was a good and honourable man—you must never think anything else—but he was very much older than me; I was only twenty-six then and he was more than sixty; and I still wanted gaiety and fun. Roland—I suppose I can call him that now—Roland was nearly fifty, of course, but he could be as lively as a boy and as mischievous as any under-graduate or medical student. I used to tell him so. But I loved him for it. I adored him. We fell most terribly in love. . . .'

'Yes?' encouraged Gael.

'I don't know how one avoids these things. I don't know what good it is telling people that they shouldn't do them. It always seems to me like telling one that one shouldn't sicken and be ill. Something happens within one that one has no power over at all.'

'Oh, *yes*,' Gael confirmed, as if she knew the truth of this from experience.

'Yes . . . yes,' agreed Auntie Flavia, desiring, though forty years older, to be no less romantic about young love, or about such as hers, at any rate. 'It happens like that. If it is real, it happens like that. Always.' And she began to speak of their first meetings in London. But she said no word about that back room among the old junk shops in Rufus Street, Somers Town. Then she came, hesitantly, diffidently, to the house at the top of Roehampton Lane. Indeed she stopped completely here, the ancient shame perhaps constricting all mention of the Colonel's goodness in giving her that house, wherein she had betrayed him.

'Do go on,' Gael begged. 'You used to meet him there? He used to come to you there?'

She sighed deeply, her eyes still on the fire with its orange-gold caves.

'Yes, he used to come to me there. Do you remember going to Roehampton last summer, and you played cricket on the heath? Well, he and I slipped away to look at that house and to recall those wonderful old summer days—days twenty-six, twenty-seven, years ago. Sometimes he would come to me there when he was worn out by long sittings in Parliament or by his endless speech-making all over the country. It was a wicked shame to say that it was all hypocrisy. He spoke wonderfully, not only because he treated his oratory as an art and took immense pains with it, but because he believed so passionately in all his causes and hated all cruelty so violently—whether it was cruelty to poor factory hands or poor Irish tenants—we were doing terrible things in Ireland then. The Conservatives were terrified of his meetings and would try to break them up— or they'd wait in dangerous gangs at the doors for him to come out. Sometimes he could only get from the hall to his carriage, surrounded by police. It was from scenes like these that he would come to me, worn out and white and sick. He was then—what? Fifty?—and superb to look at, taller than anyone else and splendidly built, with a face that showed no hint of fear or worry, or indeed of any emotion except a calm indifference, when the crowds raged at him, and so everyone imagined him to be a man of great toughness; but *I* saw something different. I saw him as a man wearied beyond bearing, and almost broken. I've seen him break down in tears, sitting before me by the fire. I would do all in my power to comfort him. Sometimes I would wait up for him till two or three in the morning and put him straight to bed—and he would lie there and say that I was his only comfort; that there was no comforter in the world like me.'

Here, inevitably, she must pause again, to meet and pacify the insurgent tears. And Gael waited for her recovery before beseeching in a low voice, 'Go on. Do go on.'

'It really does interest you, does it?'

'More than anything in the world.' And indeed she was leaning forward, chin in hand, eyes enthralled.

I murmured the same from my chair by the wall.

'You must remember he had no other woman to nurse him and make much of him. His wife would neither see him nor divorce him. She was a Catholic and he used to call her his Holy, Catholic, Apostolic, and Immortal Wife, and say, in his very naughty way, that the sainted woman was as tough as a turtle and would certainly live for ever. After a long night's rest he would be full of high spirits again in the morning, and if it was summer and fine weather I would perhaps drive him out for miles over the Heath or through the Park, and we would put the horse up at an inn—or even tie him to a tree—while we walked away, out of sight of all the hateful world and found some lovely place to sit together under the trees. Whenever possible I used to drive the phæton myself, but sometimes we took Loveridge, the groom, and would leave the carriage in his understanding care, while we wandered off through the bracken and the gorse . . . miles away.'

In my place against the wall I remembered the witness of the coachman as to what he had seen in the bracken. His name was not Loveridge, and I was glad of this.

'Sometimes when he'd been speaking in the north and come back by the last train, I would wait for him at Euston, and we would drive all the way home through the night in a hansom. I loved those drives when all the world was asleep, and perhaps the summer sky was a mass of stars, and he and I were happy together. We went by the same way that we all took that afternoon: over the river at Hammersmith—though the bridge was much smaller then —and so on to Barnes and up Roehampton Lane. You can imagine how we were remembering those old rides that day when you sat before us in the carriage, and Travers was on the seat with the driver. . . . Wonderful days . . . easily the happiest of my life.'

Turning towards the table, and with no thought of what she was doing, she picked up a fragment cut from her sewing and rubbed at a stain on the mahogany; then began to clean other parts.

'But it wasn't all happiness by any means. He could be very irritable when worn out, and in moods like that he was much too easily hurt. I would try to soothe him, but he would stab at me with the most wounding words, and then there'd be a terrible row between us, neither speaking to the other at all. Oh, he knew how to wound. That was what made him so many enemies. He had a power of silence which could reduce any woman to a wreck. You see, if he loved you, he turned you into some-thing so big in his life that it was agony if you seemed to fail him. The more he loved you the more wretched his silences would be. They frightened me, his silences, and made me dumb, too. I couldn't speak, but would sometimes put a letter by his bedside, begging that we might be friends again. But he couldn't bring himself to speak. Only after days did he get the better of himself, and then perhaps he'd come home from a lonely walk, bringing me expensive flowers as a peace-offering.'

Kensington Gardens . . . Kensington High Street . . . the large pleasant lady at the florist's. . . . I leaned forward in my chair and, elbows on knees, played with my fingers.

'Still, those years at Roehampton were the happiest I've ever known. The time when you're in love, Gael, may be full of torments and yet the most wonderful of your life. I'd known nothing like this with Colonel Morris, though I was fond of him. Can you understand?'

'Oh, *yes*. Yes, of course!'

'Yes, they were happier even than my childhood days when we were all girls together, and dear Father was alive. But of course they couldn't last. People guessed who he was and began to talk. We saw people prying in at the windows and newspaper reporters slinking round the house or waiting in ambush for us when we rode out. Some people, you can be sure, were kind enough to write anonymous letters to my husband. His fury when he learned the truth was something awful to see—rightly, of course; oh, yes; he'd been tricked and deceived and lied to—but I don't know what else one can do when an overhwelming love comes into one's life. It was really to spare him that I lied and lied. I couldn't bear to hurt him.' She looked up from the table at Gael. 'Is all this a great shock to you?'

'Oh, no. I'm just feeling glad that he was my father . . . and that you . . . ' But she didn't complete that sentence. I could see what was happening to her. She felt that she ought to run from her window seat and put an arm about her mother's shoulder and perhaps kiss her; but she just couldn't do this; not yet; she was held tight to her place, chained to it, by the difference between the beautiful Lottie Morris of her imagination and Auntie Flavia sitting there, slumped and bunched and untidy, with her face all marred by recent tears.

'I begged him to spare Roland, but he wouldn't hear of it; the fury of a quiet man can be a terrible thing. He said, "Not for one moment. His deluded followers shall know him for what he is. He's given me ammunition enough and I'll fire with every gun I've got till he's not a shred of reputation left." And he did this. I remember the Solicitor-General said—you say you've read the divorce case? Oh dear! you shouldn't have at your age. He said that the Colonel had laid his sword between us and that it represented the Law. But I always used to say that he used it to far greater purpose than that. It slew my life for me: it was even more terrible to be a divorcée then than now. And it slew Roland's career at a blow. The message from the lawyers was delivered to him at the moment of his greatest triumph, when his party, largely as a result of his wonderful speeches, had been returned to Parliament with a majority over all other parties, and now there seemed no position too great for him. But he received the message as he was dressing for a big dinner at which he was to be the guest of honour, and he knew at once that all was over. It meant total ruin. The end of everything. But he went to the dinner and made his speech; a brilliantly amusing one, so I've been told. Total ruin it was. His enemies came down upon him from every quarter like yelping dogs. He appeared once again in the House of Commons to make his speech of resignation and stood unmoved while they howled against him. They raised a storm of cheers when he said he was going; and I'm told he showed no emotion. He only raised an eyebrow and faintly smiled. But when he got to me that night he just laid his head on my breast and cried, while I stroked his hair. They got him solemnly expelled from his clubs—clubs which had been only too proud to have him a few days before. They ran a violent campaign against him in the Tory press. Oh, how people love to add to the pain of anyone in disgrace!'

'Beasts! Beasts!' muttered Gael.

'Yes, and some of his own party were among the best pleased to see him go. They'd always disliked his extreme views and jeered at his success, calling him "Radical Roley." So they were only too pleased to lift up holy hands in horror and then to help in hounding him out. In his bitterness he used to say to me, "It is natural, my dear: marital fidelity has always been an outstanding characteristic of politicians. That, and a scrupulous regard for truth." But there were many who still loved him and were heart-broken at his going. He got a letter signed by hundreds of them and ending, "Farewell, our chief, our dear chief, farewell." He keeps that letter in his pocket to this day.'

'Oh, my poor Uncle Lucy!' said Gael, forgetting for the moment that he was her father.

Auntie Flavia nodded and sighed. 'At first he went and hid himself among the mountains. I went with him to try and comfort him. But then he decided to leave England for ever and go and live in Paris, which he'd always loved. As he used to say, "England has seen the last of me. I come not where I am a by-word and a hissing." But I think, too, that a kind of ceremonial departure appealed to the old aristocratic de Brath in him. He wanted me to stay in England, saying I could live it all down and find friends again; but I said No, I would go with him into exile, anywhere, everywhere, and share everything with him.'

From my chair I saw that she enjoyed recalling this fine declaration, and I guessed that she had enjoyed uttering it even then. And I was glad that she'd had this one sweetened taste in her great meal of bitter herbs.

She pursued the drama of it still, and tasted the old sweetness still. 'How could I desert him? I never loved him so much as then when he was in disgrace and people were being cruel to him. And, anyhow, I had given him my love of my own free choice, and I wasn't going back on it. He must never think I regretted it—and I didn't; I didn't. Oh, *no*. And I don't think he ever regretted his love for me, though it cost him so terrible a price— though it cost him all. I would ask him if he regretted it, and he would only smile and say, "*Quand on n'aime pas trop, on n'aime pas assez.*" Ah, but you don't understand French.'

'I understand that,' I said.

'It is so true. . . . In Paris we lived as Mr. and Mrs. Grenville and were very fairly happy, because he always had a gift of high spirits and would quite often scatter all melancholy to the winds. But at other times he would be very silent, and I knew he was thinking of the splendours of the past which would never come again. He wasn't being silent because he was angry with me. We had far fewer quarrels after his disgrace. I suppose he'd lost some of his great pride and was feeling his dependence on me for love. I tried with all my heart to give it to him. I tried never to fail him. And after a time you were born there, in Paris—as you know. . . .

'That is really the whole story.'

She stopped; stopped as if there were nothing more to tell; and it seemed to me that she had told these things as if they were simply a matter between herself and Gael, and that I had been forgotten. So after a minute I asked, 'And me? What about me?'

CHAPTER NINETEEN

THERE was silence in that room while, once again, Auntie Flavia struggled, tight-lipped, with tears.

At last she began, sighingly, like one in part bemused, and stretching a palm towards the flickering fire as if its warmth would strengthen her. 'I don't know . . . perhaps with the passing of the years his memories of those dreadful days dimmed and lost some of their power to hurt, and so he felt the need of me less, because he was now enjoying quite a little the social life of Paris; and he could always feel, of course, the admiration of all the women. He was nearly sixty then, but still tremendously attractive to them, not only because he was still so handsome, but because his manner towards them was always so wonderful—so courteous and tender and obviously admiring. That is what women like. They could feel a kind of overflowing tenderness coming from him—especially if they were beautiful.' She breathed out a further sigh. 'Well, in the Rue François Premier, not far from us, there was a Josiah Waybon'—my heart stopped at the name and then began a sick acceleration—'he was something to do with Homard's, the great parfumiers—their English director or something—and his wife Peggy was certainly one of the young beauties in the English circle. He was nothing; just a wealthy business man. The title was hers; she was the youngest daughter of the Earl of Morry. I suppose she was under thirty at the time—just as I was when your father first met me. He saw her first in the British Embassy Chapel where we would go to church on Sunday mornings like most of the English residents. In any church, as you know, he likes to take a humble place at the back and we were sitting in almost the last pew of all. His humility and devotions in a church are very genuine, I'm sure, but they didn't prevent him, that

morning, from staring during most of the service at a
pretty face just ahead of us. She was certainly rather
beautiful.'

She said this as if it hurt to admit it but she must be
generous. For me—I saw a vision of my mother, and loved
her. Having known no mother, I chose to think this one
very lovely and lovable. That drab suburban room was
darkening, and I sat in it, against the wall, delighting in
my picture of her, as she had been when alive. I wondered
where she was now, and thought of speaking to her, in case
she could hear.

'He admired her from that first moment. I remember
him mentioning her as we came out of the church with the
crowd of people. And it was altogether too much for him
when we met the Waybons at a soirée, and she made it
perfectly clear that she had admired him from the first.
I don't say she did this deliberately; she was just young
and simple and couldn't help it. She became so interested
in him that, somehow or other, she found out all his story;
and she managed to let him know this one day when they
met in the Bois and were walking by the lake. She wanted
him to know that he had all her sympathy—that she was
"on his side" in everything—and he was so grateful for
this that he kissed her—a silly, fatal thing to do, for from
that moment they were in love. He sixty, she thirty.'
In those words the old bitterness peeped. 'It was all very
terrible because it was only a month or two before Gael
was born. Perhaps I had no beauty just then and no
attraction for him. I was forty and shapeless and—oh,
I don't know—he was always as weak as water if anyone
beautiful offered herself to him—as I suppose I had done,
and, of course, this child did. For my sake he tried to
hide it all from me, just as I had tried to hide everything
from my husband, and he was certainly very gentle and
sweet to me when you were born. Turn on the light,
Travers; it is getting very dark. Some months later it
was obvious that Peggy Waybon was going to have a child
by him, and old Waybon vowed that it couldn't be his.
Poor man: he was my husband over again. Perhaps it is

a mistake to love. He insisted on a separation there and then, and Roland took her away with him to Italy that the child might be born somewhere where they were not known. To Florence. Even then I didn't know all that was happening—he told so many lies to me, and, in any case, one won't believe what one doesn't want to believe. He pretended that he'd best go alone to Florence while you were only a few months old, and that after a time he'd send for us both. All lies, of course. Lies so that I shouldn't be hurt. He confessed it all in a letter from Florence. It was a letter full of love; almost as if all the old love had come back again, now that he was parted from me. He promised that he would always do everything for you and me—as indeed he always has. But it nearly killed me. I had thoughts of drowning myself in the Seine.'

Oh, my dear, my dear, that you should have done this to me!

'I actually walked to the Pont Neuf to do it. I walked down the Champs Élysées and through the Jardin des Tuileries—all the places where we'd been so happy and loved each other—and so I came to the Pont Neuf and looked down into the water.' She extended a hand towards the fire again, to feel its presence and comfort. 'I had given up everything for him, gone into exile with him, shared everything with him—and now this! With Gael hardly weaned. And I'm sure I'd been at death's door when she was born. But there! The old pattern repeated itself. . . .

'He loved quoting "*Je l'ai trop aimé pour ne le point haïr,*" but the worst of it was I couldn't hate him; I had never loved him more passionately than then. And I wanted to die. I went to the first recess on the bridge and to the stone seat where he liked to sit in the sun with his arm about me, and I gave one look at Paris and then looked down into the water. But it seemed too close, so I went to the next recess which was higher. Death looked to be surer there, and easier, perhaps. And I looked down and remembered a day when we'd thought of throwing ourselves from a great precipice among the mountains. But we'd have been together then—and there on the Pont Neuf I was alone.

I couldn't do it alone.   It was winter, and the water seemed so dark and cold, and after a long time on the bridge I just came away.   I walked home by different roads—strange roads—but it was no good; all Paris was full of him.

'Travers was born in Florence.   They lived together there for more than a year, in a large apartment in the Via Maggio, not far from the Casa Guidi, where the Brownings lived.   But she was never very strong—and I've never thought these Italian cities healthy—I'm sure the famous Arno looks like a river of yellow mud, and their palazzo was quite close to it.   Whether that was the cause or not, she contracted typhoid fever, which was followed by low pneumonia.   I believe he nursed her tenderly, often all through the night.   I'm sure he did.   He has always told me that she died in his arms and that her last words as she settled her head against him were, "That's beautiful.   Please keep me there."'

For a little she could not go on, because she was weeping internally at this picture of a beautiful death, even though the dead had been her rival and wronged her.   After all, it was all so long ago now, and the victory was hers, since there is no conquest so complete as to be alive when your adversary has surrendered to death.

Uncle Lucy in the tea-shop, sadly, '. . . Queens have died young and fair.'

'He wrote and told me all about it in a most pitiable letter and—well—it was two years since he had left Gael and me, and after that time one has got used to things and is able to forgive, so I hurried to Florence to help him, leaving you in Paris, Gael, with your French nurse.   I found him abjectly miserable: he kept declaring that he'd ruined my life and ended hers; that he brought nothing but disaster to everyone.   I tried to tell him that he'd once brought the greatest happiness to me that any woman could know—something that I would never, never want to have been without—and that I expected this was true of her also.   But he only shook his head, not wanting to be relieved of any blame or any misery.   He took me to her grave in the Protestant Cemetery, where so many English poets and others of the English colony are buried. It was as we stood looking down upon her grave that he asked me if I could forgive him, and I said, Of course I would—it didn't seem possible to say anything else just there. And that evening in his apartment he said he didn't know what to do with a little baby like Travers and made the suggestion that you and he should be brought up together in England by me. He promised to provide an income that would be enough for us all and to buy me a house somewhere where I was not known and where there'd be good schools for you both. I consented to do this for his sake, whom all my life I'd tried to help, and for Gael's, and for yours, too, poor little Travers. I decided to devote my life to you two children—to make you the one object of my life——' As she said this a thought stirred in me; an ungrateful thought, perhaps, but not to be stayed. Were her motives for consent really as unselfish as she wished to proclaim now and to believe? With middle age at hand, had she not instantly perceived the advantages of a secure income and her own home? I knew my Auntie Flavia well.

Her next words seemed to reprove this very thought. 'He was so grateful, saying that there'd never been anyone like me for comforting him and helping him when he was feeling utterly defeated and in despair. And so all was settled. As soon as we could we came to England. He came with us as far as Folkestone; I have never forgotten how, after he'd kissed us all for the last time, he suddenly turned round and walked quickly away, without daring to look back.

'When we all arrived in London, myself, you two babies, and the French nurse, who do you suppose took us in and looked after us and couldn't do too much for us? Who do you think?'

'Who?' we asked.

'Gloria.'

'Auntie Gloria!'

'Yes. She'd never had a good word to say for your father and, being a woman happily married herself, could never find words severe enough for all that I had done, but now she said that if an elder sister couldn't stand by a younger one and do everything for her, she'd like to know who would. You can imagine her saying that in her loud domineering voice. She said also that she'd nothing, thank God, against you "two poor little mites," and she welcomed you both in and kept you in her own home for months. She helped to find this house for us, near to her, because as she said with one of her loud laughs, "she'd have to keep an eye on us." Poor Gloria: her manner is against her—but she is a good woman. Probably the best of us, really.'

This revelation about Auntie Gloria left us empty of words. And Auntie Flavia, idly lifting cotton reels an inch and dropping them, without sense of what she was doing, went on, 'And now he just sits alone in that great apartment in Paris, thinking, I suppose, of the past. I'm sure he thinks often of you in England, and that's why he feels driven every now and then to come over and look at you. Oh, I only wish he'd come now and stay for ever.'

'Oh, *yes!*' we both murmured.

'Surely all is forgotten now, or it's all too far in the past to worry about any more. But no: he still can't conquer his pride and come back. But it's sad: we three are really all he has to love.' She paused and, turning the restless fingers from her cotton reels to the hemmed garment, said, 'That is really all, my dears.'

She drew her needle from its cushion and gathered up the sewing to begin again.

I saw Gael rise to her duty. I think that both of us, in this last hour, had made a leap in growth. Between early evening and late, in this small drab room, we had stepped from the self-absorption of childhood into the responsibilities of adolescence. I saw Gael complete the step now. Overcoming any recoil, she went forward, rested a hand on her mother's shoulder and kissed her forehead. 'It's all so wonderful,' she said.

§

Gael's kiss had set Auntie Flavia's mouth quivering in front of tears, and started Gael crying, too. Doubtless,

Auntie Flavia thought Gael's emotion merely sympathetic, but I suspected otherwise, and more so when Gael suddenly ran from the room, dragging the door so sharply behind her that it didn't latch, but rebounded open again. I heard her running up the stairs like a child who takes an anger or a hurt into a far solitude. High upstairs the Playroom door banged sharply.

Since Auntie Flavia had resumed her needle and was not looking at me, but coping with tears, I too went from the room. I walked up the stairs slowly, very slowly, because I was accompanied all the way by a ghost. A ghost slender, graceful and kind, because it was Lady Peggy Waybon as I wished her to be. Once or twice I halted on a step, trying in the darkness of the staircase to see her more clearly. I gave no thought to her sins nor to any agonies she'd caused to her husband, who was but a feature-less name to me, or to Auntie Flavia, standing alone on some bridge in Paris. I saw her only as slim and exquisite, loving and lovable.

And in truth the illusion which I was making for myself on the stairs is the one with which I have chosen to live from that day to this. It is with me this evening as I sit here and write. Probably the real Peggy Waybon was very different from my happy creation—I have since heard her called 'a sensual little creature,' and even 'a lecherous young woman,' but all such words strike against some dull armour on my breast and fall frustrated. She is but a dream-figure like the lovely phantom of Lottie Morris in Gael's mind; but, unlike Gael's figure, she was never destroyed before my eyes; because she never grew to be old, and seen.

On the upstairs landing I saw that Gael, once again, had flung the Playroom door behind her so violently that it had failed to latch. It stood two inches ajar and I was able to hear a sobbing beyond it. Well set now in my eavesdropping ways, I peeped through the aperture. One gas-mantle lit the room, and from my dark passage I could see Gael in her favourite chair with her arms spread on the table and her head thrown on to them, much as Auntie

Flavia's had been an hour before. One elbow, impatient for its comfort, had thrust aside the toy bagatelle-board on which we'd been happily playing before we decided to take our question to Auntie Flavia. Her back trembled as if the sobs were tearing the young breast beneath.

To warn her I was near I began to hum. What the words were didn't matter, and I heard myself singing softly, 'De Camptown race-track five miles long, Oh, doodah day' before making the door handle rattle at my touch. Gael leapt up and, keeping her back to me, walked to the window and pretended to be looking out, a poor pretence, because the street was dark. Useless, too, because she had to spoil it by lifting a knuckle and brushing both cheeks under her eyes. That this action might seem of no moment, she leaned forward as if recognizing someone in the dark, empty street.

To help her I hummed, '"I come down dah wid my hat caved in, Doodah!"' and asked, 'What's the matter?'

'Oh, nothing. Nothing.' Since this was exactly what I would have said if caught in tears, I knew that Nothing meant Much.

'Oh, come on! Tell us,' I urged, and to make her feel less alone, submitted, 'We've all had a bit of a shaker. So tell us.'

A long moment, and then, half turning her face to me, she said, 'It's all right for you.'

'For me? Why?'

'I thought Peggy Waybon sounded sweet. Adorable.'

'Well, but she . . .' I was wondering whether to comfort her with a mention of Peggy Waybon's sins, but before I could do this she said, 'I wouldn't have minded having her for my mother.'

'Don't you like the idea of having Auntie Flavia for a mother?'

She turned her face away again and stared at the night sky, flushed with a saffron glow, above the roof-tops opposite. 'I'd got it into my head that it was all so different.'

'I know.' I wanted much to comfort her, but it was difficult for a boy of fourteen to speak any tenderness, so

I could only offer in some unembarrassing slang, 'It was all a bit of a staggerer, I admit.'

She came away from the window and stood gazing instead at one of the room's blank walls. Her teeth crunched on to her lower lip, and she said, 'I don't love her. I can't. I can't. I've been trying to, up here, trying hard, but I can't. She's so . . . so different from anything. . . .'

Longing to show sympathy, I thought of saying, 'I shouldn't be awfully keen on her for a mother myself,' but decided that these words were not such as would carry comfort; so I just murmured, 'I see what you mean.'

She sank into her chair and rested her arms on the table, hands overlapping. 'Gosh, you're lucky!'

'Me?'

'Yes, you have all the luck always. Uncle Lucy loves you better than me——'

'Oh, I don't know. I don't see why you should think that.'

'He does. And now you've a mother you can love. I should have adored Peggy Waybon. She sounded sweet. An earl's daughter, too; golly!'

Hastening to make things level between us, I reminded her that Lottie's father was a bishop.

'What's a bishop?' she objected contemptuously.

So, seeking surer ground, I touched upon my mother's undoubted sinfulness.

But she only interrupted, 'Oh, what does that matter? What on earth do I care about that?' And where all her churchgoing was in that moment, and her Mr. Appledore, and her *Garden of the Soul*, I do not know. 'And in any case,' she pursued, 'Auntie Flavia—or Mother Mine, as I suppose I must now call her—was as bad. The only decent one in the whole story seems to have been Auntie Gloria.'

'Yes, our Auntie Gloria was a sport, certainly. When I have time I must really sit down and do some reconsidering of that good woman.' To leaven the air a little, I might pretend to jest like this, and be at ease, but actually I was searching for better words of comfort; and the best I could find were, 'At least your mother is still alive.'

'Yes,' she said, 'that's it.'

'And perhaps,' I added, though I didn't want to say it, I recoiled from saying it, 'if Peggy Waybon had lived, she'd have got like Auntie Flavia. She'd be nearly fifty now.'

'Yes, but . . . she didn't. . . .'

'No,' I agreed; and was glad to agree.

'Oh, well, I suppose I shall get used to it. One gets used to everything. Maybe I shall grow to love her. I'm fond of her in a way, and I *do* understand all she's suffered. I do. But, oh, gosh, how I envy you!' And suddenly, as she said that, she cried out defiantly, 'At any rate I'm happy about my father . . . ever so happy . . . never so happy . . .' and bursting into tears, she buried her face in her arms again.

CHAPTER TWENTY

'As you wish, my dear.' It was Auntie Flavia who said those words, when she was the young Lottie Morris, and my father held her poised over death. It is a strange thing, but though I have been climbing mountains for forty years, and many of them in the great Cumberland series, it was not till three years ago, and all of seventy years since these two considered death together on Pisa Crag, that I found myself in Emberdale and saw that splendid mass of rock. Perhaps this was because, as my father said in his diary, Emberdale is not easy of access, and I loathe long hours of fell-walking before beginning to climb.

But it chanced that on this occasion I was on business at Whitehaven in Cumberland, and so within twenty miles of the famous rock. There was indeed a picture of it in a geological study of Cumberland which I found among my hotel's books. As I turned the pages and saw the picture, an eagerness came upon me to go and gaze at the rock, just as fifty years before I had been driven to gaze at that house in Roehampton which had known such scenes of joy and fear and disaster. My business done (and to my great profit), I drove to the little Eel Sike Hotel in Emberdale and there from my room window I could just see far up the valley, far beyond the head of Emberdale Water, high above the desolate upper end of the valley, the giant rock abutting like some grey towered castle from the mountain's breast.

In the morning, almost as excited as when I was a boy stealing off to Roehampton, I walked the long miles to Bottom Wood and began to paddle upward through the dead tawny leaves beneath the oaks, the feathery birches, the larches and pines, of which my father had written. Since there was but one natural way I must have got my feet in the tracks which he and Lottie made seventy years before. But it was June now, and instead of the rowans by the waterfall being on fire with berries they gave forth a sweet pungent scent that climbed with me much of the way. The larches were not old and dying as when he and Lottie came by, but young and light and feminine, in contrast with the sombre pines. At the top of the wood I came upon a true sight of the rock and stood amazed that so huge an outcrop could issue from the breast of a mountain. It was so high, so thick, so bare, that my first thought was an unexpected one. I thought, 'When I came to that house I half imagined that the sufferings it had known might somehow have changed its face, saddening it. I have no such feeling about this terrible buttress of primaeval and everlasting rock. Obviously it stands haughtily indifferent to all the ant-like troubles of men.'

Determined to stand on its top where they had stood, and to look down, I climbed the steep fell-breast which, as I remembered (and well understood) all the fell-walkers called the Grass Wall. There were far more flowers on it in this June month than when Lottie paused to gather her hawkweed and harebell, but what pleased me most was to see, just as my father had said, the tiny yellow tormentil 'climbing more bravely than they all.'

With much panting, and many halts to fetch my breath, and not a few blasphemies, I got to that point where, 'with a glory of achievement,' I could step on to the mossy arena which was Pisa's summit.

At first I sat for a space on a green-shawled rock which, because of its broad invitation to comfort, was almost certainly the one on which they had sat or reclined. Then I walked to that edge where alone the precipice seemed vertical. This must have been the brink where, momentarily, the death-wish seized them. 'As you will'—aye, it was a large word that our Auntie Flavia had spoken after she'd looked down and seen, far below, that spawn of rocks and scree.

They were long dead now, those old lovers; and they did not die together as for one moment up here they had wished to do. Their deaths were sundered by many years, for Auntie Flavia, living to be seventy-two, did not die till fifteen years after him. They lie far apart, he in the private chapel of the Marquesses of Hayle and Ensor, in the great Longchambers Park, she in a distant, and, I am afraid, neglected grave, crowded about with others, in a little French churchyard over against the Forêt de Meudon.

Well, just as I found it difficult to drag myself away from the front of that Roehampton house, so I didn't want to leave, probably for ever, my storied summit of Pisa Crag. I sat looking at the wonderful prospect and thinking that, only in colour, this June day, was it different from the far-flung beauty in which they had found some assuagement of their heartache and despair. In the deep of the valley some of the fields were more yellow than green with butter-cups, and others were powdered white with daisies or washed purple with meadow cranesbill. The bracken across the valley—was it a lineal descendant of the dead and rusty bracken they had seen?—flushed all the hill-cheeks with a bright young green. Seventy years ago. Twenty-five thousand days and their nights had awakened and brightened, then darkened and slumbered, over this mountain scene, and yet my fancy could stretch forth its hand to that past day and hold it here beside me. As if it were now: this day. . . .

I had to come away at last, so I walked once more to the place from which they must have looked down, and I stood there and said a prayer for them both, wherever they might be.

CHAPTER TWENTY-ONE

AFTER that unveiling of the past to us, a new and continuing gentleness appeared in Auntie Flavia's manner; and a new friendliness sprang up between us all, as if the forty years separating her age from ours had narrowed, and we were now almost contemporaries together. More often than before we would go on wet autumn evenings upstairs to the piano in the sheeted drawing-room, and she, having pulled back the piano's shroud, would sit herself on the stool before the book, *Old Songs of England*. And we, standing on the drugget to either side of her, would sing the old favourites one after another, while she hammered out accompaniments with the sides of her little fingers, and sometimes sang, too, in that ageing voice of hers of which the middle notes were still sweet. We sang 'The Lass of Richmond Hill' and 'Scenes that are brightest.' We roared out 'Nazareth' because Uncle Lucy used to give it so much voice and gusto: 'Though poor be the chamber, Come here, come and adore; Lo, the Lord of Heaven hath to mortals given Life for evermore. . . .'

It was on one such evening, a wet October evening when the dusk had fallen early, and our candlelight fell on the music-book, that Gael, probably because our bellowing of these words reminded her of Uncle Lucy's full-throated joy in the same, asked Auntie Flavia even as she lifted her hands from the last chord, 'Have you written and told him we know?'

'No. No, not yet.' By her hesitation in the words I discerned that Auntie Flavia, never wholly without fear of Uncle Lucy, didn't want to tell him that she'd told us. 'Perhaps I'll tell him next time he comes.'

We said nothing, the subject being still uneasy; and she, partly providing an excuse and partly in pity for him, explained, 'I don't think he wants to think you know.

Inevitably he'd be a little ashamed before you—and he's had so much shame in his life.'

'But how can he imagine we don't guess?'

'How? By living in a fool's paradise and preferring not to think properly. As I did, as we all do, till we're driven out of it.' Loving dramatic utterances, especially if they were words from the Bible, she added, 'Driven out with a flaming sword. Do we want to do that to him?'

Neither of us answered, and she, turning a page of the music-book, perceived our greatest favourite, 'Early one morning,' and began to play it. We were half-way through the first verse—we children far more interested in our voices than in the maiden's pain as we sang 'Oh, never lea-eave me, Oh, don't decea-eave me' when the door-handle turned and Lizzie entered.

'Just one moment, Lizzie,' Auntie Flavia warned, and we all three sang the last words, myself with an especial *élan* and, as I hoped, no small effect, 'How can you treat a poor maiden so?'

Auntie Flavia hammered one good final chord and asked, 'Yes, Lizzie?'

'Lord Roland is here.' Ever since Auntie Flavia had told Lizzie, her one confidante, that we children now knew all, Lizzie had been more than pleased, in her simple snobbery, to give him his title again. 'He's downstairs.'

'Lord Roland! But he's said nothing about coming.' Auntie Flavia stared at Lizzie as if thinking she must be mistaken in the caller downstairs. 'We've nothing ready for him. There's nothing nice in the house. Oh, my goodness, why didn't he write? Why didn't he tell me?'

Gael shouted 'Uncle Lucy?' I, trying to be clever, demanded of them all, 'How can he treat a poor maiden so?' but no one listened to me, or admired.

'Yes, he's there downstairs, his lordship. And the cabman's bringing in heaps of baggage, ma'am. Stacks of it.'

Gael rushed to the door; I had no intention of letting her get to him first and raced after her; Auntie Flavia followed hardly less fast.

He was seated on the only chair in the hall, side by side with the hatstand. He was slightly panting, with lips apart, as if our eight front steps had pumped him nearly breathless. His stick, like that of an invalid, was between his knees, and his palms at rest upon it. From this bare seat between wall and stair he was delivering a sufficient farewell to the cabman, an old grey man, heavy and bowed.

'That's all, cabman, and I thank you very much. Change? Good gracious, no, sir. No, no. The labourer is worthy of his hire. More than usual? Well, maybe, maybe. Then give an extra feed to your admirable horse. I trust that you will forgive me for not having borne a hand with those bags, but just now I am under the doctor's orders. A very good evening to you. Lizzie—where is the excellent Lizzie gone?—oh, well. . . . Win—good evening, Win—show the gentleman out, will you?'

The cabman touched his hat-brim; Uncle Lucy raised a hand in friendly acknowledgment; I held back the door and was about to shut it directly the old cabman had passed me, but Uncle Lucy called out anxiously, 'No, no, Win! Wait till he's gone farther than that. Wait at least till he's off the last of our steps. Good evening, Gael dear. And even then shut the door quietly and with magnificent unwillingness. Never speed a parting guest. Least of all, one who has just served us well.'

What further instruction he would have given me, on this subject of courtesy, I do not know, for now Auntie Flavia was at the stair's foot and exclaiming, 'Marcus! How is this?'

He inquired first, in politeness, 'How are you, my dear? Good evening,' and then began apologetically, 'You were singing your hymns, Lizzie tells me. "The day thou gavest, Lord, is ended." Please go on. "Abide with me." I can find my way alone. The old prophet's chamber, I am sure. That dunderhead of a doctor——'

'What doctor?'

'Your doctor. The nincompoop in Wimpole Street. I forget his name, and I've no desire to be reminded of it. The silly trifler who imagined that all I needed was rest and good food. The fellow who made stupid jokes about living to be ninety-two. I did everything the buffoon said and the only result is that I'm in worse pain than I was before. Of late every movement has left me breathless. I don't understand it. I went to an excellent French doctor, and he foretold an early and sudden death.'

'Nonsense!'

'Well, he practically said it, and I've felt much worse ever since. He told me my heart was not only enlarged; it was displaced. A whole long way to the left. Or right; I forget which. I've had stomach and liver troubles, too. Complications. He suggested I might have them, and I promptly did.'

'Yes, but one can imagine——'

'Yesterday it seemed for a moment as if I wasn't breathing at all, and I wondered if I was already dead. Who else is dead? I never come back without hearing that someone is dead. I was walking in a singularly beautiful part of the Jardin des Tuileries; it was very empty, and there were strange white statues like ghosts among the trees; and I wondered, for a second, if I was dead and this was Paradise. But I decided it wasn't, and that, anyhow, I wouldn't have deserved an instant translation to Paradise like this. A thousand years in Purgatory first, perhaps. A hundred certainly. And then I thought how extraordinarily unhappy it would be to have died without saying good-bye to you and Gael and Win. So I decided to come here and die. Oh dear, oh dear.' His breathing was palpably disturbed; a low hiss accompanied each in-taken breath. '"My race of glory run, and race of shame. . . . And I shall shortly be with them that rest." Samson, my dear. Samson Agonistes.'

'You're not going to die. Don't talk all this graveyard stuff. We'll look after you, won't we, Gael? You've got years before you yet.'

'I gathered from the Frenchman that I might have a year,' he agreed, his eyes seeking for hope and endorsement in Auntie Flavia's eyes. 'Possibly a little more. With care.'

'A year? Ten years. You were always as strong as a horse. You know you were. Now, come, Marcus dear.'

And, as always, she fussed over him, helping him to his feet, removing the silk scarf that muffled his throat, and taking off the heavy fur-lined overcoat. I, proud of my strength, began carrying his bags upstairs, while he called after me, 'Be careful, Win. Don't you strain your heart, too. We can't have two weaklings in the house. I shall need all your auntie's kind attention—good heavens, the child has gone! Well, he is at the beginning instead of at the end.'

That night, wearied by his journey, he very willingly obeyed Auntie Flavia's counsel and went up to bed even before we did.

This left Gael free to ask, 'Auntie'—she used the old address, in part from habit and forgetfulness, in part because she could not yet say 'Mother'—'Auntie, are you going to tell him?' to which Auntie Flavia answered, 'No—oh, no. Not while he's feeling ill. I'm sure he doesn't look at all well. I don't like the look of him at all.' And I knew that she was glad of this excuse to stay silent.

§

Marcus . . . she had told us now why she slipped so often and so easily into giving him this name. In the first years after their joint catastrophe she liked to tease him by calling him Mark Antony, and Marcus, because he had thrown away the crown of the earth by loving her. Both, she said, drew a small assuagement, a very slight salve for their wounds, from this mutual jest.

§

In the morning light we saw with distress that he seemed to have aged six years in as many months. His face was grey, with the cheeks more sunken and the eyes more recessed. The grey skin was taut over the strong bones; the tall body had shrunk within the expensive clothes. In his eyes, no matter how he essayed the old jesting, always that *timor mortis* followed swiftly on the old slow smile.

And as if some mental wheel had worn smooth, his talk was not only more continuous, but somewhat loose and straying, and often lost to caution. This first morning at breakfast he talked as if forgetting that we children were supposed to know nothing of his career. 'All my life,' he said, his fist in its perfect white cuff resting on the table as he forgot to touch coffee or toast, 'I have wanted to do all I could for the people. The life of the working man, it seemed to me, was often a wretched climb up ever-steepening rock—like our Pisa Crag, my dear—and at the top what does he find? No well-earned rest in the midst of beauty—no, he finds a workhouse. It's not good enough; and so I was on his side from the beginning. I sincerely wanted to help them while I had time. . . . For this purpose, Win, I was ready to put on the abominable stiff mask which our bourgeois demand of their leaders; I—what I mean is, I was ready to appear as pure and prim and churchgoing as H.M. herself. But behind this façade of exemplary dullness I was determined to be myself and live my own life just as fully as possible.'

I said nothing. I'd heard so much of it before. Auntie Flavia watched him, plainly worried as to what he'd say next.

'They were both myself: the man who intended to live as abundantly as possible, and the man who had this odd but very real longing to serve the people—the man in the iron mask, Win. Your timid and conforming English Gentleman——'

'Drink your coffee, Marcus. It's getting cold.'

'Eh?—what?—no, just let me finish. One thing I didn't do, Win. I refused the aristocratic embrace. That is to say, I refused to let my labours for the poor be corrupted by the house parties and the dinner parties of the rich. Blenheim Palace never saw me at one of its great garden fêtes. . . . No wonder they called me a renegade.'

'Let me give you a fresh cup. Pass his cup, Gael.'

'Yes, well, there's no point in talking now. Those things are all over. And, for me, everything else will be over soon.'

'Rubbish,' said Auntie Flavia, filling his cup; and I think I said 'Rats!' Or perhaps 'Piffle to that!' or some similar confutation from a schoolboy's argot. Not but what his words had contracted my heart, and left a sickness in it.

'But it is so, Lottie——' At the name her eyes shot towards us. 'The End creeps upon me. And it's funny, but however my country may have treated me, I seem to want to die in it, and lie in it, at the end.'

'Do stop talking about death.'

'Hear, hear,' Gael endorsed.

'But, Gael, my dear child, I am seventy-eight. Seventy-eight, and I'm told to keep quite still or I shall go out like a candle. Or off like a bomb—I forget which the Frenchman said. And as the excellent Blaise Pascal puts it, nothing is so insufferable as *plein repos*. *Plein repos*, without passion, without excitement, without work. One sits with it and becomes aware of one's forlornness, one's dependence, one's final and fundamental loneliness. Oh dear!' He sighed heavily as if his *plein repos* had already the pale quality of death.

§

But if at last his strong intelligence had softened a little, loosening his talk, there was no such slackening in his outward dress. I think he never took more care, and never looked more splendid, than in these last days. He wore now always an expensive orchid in the lapel of his frock coat, and Auntie Flavia whispered to us that in his great days he would wear it deliberately, like the Napoleonic imperial, as a kind of recognition-mark for the cartoonists to seize upon and the public to laugh at and love. Now, driven by some motive beneath our sight, he had run up this old flag again. The imperial was now white and sometimes unruly, but he was forever shaping it with his long fingers, and smoothing the white moustaches above it, lest they, too, were being unceremonious. He still smoked a fine cigar in the streets and passed it back and forth beneath his nose to enjoy its aroma.

Yes, his hand upon his controls was weakening. Always he had been touchy and easily hurt, but not so easily as now. One Sunday at dinner, our church duties done, Auntie Flavia was unwise enough to say the following, after he'd been merely joking about his 'imminent and long-overdue demise'.

'Don't you think,' she said, 'that you'll make your condition worse by constantly harping upon it?'

Instantly—as instantly as the silence that stills our island on Remembrance Day when the maroon has sounded in the sky—the old familiar and awful silence turned him into a statue in his chair. We always knew at once—I know not how—when some small, untoward phrase had transformed him from a lively, joking companion into a monument of sadness and long-suffering. Auntie Flavia looked at him over her fork; we looked across the table at him; and we all went on eating. None of us spoke. None of us dared speak. We just continued our meal—all of us—even Uncle Lucy. Frequently he sipped his wine. Only after five minutes did Auntie Flavia ask, 'What is the matter, dear?'

'Matter?' You would have thought no question could be less warranted.

'Yes. You've gone so silent. What is it?'

'Nothing. Nothing.'

'Oh, but that's silly. It must be something.'

'Oh, please don't worry me.' He beat his finger-tips on the table.

'Worry? I'm not worrying. I was only asking a simple

question. I suppose one can do that. Did you have a bad night? '

'Night? Good gracious, no!' Clearly the last thing he desired was that the responsibility for his silence should be removed from her and attributed to the night.

'Well, what is it? Can't you tell me?'

'Please don't go on and on.'

'Well, I like that! On and on, when I've asked precisely two questions!'

'Two questions can sometimes be one too many.'

'And I don't consider that a very nice remark. Or very polite either.'

'The truth is not necessarily polite.'

'Nor is that very clever.'

'But who said it was?' He raised his thick white eyebrows, as in weary surprise at her statement. 'One claims no cleverness when stating a simple truth. One realizes that it can be but trite.'

Auntie Flavia put knife and fork together, shot up from her chair, and went in tears from the room.

Uncle Lucy only sighed as if he were the injured party. And as if the behaviour of all women were incomprehensible. And shortly after this he, too, put knife and fork together, and without any reference to the pudding now due, went his own way from the room. He went slowly and with far greater dignity than Auntie Flavia.

'Well, I suppose we children can have some pudding, anyway,' said Gael, and rang the table bell.

Averil, our latest parlourmaid, a rosy girl, bringing an apple pie through the door, stopped in surprise to see only two persons at the table where lately she'd left four. Still in her morning wear of pink print frock and long apron, she stood in the doorway, plump and rosy and astonished. 'Have they gawn?' she asked.

'Don't ask me,' Gael retorted with a shrug.

But I, confident that neither of them would come downstairs again for their share of the pie, assured her, 'You bet they have! There've been Words.'

'Words?' Averil was much interested, as she piled up the used plates.

'Yes. And now there's a general ungladness abroad.'

'Lord! A real old set-to, was it? What about?'

'Lord only knows,' replied Gael. 'I don't.'

'I do,' said I. 'I know very well. Uncle Lucy said what it was about.'

'He didn't.'

'Yes, he did.'

Averil laid down the piled plates to hear what he had said.

I told her. 'He said it was about nothing.'

'Oh, but it can't really be about nothing,' submitted this wholesome girl.

'You don't know my Uncle Lucy,' I reminded her. 'You haven't lived with him as long as I have.'

'No, but the truth is he's not at all well,' she offered, generously. 'That's my opinion. He looks really bad, and one's easily aggravated if one's feeling poorly. I am meself. I'm all on edge. And if I'm like that at eighteen, what's he like at seventy-seven? Or seventy-eight, is it? Don't they want any afters?'

'I doubt it. There's nothing like Words for spoiling your appetite for afters.'

'Law . . . Words between them! And he's ever so fond of her really, as anyone can see. Oh, well, it's just that he's ill. I'm sure nobody could be nicer than he is when he's all right. I was saying so to Lizzie, I said, if anybody was a gentleman, it was him, and Liz said there was every reason why he should be. She says he come of a real aristocratic family, but she won't tell me which.'

Nor did we tell her.

'Of course he's only a Mister, but she says that don't necessarily mean nothing. And that he was once in Parliament for quite a while.'

'Yes, he was in Parliament,' I said, since someone must say something. Besides I was proud of it; it was the only thing left to be proud of.

'Well, I never! Your Uncle Lucy in Parliament. Go on! No wonder he behaves so perfectly and is such a gentleman. Why, yesterday he held open the door for me and bowed, as I went out of the drawin'-room. And he always calls me "Miss Averil", like I was a lady visitor or someone. I love him, I do. If he sees me in the street he always takes off his hat and does his bow. He does; straight.'

'He would,' said Gael. 'He always does to me, and not in joke either. The other day he took it off to little Edie Nelson, who's not yet nine and who'd nearly hit him with her hoop. He swore rather awfully at first, but he took off his hat as they parted.'

'Well, that's what I call being a gentleman,' said Averil firmly. 'He'll come round all right; don't you worry. He'll be his old self again. In time.'

'Yes,' I agreed. 'I put the visit to the florist's at about two days from now.'

Gael accepted this estimate. 'That's about it. I don't give it more than two days. This is only a mild ungladness, Averil, compared with some we've had.'

When we had eaten our apple tart, unimpeded by manners because unwatched by adults, we left the room and started to go upstairs, but were driven back by Uncle Lucy coming down. Tall and wide-shouldered, he filled the staircase, descending slowly and heavily, hand on the banisters. Still wordless, he took his heavy coat from the hat-stand. We did not like to speak, feeling that the Order of the Day was Silence, but Auntie Flavia came rushing with her tears from the drawing-room above, where she'd hidden herself, and as he drew on the overcoat said, heedless of our presence on the hall tiles, 'I don't think you're being at all nice to me.'

He stopped all movement. The coat stayed over one shoulder and under the other. Then he seemed to master anger and, drawing on the coat and dragging out his stick, he walked to the door.

Auntie Flavia, in a helpless small frenzy, besought him, 'Listen, please listen. Don't go like that.' But he could always hurt cruelly if he thought himself hurt, and he just opened the door and began to shut it behind him.

But Auntie Flavia rushed to its handle and prevented this. 'Oh, don't, please don't go like that. You're making me so miserable.'

We two forgotten children watched with interest and not without distress.

He went on down the steps. Using the stick like a limb, he descended heavily, his breathing short.

'Roland! Roland!' she cried—the first time she'd called him this in our presence.

He was undisturbed by the name because he had forgotten us. 'Please don't row me,' he said in a voice deliberately quiet so as to contrast with her excitement and rebuke it. 'I can't stand it. I am in pain. In great pain. Every breath. Let me be, if you would be so kind. I desire to go out because I breathe easier in the open air.'

With her lips clamped over her tears Auntie Flavia shut the door behind him. And still without heed of us, but addressing rather the stairs as she hurried up them, she lamented, 'Oh, why does he go on like this? Why? Why?' We heard her room door bang and her steps creak up and down, up and down.

It may be that he exaggerated on this occasion when he asserted that every breath gave him pain; perhaps he said it only because Auntie Flavia had suggested that he talked about his health too much; but it seemed certain on the next day that his breathing was hurting him enough to force him, soon after breakfast, to go up to his bedroom, in his silence and loneliness, and lie down.

This was more than Auntie Flavia could stand. She sped up to him in his room, and we who had followed her excitedly and inquisitively, watched them through the open door. He was lying flat upon his back, his half-closed fingers touching and pressing his breast as if the pain were there. She rushed and knelt by the bed and laid a hand

238

on his fingers. He patted this visiting hand in a word-less gratitude, and we saw that the quarrel between them was fading away like a mist in a break of the sun.

'Oh, my dear, my dear,' she said. 'You were in pain. And I——'

'Not really much pain yesterday,' he corrected her, for her consolation. 'A certain amount of play-acting then. Unpardonable play-acting. Amateur theatricals, my dear. But not quite all of it,' he hastily added, in justice to himself. 'I was really suffering a little.'

'Oh, and I didn't understand! I was unkind——'

'No, no. There's no one like you.' He gathered up her hand. 'There never was. And never will be. The kindest and best. Yes, yes. The warmest heart that ever woman had.' He was now patting her hand again, grate-fully. 'It is I who can be cruel. And it's late to be cruel now. I am sorry. Try to put it down to my being rather worn out, and in a little pain. It wasn't that, really, it was just my natural beastliness; but try to think it was.'

'Yes, but *now*? *Now*? How are you feeling now?'

'I'm in a little pain now. Yes, a little pain. And Lottie, my dearest, I'm so afraid. . . . But there . . . it is nothing. *Ce n'est rien . . . Ce n'est rien.*'

Later I learned that this was what Henry of Navarre said of Ravaillac's knife-stab that killed him.

§

Since death was still hateful to him, he had reason to be afraid. This attack was real, and it was followed by others at diminishing intervals, each worse than the one before, till at last he was driven finally to his bed, with little to do but stare at the ceiling and finger the bedclothes, and hope. Gael and I went often into him, and he would smile a welcome, but the smile could no longer, even for a moment, displace the fear in his eyes.

Does one cross a bridge on one's fifteenth birthday, or thereabouts? I'd had my fifteenth birthday some weeks before, and I think that this was the first time in my life that I felt a compassion so complete that it seemed it must burst my heart and fling me to my knees at his side. I did not do this lest it seemed unmanly, or weak, or childish —or something like that—but when I left him I would rush up to my attic bedroom, shut the door, and throwing myself on the bed, let the bitter tears run. I prayed, but I did not believe in my prayers, because I had no hope. The doctor had told Auntie Flavia that the time for such illusion was past. I could only wrestle with my misery till I had thrown it like an opponent, and was free to come downstairs again with my eyes rubbed clean and my face restored.

§

Then came that brown and blown November day. Dr. Temple had been summoned and was closeted with Auntie Flavia in the drawing-room. We stayed in the dining-room downstairs, Gael at the table among the ruins of breakfast, I at the bay window, gazing out at the long grey road which had held all our remembered lives till now. Rain had been falling softly all night, but had just stopped. After the rain the pavements stretched away, stained from end to end a snake-skin grey. Oh, how I remember it all. I remember their flags were greased with arabesques of mud, and looked slippery. The long metalled roadway, wet and pooled, glistened under a sky that was cloud from zenith to rim. Beneath this sky the wet slate roofs shone blue. Such leaves as had been shorn from the trees by autumn gales and not yet carted away by sweepers, lay along the gutters like a torn embroidery of green and lemon, russet and gold.

Because of the late rain the road was empty and silent. Only the doctor's brougham (he was an old bearded man with no interest in motor-cars) went round and round on the camber, the coachman exercising the horse during the long pause.

But now a figure before me: Don Francesco standing on the steps of his house and watching. Watching our door, our windows, the brougham. More than once of late I had seen him studying, scrutinizing, from his curtained window, or from the pavement, if he was strutting along it beneath his broad Quaker hat, Uncle Lucy's worn, gaunt, wistful figure; with an especial interest perhaps in the orchid now flying from his buttonhole. For Uncle Lucy in these last days had seemed to care not at all about showing himself in our streets to the unmasking light of day. He had observed Don Francesco once, goggling from the opposite pavement, and had asked me simply, 'Who is that Portuguese ponce?' 'What?' I asked, not knowing this word. 'Who is the assassin in the sombrero who seems to want to shoot us?' I told him.

Now the doctor came down our steps, consulted his gold hunter watch, and entered his brougham. The brougham drove away, and Don Francesco, though half-turned back into his house, followed the carriage with his eyes till it was gone from sight by the red walls of my school. Then he went in and shut his door—so quietly that I did not hear a sound from it.

At the same minute Auntie Flavia came in to us. Strange, but Auntie Flavia, whose lips could shake so readily, and her eyes flood, at any facile sentiment, showed now no hint of tears. Her face was white, but steeled in calm. I'll swear that she was holding her large full-breasted body, though it was still in its morning untidiness, straighter than ever I'd seen it before. It was as if she'd resolved to look despair in the eyes, and to stand, not fall.

Perhaps she was not the good bishop's daughter for nothing, and so had found a grandeur to meet this day. For once, too, the old sense of drama would come honourably to her help; since now, indeed, heroism was the only wear. Her voice, which as a rule she so loved to raise in excitedly dramatic or pathetic utterances, was now level and quiet. 'Dr. Temple has gone.'

Gael asked miserably, 'Yes?'

'He doesn't know for certain, but he thinks it'll be all over soon.'

'Oh. . . .' So only can I set down Gael's low cry, but if ever anguish and love and defeat were heard in a single syllable, I heard them all then.

For my part I allowed no show of grief to pass my lips, but said only, and woodenly, 'What does "soon" mean? Today?'

'It may be so. He is lying there and hardly breathing.'

'Oh . . . Mummy!' In her misery Gael was able to speak this name. 'Is he conscious?'

'Oh, yes. Only very quiet.'

'What time today?'

'Who can say? Any time, Gaelie.'

'How do we go into him without letting him know we think he's dying? He's so frightened, poor darling.'

'We must go in naturally and easily,' I advised. 'Just as if it was an ordinary day.'

'Yes,' said Auntie Flavia. 'Just as if it was an ordinary day.'

'Can we come now?' asked Gael.

'No. Not quite so soon after the doctor has gone. He might suspect something. I will call you if——'

'I see,' said Gael, to save her saying more.

Still in her armour of calm and acquiescence, Auntie Flavia went slowly from the room. Gael just sat there, and I remained at the window, playing with the lead-weighted tassel of the holland blind. I watched a woman go by with her umbrella up, either unaware that the rain had stopped or providing against its return. An errand boy cycled past, basket on arm, and I listened to the whistling of his tyres on the wet, greased road.

Averil came in to carry away, very quietly, and with a sudden controlled sob, the piled breakfast things; so, pretending not to see her swollen eyes, we went upstairs to the Playroom. But here we could settle to nothing. It was no hour for play. Gael, after idly turning the pages of an ancient picture-book, let her hands tumble to her lap and lie inanimate there. I walked up and down between window and doorway. The doorway looked straight across the landing at his shut bedroom door. Behind that door I could hear Auntie Flavia's steps sometimes, but her voice seldom; his not at all. She came out once, saw me in the doorway, and smiled tenderly. After fetching something from another room, she went in to him again.

Most of an hour passed, and then, just as I in my wretched sentry-go arrived at our doorway, she appeared in hers. She raised a finger as if she'd rather beckon than speak, and said only, in a low voice, 'Come.'

'Gael,' I said. 'Come on'; and I went forward, humming so as not to frighten him, but there was no need of this. He had sent for us. His eyes were watching the door for us. They tried to smile their usual welcome, and I thought the fear in them had gone—or almost gone. He said, between laboured breaths, 'Gael dear . . . Win . . . come close.'

We obeyed and stood side by side against his bed, I sometimes leaning forward and back, as a child will, and feeling its soft pressure against my knees. Auntie Flavia kept in the background, as if this moment must be given to us.

'I am in a very precarious condition . . . I know it . . . I'm not such a fool as not to understand that. . . . And I . . . I accept it. I don't know when the end will come, but it is not a long way off. . . . So I want to look at you again . . . Gael dear . . . Win.' His worn and feeble white hand felt for mine and pressed it; then sought Gael's and did the same.

He smiled again. 'I have been very fond of you, and . . . and I'd like you to stay here for a little. Will you stay? Only for a little?'

I said, 'Yes, yes,' so far as I could for gulping; Gael, too.

'I'd like to see you there,' he repeated, smiling apologetically, and finding my hand again. 'But not if it takes too long. . . . Lottie, my dear, let them sit down. Perhaps they'd like something to read . . . or is it perhaps selfish to keep them here?'

'No, no, no!' I cried. 'Let me sit here.' And I sat myself on the foot of the bed. Gael went round its wide brass end and sat at the other foot. And he smiled gently to see us both sitting there. We sat silently, awaiting we knew not what.

In the silence let me interrupt.

CHAPTER TWENTY-TWO

WHEN the once-famous Lord Roland de Brath, son of a great English house, died in our small suburban home, there was no longer any possibility of concealing his identity. No sooner were our blinds down and Uncle Lucy's death bruited in our road than Don Francesco ran headlong to Fleet Street and informed his friends there in whose house and in whose care a once-great statesman had died. Don Francesco had completed his identifications and packed up his pleasant game of detection many days before. You will remember that Gael had given him the name Flavia Middian when he challenged her in the street and that the name had seemed to stir a memory in him. It was not difficult thereafter to rake among old files in Fleet Street and learn again that the lovely and notorious Lottie Morris had been a daughter of Canon Middian, later Bishop of Chesterfield; nor, after researches in Somerset House, to learn—doubtless with delight—that she had been christened Charlotte Gertrude Flavia. Only one more confirmation was necessary, and he got this when he joked us in the street about the 'deputation of political ladies,' and Gael revealed that they were our Aunties Gloria, Evelyn, and Primrose. These he quickly ascertained—with some elation, no doubt—were the names of other daughters of the saintly Bishop Middian.

And no sooner had he run to Fleet Street and fired this fuse than our house, with the once-great tribune lying dead behind its walls, was besieged. Reporters and press photographers stood watching its front door and windows from both sides of the street, and its back door and windows from the gardens of North End Road behind. There were old stout trees in these back gardens (some are there still) and the photographers climbed into their upper branches to make pictures of the house-back and especially of the window behind which he lay. Patient creatures, they sat on their branches like cloak-winged and shaven-necked birds of prey. In front, if Averil for a second pulled up a blind, the reporters leapt on to the dwarf wall of the area and, holding on to the lime trees, peered into the dining-room. They sought interviews with our neighbours on either side and opposite. They rushed with their note-books to ask· questions of every caller or tradesman who approached the house, and of Lizzie or Averil who answered the door to him.

Lizzie defended her castle gate frantically. 'Go away! for shame! Have you no decency?' she fired at them, and slammed the door in their eyes. 'I never heard the like,' she muttered to herself as she went down to her kitchen. 'They're beyond anything. Ought to be locked up.'

Next day the half-penny morning papers and all the nine evening papers made it their lead-story under such headings as 'Lord Roland de Brath Dies in the Arms of the Woman He Loved', 'One of the Love Stories of the World', 'A Great Tragedy of Our Time', and 'A Romance World-famous Ends'.

The Liberal papers were very gentle to his memory. Their headlines ran: 'A great Tribune of the People Passes'; 'A Patrician who Loved the People'; and 'The Lost Captain'. A Socialist paper, the *Clarion*, remembering his battles for the oppressed, headed a generous tribute, 'Lest we Forget'.

The cheaper papers retold, with the relish and ex-travagance of their kind, the whole tale of 'a world-shaking scandal', the flight from his country of 'one of its greatest and most controversial figures', his disappearance for a quarter of a century from the sight of all who had known him, the secluded life of 'the lovely Lottie Morris' under a changed name in a quiet West London street, and, of course, his 'coming home in the end to die in her arms'. With the photographers' aid they made much of the con-trast between Longchambers, the stately home of the Marquesses of Hayle and Ensor 'with its broad terraces and its spacious, deer-filled park,' and our small suburban house 'in a road of fast-fading gentility.'

And all that day the readers of these stories bore down upon our Edith Road, from either end and every corner, so that they could stand and stare at the house. They watched the undertaker's men going up the steps and the reporters pestering them for 'a story'. From windows opposite eyes gazed at the house and at these people standing about it.

All the Paris papers carried the story, and the lovely French language gave it grace.

More than once that day the reporters, trespassing on our steps and violating our door with their knocks, got Auntie Gloria instead of Lizzie. She had arrived with the first morning light to help us all. Knowing now that we children knew it was our father lying dead upstairs, she said, 'Poor mites', and dealt with us very gently. To Lizzie, when some pressman knocked, she said, 'Let *me* go to him;' and to the door she went with a steaming indignation and its inseparable partner, joy. 'I have sent for the police,' she told the man before he could open his mouth, a statement which was quite untrue. 'Be off with you. And you others, too. Go on! Away with you, all!'—as if they were street urchins. 'Have you no shame? Why, a dog behaves better than you in a house of mourning. This is a house of mourning. Can't you understand? There are children here. Can't you respect *anyone's* grief? Banging on the door! Poor little bairns. Lizzie, how soon did the police say they'd be here?' Nor did she shut the door till she'd shoo'd away with her hand all the people on the pavements, as one shoo's the fowls from the farmyard. 'Be off with you! Go on! The police are coming.'

None the less, again and again that day some new pressman, refusing frustration, knocked at our door. These recurrent knocks went on far into the night; there was one at two a.m.; and I have always thought of them as the first touches of the future beating on the door. Because if the world showed Uncle Lucy small mercy in life, banishing him to a desert for his sin, it made him some recompense after death by bringing him back in triumph as a popular romantic hero. Early symptoms of this appeared in that evening's post. Auntie Flavia received from a Sunday paper an offer of a large sum if she would 'tell her story' for serial publication. Lizzie, too—Lizzie received an offer from a woman's journal for her story of 'My Life with Lottie Morris and Lord Roland de Brath.'

Then thirty-three years after, and eighteen years after Auntie Flavia's death in France (she died in 1921) a dramatist of some note made the first play about them. It never reached the footlights because this was 1939, and in September the war broke. Its film rights had been sold but because of the war and the subsequent depression work on the film was postponed and postponed, and to this day it remains only as a script in a drawer. But they will make it yet. With wide screen and full colour.

Neither Gael nor I had any legitimate position from which to stop the play, even if we'd wanted to, but it was shown to Gael in courtesy; Gael summoned me to share it with her, and a strange experience it was to sit together by her fireside and read it.

The last minutes of the play show the hero's death. He lies, fully and handsomely dressed, on the sofa in our drawing-room, on to which he has collapsed after a spasm at the heart. The room is described as 'overloaded with small furnishings, most of them tired and shabby, and with palms and ferns and peacock's feathers—a typical suburban room in the later Victorian style.' On the other hand, the play's heroine, Lottie Morris, or Flavia Middian, is set in affecting contrast with this shabby chamber—'a tall, slim, white-haired lady whose aristocratic air, quiet voice, and elegant, tasteful attire remind us of her origins in larger and happier rooms.' Only one other person enters on the scene, the 'stout and grey' old servant (Lizzie) to whom, because of her long loyalty, the dramatist has allowed a large and appealing part, though mainly a low-life comedy one. It is made clear that, except for these three, the house is empty. There are no children. There is no mention of the bare-armed Averil going about her labours in the kitchen below, and steadily, if quietly, weeping.

And Lord Roland says, 'Try to go on loving me, my dear, however long you live. Don't grow to hate me for having ruined your life.' At which the heroine drops to her knees at his side and, throwing an arm about him, declares, 'It was I who destroyed yours, my love, my only love.' The dying man shakes his head and smiles. 'You couldn't help being everything I wanted. I took what I wanted, and that was the end. But, oh, my dear, it was very lovely while it lasted.' Whereon they speak for a while of the old Roehampton villa and their happy rides on heath or common in the bright summer days.

Then, falling into a reverie, he murmurs, 'There was a storm of cheering in the House when the Prime Minister invited my resignation. I tried to stand unmoved before the tempest, but it was not easy. . . . It hurt like a death. . . . Though that's not right. . . . For death hurts less.'

'I know, I know, my precious. They drove you out with every cruelty. For loving me.'

'Yes, and the people made a joke of me.'

'Of me, too, my dear. They sung their dirty songs about me in the streets.'

'It was only their rough fun, I believe. They have to joke and be lewd because their lives are so harsh and empty. I can't think the common people ever really hated us.'

'They loved *you*.'

'Once they did. . . . But my own people didn't. How they seized their chance to blast me with their vengeance. . . . Ah, well, it's all so long ago now. So long that I can hardly remember much of it. It's fading from me.'

'That is best, my dear.' The heroine kisses his brow. 'Let it go. It's none of it worth remembering any more.'

'But you? You have to live with it for many years yet.'

'Don't think of that, my darling. Already it seems

powerless to hurt me any more. Twenty-six years have gone and soon there will be no one to know of it. We shall both be forgotten, completely forgotten, by all the world.'

On which words the curtain falls.

CHAPTER TWENTY-THREE

But Uncle Lucy's last hour was not like this. Not at all like this. We two children sat at the bed's foot. Auntie Flavia, resigning him to us for a little, sat at a distance on the arm of an upholstered chair. Because it was morning and early she wore a slack blue dressing-jacket, loosely open, her greying hair was in slight disarray, and her feet were in bedroom slippers, worn and crumpled. Her face was still raddled by the tears she had shed before resolving, in some lonely moment, to gird on strength and courage and be mistress of the end.

Now she went out while we were seated there and all was quiet in the room. When she came back she was robed in a beautiful tea-gown all draped with fine lace about the breast and adorned with silken bows from throat to hem. Her hair was carefully arranged and her face restored to its very best with powder and paint. Her feet were in her best house-shoes.

I think she wanted to be beautiful, if possible, for his last sight of her.

The great bed extended from the wall between door and window so that in the many times of silence I found myself gazing across the bedclothes towards a back garden and an old tree which was but a pencilled trunk and branches now, but would be alive again in the spring. The air above those rain-drenched London gardens smelt clean and washed and pure, like the air of a new beginning.

As I was thinking something like this I felt his eyes on me. He smiled and said with difficulty, 'It seems but yesterday that I was a child at home like you two. . . . Gael dear. . . . And now it is all over. . . . One thinks one has all time before one, but in such a little while it is gone.' He paused, perhaps to rest the struggling breath, perhaps to think of the past, so much of which had been splendid, but all of it, good and bad, now gone. 'Make the most of it—your time, I mean. . . . It's stopped raining, hasn't it?'

We all agreed that it had stopped raining.

'It'll be a fine afternoon, I think . . . or evening.' An evening which could matter only to us, since he would not be there to see it. 'Time gathers such speed as you get older. Ever faster and faster as it gets nearer the end.'

For the first time I heard the clock on his chimneypiece. 'Tick teck, tick teck, tick teck,' it commented, keeping a slow level pace, with never an increase. 'Tick teck, tick teck.' It could hardly beat for a slower march. Beyond the windows the pale November morning was like a still picture that cannot change. One could imagine—or at least a child could—that out there in the gardens duration had ceased. But then one heard the rumour of jarring wheels in the North End Road; and it was like the sound of Time itself running at a distance and heedlessly by.

When he could speak again he sighed and said with a small resigned smile, 'This world's praise matters so terribly to you, Win, right up till you know you're in your last bed; and then, suddenly, it is nothing. Nothing. Once it meant everything . . . it meant the whole world . . . and now'—so far as they might, his shoulders shrugged on the bed—'now . . . well . . . what does any of it matter, Win? . . . *Je la quitte maintenant.* . . .'

Win. As he said the name, the look in his eyes changed from one of memory to a question. A question for me. A question that even now he dared not ask. But I saw it in his eyes and answered it at once with an affectionate smile, whereupon he stretched out his hand, and I shifted along the bed that he might take mine. He took it and pressed it as hard as he could in his weakness. Such was his unspoken confession, and his *tu propitius esto.* Never a word from either of us as to what he was to me, but our knowledge was exchanged, and our love accepted and all my rushing forgiveness. He smiled in gratitude for a child's mercy, and continued to stare at me, thinking, I dare say, of Peggy Waybon.

One must begin some time or other to bear one's share of our human pain, and this was certainly the first moment that my schoolboy heart was ripe for bursting. Selfishly, because the pain was so great, I had to tell myself, as I used to do when they made me wear a top-hat in the streets, 'All things pass.'

Then there was Gael. He looked towards her, raising his eyebrows in the same question; and she it was who, as in the play, flung herself on her knees beside him and laid her arm across his breast. He patted the arm gratefully, and if he dared not speak of his fatherhood, he was able to turn his eyes towards her mother and tell Gael, 'Always be very good to her'. ('To her'; no more 'To your kind auntie'.) 'She was always so good to me.'

Gael nodded and nodded, to assure him passionately that she would honour this request.

So, comforted, he lifted his hand from Gael's arm and extended it in invitation to Auntie Flavia. We rose from the bed's foot and stood aside for her, apprehending, as she had done for us, her right to have him to herself. We stood at each corner of the bed's wide end and watched.

He grasped her hand and said, 'Let me hold it, Lottie my love. Let me keep it. May I?' In answer, sitting on the bed's edge, she gave him her hand, and he weakly held it, lifting it up and down sometimes.

This was as good as speech between them, and it was some while before he spoke again. Then he said, 'Come and join me one day. . . . But not for a long time yet. You are young.' Perhaps these words reminded him that the judgments of men could still matter to her, for he said, to no one in particular, his eyes shut, 'It is a pity. . . . It was cruel. . . . She was made for happiness and praise.'

The eyes remaining shut, Auntie Flavia, turning, whispered to us to go.

I shook my head.

And she, feeling, I am sure, that we were too young to see anyone die, rose and put her hand on my arm to lead me from the room.

I cried, 'Oh, no, *no*!' like an angry child—but not too

loud. 'No, please, *please*!' I insisted—only just this side of
furious tears. And I snatched myself free and went and held
tight on to the brass rail of the bed. It was inconceivable to
me in that moment that I should not be allowed to stay with
him to the last—as a mother would be, or a grown-up son.

He heard the slight scuffle, opened his eyes, and seemed to
understand. 'Let them stay if they like,' he said. 'It is good
of them to want to stay.' He looked towards us with a smile.
'They are growing up now, I think, and will not be afraid.'

I went back to my seat on the bed's foot, and Gael found
a chair and sat beside me.

Half-forgetting us there, he began to speak to Auntie Flavia
of things that must have happened in days before we were born.

'Remember the Allée de Flore et de Céres? . . . And
the Bassins du Printemps et de l'Été?'

'Oh, yes, yes.'

I conjecture that one happy summer day, wandering
among the tall plantations of Versailles, they came upon
these two secluded basins in the Allée de Flore et de Céres,
and that they embraced there in the great silence between
the trees. And if I know my Uncle Lucy, he jested that
she was Springtime and he Summer—late summer fast
rusting into decay.

'And the Bois? Remember the Châlet des Iles? And
our little café in the Rue de Passy?'

'Oh, I do.'

'Ah, Paris. We were happy there sometimes . . . even
after that. . . . Win must go to Paris one day. And Gael.
I always wanted to take them there . . . and to the valley of
Port Royal. Pascal's valley. . . . Yes, it's stopped raining
now. It was raining in the night. Gently.... The excellent
Lizzie, you must say good-bye to her for me. Say good-bye
and thank-you to her. . . . And to the child Averil, too. . . .'

His breathing was very laboured now, and he would
often close his eyes, as if it racked him. But he would open
them again, and smile, as much as to say, 'This can't be
helped, my dear.' Once he shook his head, smiling, and
said aloud, '*Ce n'est rien.*' Later, and almost with an amusement at play about his lips, he struggled to say some other

words in French (I found them years afterwards, with a leap of recognition, in his beloved Pascal). *'Par sa grâce, j'attends la mort en paix . . . moi . . . un homme plein de faiblesses, de concupiscence, d'orgueil et d'ambition . . . par sa grâce. . . .'*

For a time they seemed to comfort him, and he lay still, repeating *'par sa grâce'*; but then, gazing before him with speculative and doubting eyes, he murmured, *'Mais . . . je ne crois pas tout cela . . .'* only to add a little later, *'Cependant . . . peut-être . . . peut-être.'*

As the murmuring grew less, Auntie Flavia, without loosing her hand, leaned forward to look at him, wondering if he was still conscious. Forgetting us, maybe, she whispered, 'I am still here. I am with you, my dear, my very dear;' and at her voice, he raised his eyelids a little way to show her that he heard. The old receded eyes, like marbles of Arctic blue, gleamed for a second beneath those half-lifted blinds, and his lips moved as if in recognition and thanks, but no sound came, and the lids dropped again. Once more, however, he opened them and, looking into her eyes, said, 'Good-bye, my dearest and best . . . and thank you.'

He tried to say more and smile at her tenderly, but weariness closed the eyes. He repeated 'thank you', halting as if the sense of the words were dimming; and he did not again open his eyes. His last breath, coming soon after a small, private smile, was like an unfinished sigh whose meaning can never be known.

§

Still tearless, but with lips beginning to totter, Auntie Flavia laid a formal farewell kiss on his brow. Turning to Gael as if I were not there, she said simply, 'I did my best for him.'

Gael, who could not speak, nodded to comfort her.

'It is what I tried to do from the beginning, Gael dear. He seemed to need me so desperately then, and . . . I loved him, and, oh, I wanted to help him. But people don't understand.'

'I know, Mother dear,' said Gael.

'In some ways he was weak, I suppose,' she said, looking down upon him with eyes still dry and head shaking and Gael at her side stroking her hand, 'but there was much in him that was rather wonderful, too. . . . You never saw him in his great days. . . . Oh, I hope I made him happy . . . sometimes.'

'I'm sure you did. He always said you did. He always said there was no one like you. Don't worry, dear. . . .'

I didn't mind being apparently forgotten, because Auntie Flavia needed all the comfort that could be given her; and, for me, nothing mattered just then, as I looked on that stilled grey face, now splendid as a king's in marble, but my heart's first realization of death. That what was, now was not. That Uncle Lucy was not, and death made trash of all our worldly ambitions, and dust and wind of all our loves. That he was gone into the great waste of nothingness that lies—or seems to lie—around our world. That love must always look upon this in the end, and be left alone, without understanding, till death itself, perhaps, shall give the answer. And that one bears it, hoping all things.